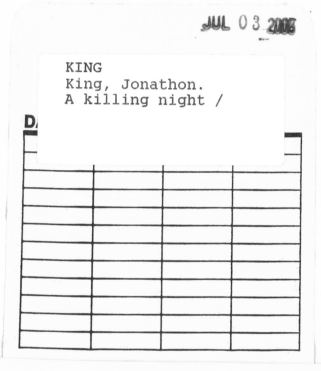

A KILLING
NIGHT

Also by Jonathon King

The Blue Edge of Midnight

A Visible Darkness

Shadow Men

A KILLING
NIGHT

JONATHON KING

DUTTON

DUTTON
Published by Penguin Group (USA) Inc.
375 Hudson Street, New York, New York 10014, U.S.A.
Penguin Group (Canada), 10 Alcorn Avenue, Toronto, Ontario, Canada M4V 3B2
(a division of Pearson Penguin Canada Inc.); Penguin Books Ltd, 80 Strand,
London WC2R 0RL, England; Penguin Ireland, 25 St Stephen's Green, Dublin 2,
Ireland (a division of Penguin Books Ltd); Penguin Group (Australia), 250
Camberwell Road, Camberwell, Victoria 3124, Australia (a division of Pearson
Australia Group Pty Ltd); Penguin Books India Pvt Ltd, 11 Community Centre,
Panchsheel Park, New Delhi - 110 017, India; Penguin Group (NZ), Cnr Airborne
and Rosedale Roads, Albany, Auckland, New Zealand (a division of Pearson New
Zealand Ltd); Penguin Books (South Africa (Pty) Ltd, 24 Sturdee Avenue,
Rosebank, Johannesburg 2196, South Africa

Penguin Books Ltd, Registered Offices: 80 Strand, London WC2R 0RL, England

First printing, April 2005
1   3   5   7   9   10   8   6   4   2

⚡ REGISTERED TRADEMARK—MARCA REGISTRADA

Library of Congress Cataloging-in-Publication Data

King, Jonathon.
A killing night / by Jonathon King.
p. cm.
ISBN 0-525-94865-1 (hardcover : acid-free paper)

1. Freeman, Max (Fictitious character)—Fiction. 2. Private
investigators—Florida—Fiction. 3. Young women—Crimes against—Fiction.
4. Ex-police officers—Fiction. 5. Policewomen—Fiction. I. Title.
PS3611.I58K55   2005
813'6—dc22   2004021335

Printed in the United States of America
Set in Sabon with Grotesque
Designed by Daniel Lagin

For Jessica and Adam

Things break more in bars than they do outside—hearts, noses, bottles, promises. And in the breaking are beautiful stories.
                                                    —Pete Dexter

A KILLING
NIGHT

Man, he loved that smile of hers. It was a killer.

He could see her using it from here, flashes of the white teeth that she swore she'd never bleached. The raised cheekbones in her profile every time she turned from the bar back to the register. He was too far away to see her brown eyes, but he knew their shine and the way they laughed when she smiled that smile. It was what had captured him, what made him know that this was the one, the girl who was going to save him this time.

He saw it again but he had to lean forward into the steering wheel to keep it in sight through the window as she swung back to her customer. The guy had parked himself right in front of the taps so he'd get to chat her up every time she poured a beer. When she tossed her hair back over her shoulder, he saw the smile again. That killer smile. His smile. So why the fuck was she giving it to this guy?

"Two-oh-four? Dispatch to two-oh-four."

The radio squawked and without looking he reached over and turned the volume lower.

"Two-oh-four. Report of an assault from caller at four-twenty-four Northeast Ninth Avenue."

Assault my ass, he thought. Some old lady trying to get us to run over to her place 'cause she heard a noise that'll turn out to be the damn cat. You don't get assaults in that neighborhood at one in the morning. Waste of time. He didn't bother answering, even though he knew it wasn't going away.

"Two-oh-four? What's your location?"

"Shit," he said out loud, snatching up the mike.

"This is two-oh-four," he answered, monotone, no emotion in his voice.

"I'm in the two hundred block of South Park Road on that burglary call out. I need to check this alleyway and secure the premises."

"Ten-four."

He could hear the exasperation in the dispatcher's voice. But the hell with her.

"This is four-eighteen dispatch," came another voice on the box. "I'm clear on the last call, I'll take that assault."

"Ten-four, four-eighteen. I've got you en route at oh-one-hundred hours."

Good ol' Roger, he thought. Always the hustler. Always coming through to build his numbers. He clipped the handset back on the dash and turned back to the bar. The first few pinprick spots of rain began to pepper his windshield and glistened like sugar in the high parking lot lights. She'd be on her shift another two hours. Then she'd do her cleanup for the girls on day shift even if he did try to convince her to leave it for them. Then maybe he'd find out what the hell she'd been talking about earlier with that fucking P.I.

He rolled down his window and took a deep draw of night air and the smell of rain in the breeze. He watched an old Camaro pass slowly through the parking lot and then pull a rolling stop through the stop sign onto Federal. Oughta light that guy up right now, he thought. Even if there isn't any traffic. These punks who think they can break the law any damn time they feel like it. He watched the red glow of the Camaro's taillights wink and then fade into the next block.

He turned back to the bar and she was still talking to the guy on the end stool and he could feel the heat rise into his ears and the twitch in his back that made him shift in his seat. The leather of his belt and holster creaked. He picked his personal cell phone up off the passenger seat and hit the speed dial and watched her turn to the bar phone as soon as he heard the ring in his ear.

"Kim's, can I help you?"

"Only by getting off early," he said, using his sweet voice.

"Hi, baby," she answered, but turned away from the window, hiding the smile that was supposed to be his.

"You know I can't, even if I want to. I'm on alone."

He watched her turn and hold the mobile phone close to her cheek and then cup her elbow with her palm in a sort of self-hug. He liked the move.

"How's it going out there tonight?" she asked. "Catch any bad guys?"

He knew she always wanted to hear the stories, take her away from the boring blather in front of her.

"Not much," he said, not willing to take the effort to make anything up off the cuff. "Pretty quiet. Rain you know. Policeman's best friend. How's it in there?"

"Dull," she said and he saw her step forward and pick up a bar rag while she cradled the phone with her shoulder.

"So who's the guy you've been flirting with for the last half hour?" he said, not able to control himself.

"What? You're kidding, right?"

He could see her look up at the window on the north side of the bar where he had parked his cruiser in the past.

"Oh. Tell me he's just another old friend from high school like that last one," he said.

She kept looking north and then walked out from behind the bar over to an empty table, wiped at the clean surface.

"Yeah, old is right," she said into the phone. "He's forty-eight. He's married to my old boss out at Ranchers."

She was trying to keep an easy, teasing tone in her voice. He wasn't close enough to see the tiny prick of fear that stained the light in her eye.

He was silent and watched her give up on the table and then disappear behind a wall and then come back into view in another window. She was wearing that loose white button-down blouse, open wide down the front. She had on a cotton jersey underneath that stretched tight around her breasts and accented her cleavage.

"You gotta wear that shirt open like that all the time?" he said, watching her move close to the window and look out in his direction. The reflective paint on the side of the squad car glowed like neon under the lights and he saw her eyes stop.

"You always seem to like it," she said and cupped her hand around the mouthpiece of the phone and moved closer to the glass. Her face was shadowed by the angle of the light.

"You know I get jealous," he said. "It's just that you're so beautiful."

She knew she was not beautiful. It was a line she'd heard a thousand times from men on the other side of the bar, spoken on the scent of bourbon and beer. But his was different. He had been different. She'd liked it when he said it because it wasn't a joke, or some bad come-on. Even when he'd said it the first time, it was with a touch of passion that made her believe that he believed it. Now she knew too much about where his passion came from and she had to tighten the hold on her stomach to keep the bile from rising in her throat.

In the patrol car the radio squelched again.

"All units, officer in foot pursuit of a fleeing suspect in the nine hundred block of Third Street. Requesting backup."

The dispatcher had cranked her flat voice up a notch.

"Two-oh-four?"

His was the only specific call number she used.

"Two-oh-four responding," he answered into the set while turning the key in the ignition and gunning the engine to life. He'd left his cell phone connection open and said into the phone, "Gotta go catch some bad guys, babe," and then hit the light bar and siren and pulled out of the parking lot into the street.

He was smiling now, jacked at the chance to show off. She watched the red and blue lights flash across the south windows and felt the small jump of adrenaline nip into her blood.

"But you'll be back to get me, right?" she said, surprising herself with the coolness of the request.

"Sure, babe. I'll be back."

He cut the siren at Ninth Street but kept up the speed, taking a corner with just enough control to keep the tires from yelping on the concrete. He was listening now to the radio crackling with the sounds of the foot chase and location of Roger's suspect. He could hear his fellow patrolman breathing hard while trying to talk into the microphone that all road officers kept clipped to the shoulder lapel of their shirts.

"Suspect . . . now northbound on . . . uh . . . Thirteenth Ave approaching Fifth."

The sounds of Roger's handcuffs ringing and his baton clacking on his belt came through the transmission each time he keyed the mic to speak. This asshole was giving him a pretty good run.

He pushed up his speed and then rode the brakes just a touch while blowing through a stop sign. He was watching for the telltale sweep of headlights. Anything dark was just SOL. From other radio traffic he could tell other units were closing in like some kind of foxhunt. But he wanted to get in there first, and without announcing himself or flushing the runner into somebody else's hands.

"Two-oh-four. What's your location?" Dispatch bitch again. "We need to set up a perimeter on the east side of Fifteenth Ave."

Fuck that. Goddamn perimeter guys always miss out on the good stuff. He ignored the call and doused his flashing light bar and gunned the car up Eighth toward the park. The guy'll go into the park. They always go into the fucking park, figuring the patrol cars won't follow them into the trees.

"Suspect is . . . uh . . . in the alley moving north . . . in the six hundred block . . . uh . . . toward the park."

Nice, Roger, he thought, and cut the wheel and jumped a sidewalk onto the sod of the park's soccer field and felt the fishtail of the Ford's ass end sliding on grass.

"Description of the suspect, four-eighteen?" dispatch asked.

"White male . . . heavy, six-foot . . . wearing, wearing gray cutoff sweatshirt . . . uh . . . dark pants . . ."

Roger was doing a hell of a job but it didn't sound like he was gonna keep up much longer and this fuck is bound to go for the thick pines at the north side. If he makes that fence behind the library and across Federal, we're screwed.

He accelerated, throwing up a rooster-tail of grass and black dirt over the field, and killed his headlights. He used the spillover of light from the baseball diamond to aim for the tree line. The radio crackled again and he heard the rustle of metal clacking again but this time no one spoke.

"Four-eighteen? Four-eighteen, what's your location?" the dispatcher said, worry now sneaking into her voice.

He reached the trees and slurred the car to a stop and kept his eyes at head level, scanning the field for movement. The high baseball lights glowed up and out, leaving the grass in shadow. He opened the driver's door, congratulated himself on remembering to kill the dome light when the shift started, and stepped out. The air was heavy with the drizzle and the smell of fresh-cut grass. He unsnapped the hammer strap from the 9mm in his holster and squinted, tracking to the west and listening. His eye stopped on something on the black background, a dull flash of white that was there, then gone, then there again. He took a few steps in that direction when the radio came back to life.

"Four-eighteen. Suspect in custody," Roger said.

He could hear the crackle in both the radio on his shirt and in the air out in front of him and he started jogging.

"Ten-four, four-eighteen. Location?" said the dispatcher.

"On the soccer field, north end of the park."

As he got closer, he could see Roger, one knee in the back of a big man who was facedown in the grass, bobbing his head from side

to side and spitting out fresh clippings that were pasted onto his
sweaty face.

"Yo, Rog," he said as he reached the two. "Olympic fucking
speed, man. I didn't know you were a cross-country star, man."

Roger's face was glistening in the spare light. His breathing was
heavy and he kept his left hand on the man's shoulder blades and
wiped at the sweat with the short sleeve of his uniform. He already
had handcuffs on the man and he let a grin start on the lighted side
of his face.

"Figured he'd head this way and I knew once we got in the clear
I'd get him in a sprint," Roger said.

"Olympic fucking speed," he repeated, standing over Roger and
the suspect, watching across the park and picking up the blue and
red flashes of other units rolling up on the perimeter.

"Hear that, shit-head? Snared your fat ass with Olympic speed,"
he said and kicked the soles of the man's thick leather boots.

"Where'd you come in, anyway?" Roger said, finally standing
up. "I didn't see your car."

"I figured the park, too," he said. "But not on that speed of
yours, Rog. Thought I'd cut him off at the tree line."

The two cops talked as if there were no third party, both of them
watching the other marked cars swing their headlights into the parking area to the west of the field. They both leaned over and grabbed
an arm and brought him to his knees.

"On your feet, shit-head. Time to march the perp march,
brother," he said.

"I ain't your fuckin' brother," the man said, slurring his words,
talking through clenched teeth like his mouth didn't work right. "An'
I didn' do no felony. I was jus' walkin' downa street an' this fuck . . ."

The man snorted when the first spray of Mace hit him in the
face. The second shot of chemical started him coughing and squirming between them.

"Jesus, man," Roger said, turning his own face away from the
stinging spray and the canister that had suddenly appeared in the
other cop's hand. "Easy with that stuff. We got him."

He looked into Roger's face and gave him that smile of his, holstered the canister and looked back at the gagging prisoner.

"Hey, big man. You do have the right to remain silent," he said, and now they were half dragging the man into the cross-hatching lights of the other squad cars. Behind them their tracks were three dark stains in the wet grass.

"And if you give up that right, I'll give you another shot of that shit into that wired-up mouth of yours."

The big man said nothing.

"That's it, brother," the cop said. "Now you know who's in control."

CHAPTER 1

I was sitting in a low-slung beach chair, my legs stretched out and bare heels dug comfortably into dry sand. My fingers were wrapped around a perspiring bottle of Rolling Rock beer. It was early evening and I was drinking and thinking and carefully watching the light.

It is no new phenomenon. I am sure oceanside peoples have watched the same drift and loss and meld of color for thousands of years from their own shorelines. But for an inner city kid from South Philly who rarely saw a sunset that was not spiked with the corners and spires of buildings, the cables of bridges and the curved necks of light poles, it was a performance. I took another sip from the green bottle and watched a couple of beach walkers pass by, their feet in the run-up of surf, their bent heads silhouetted by the pale blueness still in the sky behind them. I sat long enough to watch the blue color leach away from the Atlantic and at the same time slowly leave the sky. If you watched long enough, and with patience, you could see the two sets of the world, water and air, lose their color together and blend at the line of the horizon, miles out to sea. Eventually even that border lost its distinction and gave in to darkness.

Both as a child and later as a street cop in Philadelphia I took lessons from the night. I never heard my father beat my mother in daylight. I never shot a murderer, or an innocent tagalong kid, before nightfall. I never met a woman who didn't wait until dark to break my heart. Now I was in South Florida, spending hours in the evening, almost with a need, to watch the darkness come, an event I called the "disappearing blue."

I felt the vibration on my hip and reached down to where my beeper was wedged between my waistband and the stretched canvas of the chair. I turned it off and did not bother to look at the display. It had to be Billy. No one else had the number. I spent several more minutes looking out into the now black water, watching the small winking lights of fishing boats and far-off freighters become the new demarcation of where the water met the sky. The surf made a hissing noise each time it brushed up on the sand and I let it fill my ears until I gathered the fortitude to answer the page and find out what civilization had mucked up for me tomorrow.

Billy Manchester is my friend, my lawyer, and nowadays, my employer. He is one of the most talented and quietly connected businessmen attorneys in this end of the state and is easily the smartest man I know. His heart bleeds for the downtrodden and he works the financial markets to make buckets of money and in so doing proves that the two are not mutually exclusive. He knows the ins and outs of the legal system, the players, the politics, the rules and the law. But you will never see his name in an advertisement, a who's who column, or see him in front of a jury or a news camera. The law is his passion and capitalism is his bible. We have an odd history together. We both grew up in Philadelphia, street kids on streets in the same city, but from different planets.

I was the son of a son of a cop in South Philly, a neighborhood that was white and ethnic and Catholic and often blue-collar raw. Billy lived in the black ghettos of North Philadelphia. He broke all of his stereotypes and went to Temple University Law School, top of his class. I went to the police academy, middle of my class. He went on to get an MBA from Wharton. I went on to arrest druggies on South Street, catch homicide investigations as a young detective and catch hell from supervisors for not playing the game the way it was set up. Because of an unlikely and clandestine relationship between our mothers, we finally met, as men, in South Florida and now I work as Billy's private investigator.

I walked up through the soft sand carrying my chair, my small cooler clinking with empty green bottles, and climbed the bulkhead stairs. The beach crowd had long abandoned the place after sunset. I set my things down and stood under the stairway-side shower and rinsed off the sand and salt and left wet footprints on the slate walkway to the bungalow where I was staying. It was a small, one-bedroom efficiency and a concession to Billy that had actually grown on me. I considered my home in South Florida to be the stilted research shack on a pristine river that ran along the edge of the Everglades. It was there that I'd first isolated myself after taking a disability buyout from my job as a cop up north. It had been, and still was, the perfect place to keep my head together. But as I began to do more and more investigative work for Billy and his clients, he made a convincing argument that the two-plus hours it took me to canoe off the wilderness river and drive to his office in West Palm Beach was often illogical. I agreed, even though I also knew my friend was worried that the shack had also become a hideout for me. It was time I came back into the world, even a small step back. I didn't fight it.

The Royal Flamingo Villas was yet another of Billy's finds. It was an anomaly in South Florida. For more than one hundred years the property close to the sand with a view of the ocean drew people and money. In the 1920s and '30s there were small bungalows, pink stucco Spanish-looking estates of the rich, and the low-slung motels for driving tourists. Then came the four-story hotels, the quaint pine Kester Cottages for early residents and the modern concrete mansions of the '50s and '60s.

But by the 1980s you couldn't buy a private home with an ocean view unless you were a millionaire, and even those were being squeezed by twenty-story condos set cornerstone to parking lot and blocking any glimpse of the water for anyone living even a street away from the beach. Highway A1A had become a concrete corridor for a new century, broken only by a fortuitous state park or a city beach where planners had been smart enough not to kill their future tourist business by banning development on the sand and keeping a modicum of open beach to lure more sun money.

But the owners of the Royal Flamingo Villas had been even more forward-thinking. The Flamingo had remained a group of small stucco cottages that flanked A1A in the city of Hillsboro Beach. Each place stood unconnected but for the stone footpaths that led through the property. Though they were bunched together like some close-knit village hunkered down for protection, the grounds were filled with banana leaf palms and sea grape and crepe myrtle trees that shrouded the place in green privacy. Most of the cottages were individually owned by investors who made up a small, collaborative association. It was brilliant. The only way a hotel chain or high-rise condo group could buy their oceanfront land was to convince the entire group to agree, first on selling, then on price. Billy was one of those owners. He had accepted the title to one of the cottages from a client for whom he had negotiated a deal with the feds to keep the sixty-year-old securities broker out of lockup. When it came time for Billy's fee, he took the investment of land on the beach. There were only five cottages with unobstructed views of the ocean. One was Billy's.

I propped the beach chair against the patio wall and draped my towel over the still unused gas grill and went inside. The floors were old-style polished terrazzo. The walls were painted some pale shade of foam green. A counter separated the kitchen from the living area. The furniture was wicker, and the cushions, drapes and the framed print on one wall were all done in some tropical-flower motif. The only similarity with my shack on the river was the quiet. Ever since I'd left the constant background noise of the city I had developed a deep appreciation of quiet. I went to the kitchen and started a pot of coffee in the drip coffeemaker—a blessed upgrade from my tin pot on the wood-burning stove on the river. Once it was started I sat on the wooden stool at the counter and finally dug the beeper out of my pocket to see which of Billy's numbers I needed to call. I stared at the digits for several seconds, not recognizing them at first, and then letting my memory work. It brought a scent of careful perfume, a flash of blond hair, eyes a shade of green, no, gray. I had not seen Detective Sherry Richards in several months. The number in front of me was to her cell phone. The last time we had spoken it had been on that phone and I distinctly remembered it had been late at night and it had been dark.

"Yes. This is Max Freeman. Uh, returning Detective Richards's page. I will be available, uh, well, I'll be up most of the night if she needs me, uh, if this is an urgent matter."

Shit, I thought, and then left the number of the new cell phone Billy had given me on the answering machine.

Richards and I had a history. Hell, the woman had saved my life when she pulled the trigger on a calculating asshole who had me at the business end of a 9mm during a case Billy had put me into. The guy had miscalculated that time, believing that a woman cop wouldn't drop the hammer on him. Sherry Richards was not the kind of woman afraid to drop the hammer.

We'd had a relationship. But I had slept with her in a bed left empty by a punk kid who shot her cop husband while he was still shaking his head in disbelief at the child's age. My own short marriage to a Philadelphia officer had ended when she had, well, moved on to other challenges. Even though Richards and I had carefully eased into something good, I'd opened a bit of myself to her and was dumbfounded when her heart seemed to clack shut like a vault. She didn't like the endings either of us had witnessed. They scared her, so she left the show early. I had not seen her in several months.

Now it was past midnight and I was sitting out on my porch reading a new biography Billy had loaned me on John Adams. The old fart was fascinating, innovative, maybe damn brilliant, but he was also ambitious and I am not a fan of ambitious. I'd moved a freestanding lamp with an old yellowed shade outside and run the cord through one of the jalousie windows. In between pages I was staring out at the black ocean. A night breeze had come up and the brush of waves on the sand had turned to a harder, ripping sound, like fine cloth being torn. The sharp scent of decay that came with low tide was in each breath and it created an odd mixture with the aroma of my fourth cup of coffee. My eyes were closed when the chirp of my cell phone snapped them open. I punched it on with my thumb.

"Yeah."

"Yeah?" she said. "Well, your phone etiquette hasn't changed, Freeman."

"What can I say? Evolution is a creeping process."

"Let me guess. You're reading with your feet up on that old gouged-up table and you're still working on the last pot of coffee for the night."

"You're a psychic," I said.

"You're a dinosaur."

"Thank you."

Her voice was warm and light. I was relieved, but a little set back by her ability to call after months and be so damned giddy.

"Actually, I'm not out at the shack. I'm in town on the beach."

"Billy's?"

"Sort of. It's a little oceanfront place he keeps to hide clients when they're trying to avoid subpoenas and officers of the court."

"Sounds perfect for you, Max," she said, and we both let that sit for a quiet beat.

"So, you're close by. How busy are you?" she said, her voice shifting up into a tighter, business mode. OK, it was not a social call.

"Busier than I have a right to be, but just finishing up a job with Billy. What's up?"

"I've got a case I'm working on, Max," she started. "The disappearance of some women bartenders here in Broward."

"You're working missing persons?"

I hadn't meant the question to sound like she'd been demoted.

"Not just missing," she said. "Gone. Like off the face of the

earth missing. Not runaways, or gone on a lark, or start over somewhere else missing."

"OK," I said. Her tone made me think she'd already heard one
too many skeptics on this.

"Similar circumstances? Hours? Physical appearances?" I asked,
turning my former cop process on, giving her the professional cour-
tesy she deserved.

"Yes. Thank you," she said. "Enough of a pattern for *somebody*
to take them seriously."

OK, I thought. There's enough sarcasm there to know she's been
butting heads with command.

"So, how can I help, Sherry?"

"You know a guy named Colin O'Shea? Former Philadelphia
cop. Might have worked patrol during your time?"

It didn't take long for me to come up with the face. Colin
O'Shea. Kid from the neighborhood. St. Marie's High School. Touch
of the Irish. Good-looking guy. I'd run into him on the corners and
after some football games when we were coming up. I got to know
him a little better when we both became cops. He was a third-
generation cop, like me. After a few at McLaughlin's, when the others were half bagged and horseplaying, we'd talked. He gave off the
hint that he wasn't convinced that the blue tradition was his true
calling, either.

But he was also a manipulative son of a bitch. Angry. The two
traits had come together one night in the streets and O'Shea had, in
a way, saved my ass.

"Yeah," I said. "I knew him from back then. Haven't seen him
for years. He helping you somehow on this?"

"Not exactly," she answered. "He's my suspect."

CHAPTER 2

The manager at Hammermills let her close down the bar early. It had been slow since the *Monday Night Football* game had ended in a blowout of the home team. The regulars had lasted through the hopeful first quarter and the suspicious second. At half-time the place was still upbeat and she'd been busting her ass. It was mostly a beer crowd with an occasional round of party shots. On this particular night one of the distributors had put a premium on bottled beer, two for one, so she'd been juggling them all night and carried a big chrome opener which she stuck in the back pocket of her tight jeans, and she knew the guys kept an eye on it when she walked from one end of the twenty-foot mahogany bar top to the other. The opener was like a thing with her. A girlfriend back home had given it to her for her very first bartending gig and confused her when she said it would make a difference. Now the girlfriend was long gone but she'd been working bars long enough to know there was always a bit of performance going on and always a subtle scent of sex. God knows why else she would wear these tight hip-huggers and the cotton shirt that rose above her navel and dipped low enough up top to show what cleavage she could manage to bunch together. Her boyfriend didn't like it, except for when it was just for him, but to her it was a harmless part of the bartending business.

She'd gathered some good tips from the halftime crowd, and then when her regulars started cashing out their tabs in the third quarter she looked up and saw the home team was down by seventeen and registered why the place had gone from festive to grumbling sarcasm. By one o'clock she was restocking the coolers and draining the wash sinks. By two she'd totaled out the register. She'd made four hundred dollars in tips for the shift.

"I'm heading out, Mitch," she called to the manager, who was still in his tiny office next to the kitchen. She heard his swivel chair creak and waited until he stuck his balding head around the corner.

"You got a ride, right?"

"Yeah, I do. A safe one," she said and nothing more. She wasn't the kind to share her personal life with coworkers, and for some reason she especially liked leaving Mitch out of the loop.

She stepped outside and listened for the door to snick shut and the lock to engage behind her. It was a warm night and the air was humid and thick with the smell of stale beer and discarded Styrofoam meals in the alley. There was a half moon high in the western sky, turned on its side like a white china cup. She made the corner and saw his car parked under a street lamp and she smiled. She opened the passenger door herself and climbed in.

"Hi, sweetie," she said, and his own sincere smile greeted her. "Thanks for waiting."

"You know I like to. I should take you home every night," he said, and she knew he meant that, too. He leaned over, his leather creaking, and kissed her softly on the mouth and lingered there. She opened her mouth slightly and took in his warm breath and there it was, that little flutter in her chest like a small bird's wings and she knew this was different, had convinced herself of it. God, he could be so gentle and the kisses were like, well, like some kind of chemistry between them. It had been that way from the first time and that part had never changed. Yeah, she'd seen his temper in the four months they'd been together. He'd get that macho thing going and sometimes lose it, snap at her for "telling him what to do" or condescend to her like she was some bimbo. But after their fights he was so remorseful. Those damned puppy eyes of his and they'd get tears just in the bottom wells and he'd say he was sorry over and over and tell her how much she meant to him.

She wasn't always cool with his calling her all the time and being jealous and shocking her with his anger. But god, the sex was good even if it did get a little rough. And he was gorgeous. And no one before had ever seemed to care about just her and say all those things you want to say don't matter but do. It excited her, kept her oddly off-balance and she liked it.

She sat back in the seat and took the clip out of her hair. She knew he liked it down.

"You get anything to eat?" she said.

"Not really," he answered, starting the car and pulling out onto Seventeenth Street. "Got kinda busy with some asshole thought he was king of the walk down on East Commercial."

She watched the side of his face while he drove, saw the crow's feet start to darken at the corners of his eyes, knew he was in a good mood, building a story in his head. His hands were on the wheel and she noticed the pink abrasions on his right knuckles, a light trace of blood seeping, the moisture catching the light.

"You hurt yourself?" she asked, and he turned and tracked her eyes then flexed the hand.

"Not bad. This punk is still on the sidewalk near the warehouse when we answered the silent alarm. We roll up and he's stupid enough to just stand there thinking he'd act like he was walking the dog or something. I had to drag his ass over the back of the car and give him a little attitude adjustment."

He kept flexing the hand.

"Tell me," she said, turning toward him, her back into the crease of the door and the seat. She liked to listen to his stories, even if she was pretty sure he was embellishing most of them. The perps were always bigger or outnumbered him. He always helped the victims. It was like having someone read TV to you. She listened while he took the city streets west. She never interrupted the story. He didn't like being questioned until he was through. When he went quiet she waited. He stared straight ahead, trying to outlast her.

"What?" he finally yelped, and it made her jump.

"OK. So what did you find on this guy? Like, what was he holding?"

"What did he steal? You mean how much money?" he said, giving himself time to think. "How much do you think?"

"I haven't the slightest."

"Damn right you don't." He looked over at her and let the silence return for a few moments then said: "Five thousand."

"No shit?" she said, not sure if he was lying or not.

"No shit," he said. "Here, I kept a grand for you."

He reached down, fighting to get into his uniform trouser pocket and she watched, not sure how to react. His left hand jerked at the wheel and the front tires chafed at the edge of the roadway and she snatched a gasp of air and looked up and when she looked back he was laughing, both hands back on the wheel.

"You did not!" She grinned and slapped him on the arm. "You did not, liar," and she didn't catch herself until the word had already slipped out and she saw the bunched muscles in his jaw go tight and ripple against the skin of his cheek like marbles in a bag.

Shit, she thought, remembering the last time she called him a liar. She'd gotten backhanded that time, and maybe she'd even deserved it. She'd been a little drunk at the time and questioned one of his stories, doubted his description of a fight at dinner and had essentially called him a liar in front of other people. He'd slapped the wineglass out of her hand and his fingers had nipped the side of her face. He'd later apologized, and so had she, but after that night there had been a shift in their relationship.

Now she looked away and put her hands in her lap and snuck furtive looks at his hand, waiting for the whiteness to go out of the knuckles, which now clashed against the stain of blood, which had suddenly gone a deeper red.

They rode in silence while he swung the car off a main artery and up onto the ramp to the interstate going west. The jaw muscles relaxed. He took in a deep breath and she saw his cheek go concave against a row of teeth. He blew the air out.

"OK, maybe it was a bad joke," he said, and just those words flushed the tension out of the front seat.

"No, I'm sorry," she said, going with it, letting a grin pull at her mouth. "It was, you kinda had me going there."

They were still on the ramp when he slowed and pulled over in a spot in between the freeway lampposts, and she checked his face again.

"What?"

He looked at her and arched his eyebrows the way he did when he was being mischievous and said: "You wanna drive?"

"You're not serious," she said, feeling that twinge of excitement in her stomach that always came when he did shit like this.

"Wait until there's no one coming down the ramp and switch," he said, grabbing his door handle. He looked into the rearview mirror, waited for two cars to pass.

"Go!"

He popped the door and she jumped out of her side at the same time. They were both laughing when they bumped into each other at the trunk and he slapped her on the ass as she scooted by. They climbed into their opposite seats and both doors slammed at the same time. Chinese fire drill, she thought. Hadn't done that since high school. But this wasn't some friend's hatchback. This was a "Crown Vic," he'd reminded her several times. She put the car in drive, looked over at him and when he raised those eyebrows again, she punched it.

Coming off the ramp she merged onto the westbound lanes going out toward Alligator Alley and giggled when the car on her left slowed down in deference to the decals reflecting on the side panels and let her in. It was now three in the morning and traffic was almost nonexistent and she moved out into the far passing lane and pressed the accelerator. She pushed the big modified engine up to eighty miles an hour and was already tingling when he said: "Come on. We out for a Sunday drive or what?"

She cut her eyes over to him, smiled and bit one corner of her lip and accelerated. The high interstate halogen lights were flicking by now, their orange glow brightening then dimming then brightening again like a rhythm. She was staring wide-eyed out in front of the car's headlights, watching the inside white line blur while trying to pick up any red points of taillights ahead. She glanced at the speedometer. One hundred. She could feel the muscle and vibration of the machine from her heels right up through her hands. God, she hadn't driven this fast since she took her parent's new Lincoln that first summer home from college. She could feel him watching beside her. Relaxed. She glanced over. His hands were folded in his lap and he was twiddling his goddamn thumbs!

She put the peddle to the floor. One twenty. One thirty. A pair of red dots came up in the distance and she was only thinking about slowing when they suddenly grew and rushed up on her, and before she could make up her mind they'd whipped past a white pickup truck that seemed almost parked in the middle lane. The steering was going a little loose and the sound of the wind outside was humming in her ears like they were in a vacuum.

"Whoa," she said, but the small taste of fear in her throat didn't have a chance to climb before another pair of red dots appeared. The glowing red eyes in front of her grew and shifted to the right and when they snapped by the other car she swore she saw a woman's face with a stricken look of panic painted on the driver's window.

"Whoooo-hoooo," she howled, like some kid on a roller coaster.

"OK, OK, OK, Ms. Speed Queen," he was saying, and she started to pull her foot off the peddle.

"No, no. Ease it off, slowly. Just ease it back," he said, putting his hand on her thigh and she did as he said and brought the engine down and coasted over to the far right lanes and finally onto the shoulder, where she stopped. She let her breath roll out in a long whoosh and looked at him, her eyes big like they were still trying to catch everything at high speed. He was smiling his "didn't that feel good" smile and she realized her heart was racing.

"Girl. You are hell on wheels," he said, holding her eyes.

"Yes," she said. "I am."

He leaned over and kissed her mouth and she bit back lightly on his bottom lip in her excitement and she slid his hand up onto her crotch and she squeezed his fingers there with her thighs and said: "Where to now, sir?"

They switched seats and he took the car through the toll plaza onto the Alley and in twenty minutes he had them jouncing down an unpaved road into a thick wooded area with no sign of lights. They pulled off the road and parked and she couldn't remember if she got out her side or if he'd just somehow pulled her over and out his door. They were in one of those deep kisses that always set her spinning and he was pressed into her up against the rear quarter panel of the car. They both came up for air and she leaned back and looked up into a dark sky and they were far enough away from the city lights to let a sprinkle of stars shine through.

"God that speed was something," she said, realizing that her heartbeat hadn't tripped down since he'd first asked if she wanted to drive.

"You like that don't you, baby?" he said in her ear, and she felt his hand slide up under the back of her shirt, fingers rolling over her spine and searching for her bra fastener. She knew he was no fumbler, but she'd thrown a fashion changeup at him.

"It's in the front, dummy," she said and pushed him away and reached up herself and unsnapped her bra and then pulled the tight top up over her small breasts. His mouth was on her and they both slid her jeans off and she heard the creak of his leather belt and she opened herself to him. She knew she always came too soon for him but she couldn't hold herself back and was whispering, "I got you, I got you, sweetie," when she did. He held her while she quivered and then kissed her neck and backed away. She kept her eyes closed and could feel the night air on her damp skin and was about to apologize when he took her shoulders and started to turn her. It took a second to clear her head and he pushed her chest down on the trunk of the car and she felt him step up behind her.

"Come on, sweetie. You know I don't like this," she said, but she could feel his knees pushing out on the inside of her own.

"And you know I do." The hint of a growl had come into his voice.

"Please," she said and tried to turn her shoulders and then suddenly he had a fistful of the long hair he liked her to have down and he pushed her hard onto the trunk. She could sense the heat jumping from passion to anger but she fought him just like she had before.

"What? You're not running the show? Is that what you don't like?" he barked, and she felt his other hand pull at her, trying to open her.

She thought about letting him. Then she thought about the assault classes she'd taken from an old paranoid bar manager. She relaxed her legs as best she could and tightened her arm muscles at the same time and waited until she felt him start to probe her.

"That's a girl," he said. "Just relax and . . ."

She snapped her right elbow back as hard and as high as she could and felt the point hit something that went concave and then stop solid against a jagged edge. When she felt him roll with the blow she twisted out from under him but lost purchase on the slick grass and went down.

"You fucking bitch!" he growled, and she was on her hands and knees groping for her jeans and cussing him back when she looked up.

In the light of the teacup moon she saw him step forward. With one hand he was pulling up his pants and with the other he'd come up with a small silver-plated handgun.

"Think you're the tough one now, Suzy?" he said, and his eyes were flat and hard.

The last thing she ever recorded was the glint around the .22-caliber black hole pointed in her face. Her brain did not have time to even register the flash.

CHAPTER 3

I met Richards for a late breakfast at Lester's. Turns out, neither of us would end up eating. Settled alongside of what used to be the main highway into Port Everglades, Lester's is one of those old chrome-sided diners where the coffee comes in huge ceramic mugs and the waitresses are as chipped and sturdy as the glassware. It used to be the spot for truckers hauling fuel and whatnot from the port to points north. Later it was the shift change hangout for cops when the sheriff's office headquarters was nearby. Remnants of both pasts still walked in on a regular basis. I got there early and took a booth near the back. The new vinyl crackled under me when I slid in.

"Hiya, hon. Coffee?"

The waitress was sixty if she was a day and the red shade on her lips was the color of fire engines before they went to that fluorescent yellow green. She was already balancing the birdbath-sized cup and saucer in her hand. Few people stopped at Lester's if they were afraid of caffeine.

"Please," I said.

The ceramic setup clattered like two rocks when she put it down. She poured from the plastic pitcher in her other hand and the aroma was my heaven.

"Ya knowwhatchawant, hon?" she said, like it was all one word.

"I'm waiting for someone."

"Ain't we all?" she said and slid a menu next to the coffee and winked before leaving.

I sipped the coffee and watched the patrons over the rim. Guys on the counter stools with long-sleeved flannel shirts rolled up to the elbows, rumpled jeans and thick-soled boots. Two young women facing each other in a booth. The bleached blonde was facing me and I could see her red-rimmed eyes and she kept exhaling and shaking her hand in between low words. It was hard from a distance to tell if the dark smear on her cheekbone was a bruise or a swipe of running makeup. The back of her friend's head just kept bobbing, listening. Two guys, medium height and build, slid out of another booth. They were clean-shaven and dressed in pleated slacks and polo shirts. The one with his back to me had a lump that was belt high under his shirt. When he leaned over to put a tip on the table the fabric pulled up over the clip-on holster, exposing the leather. When I looked up beyond him, his partner was checking out my eyes. Cops casing the customers, I thought. How typical.

Richards came in ten minutes late. I caught the blonde top of her head bobbing just below the windows as she walked up from the parking lot. In heels she was taller than most men. She hesitated just inside the vestibule and I couldn't tell if she was finishing a cell phone call or putting on a fresh layer of lipstick. She stepped in and turned the opposite way first. She was in a beige, silk-looking suit and her hair was longer than I remembered. It was pulled back into a thick braid that hung down her back like a wheat-colored rope. When she spun and spotted me she smiled. As she approached, I raised the big cup to my lips, uncertain what my face was showing.

"Max, I'm really sorry I'm late."

I put the cup down and started to get up to greet her but she slid gracefully into the other side of the booth. There would be no quick embrace, kiss on the cheek or uncomfortable moment.

"Not a problem," I said. "You know my motto: Have coffee, will sit and muddle."

I wrapped my fingers around the cup.

"Habits that never die," she said.

"Not until I do," I said and watched her. "You look great. Still running?"

My direct compliment, even if she got it a lot from others, brought a tiny flush of color to her cheeks.

"Cycling, actually. A friend of mine got me into it. So we put in sixty or seventy miles a week. I'm enjoying it. It's a lot less damaging on the knees. You'd like it."

I tried to imagine myself in some bold-colored, skin-tight jersey and wearing a helmet with a little mirror sticking out the side. I didn't respond.

"You look like you're still canoeing," she said, giving her own shoulders a hunch and closing her fists in a mock muscle pose. I had kept some upper body mass on my lean, six-foot-three-inch frame.

"You do still have the Glades place, right?"

"Yeah. In fact I'm heading out back out there today."

"OK." She shifted her voice. "Let me tell you about this case, then."

I watched Richards's eyes while I sipped coffee and listened to her words. She'd been working on the disappearance of three women. All of them had vanished over the last twenty months. Their only connection was that they had worked as bartenders at small, out-of-the-way taverns in Broward County, they had no local family connections and their work histories were transient and sketchy. She hadn't found any long-term boyfriends, at least none appeared to be looking for them, and there had been no apparent signs of foul play at the apartment addresses the women had given their employers.

"So where's the FBI on these cases?" I asked, knowing the feds usually get their fingers into missing persons investigations if they show any overt signs of criminality.

"No interest," she said. "Too busy looking for weapons of mass destruction."

Sarcasm did not become her.

"These are women in their mid-twenties out living on their own. They keep hours that have them in and out of their apartments at all kinds of weird hours. Folks they work with rarely even know their last names. Hell, I got one set of parents that didn't even know their daughter was in Florida."

She suddenly looked very tired.

"You talked to parents?"

She nodded and then waited, waving off the waitress who'd approached with an order pad poised.

"I've been volunteering at Women in Distress, you know, the center and shelter for domestic abuse victims."

This I knew. When we had still been dating, Richards had taken in a friend, a woman who was being abused by a fellow cop. They'd spent late nights talking, discussions that hadn't included me. There had been some kind of kinship, maybe even a shared experience. Richards had become a protector of sorts, and furious.

The boyfriend had come to an ugly end on Richards's front lawn and the angry look in her eye at the time had not left my memory. It was heated and righteous and remorseless and now as she told her story, I thought I saw it flicker behind her gray irises, under control, but still there.

Afterward she'd taken her friend to the center, and then joined as a volunteer to "do something," she'd said at the time. Several times before we finally drifted apart I'd tried to ask her out and she'd begged off because she was "at the shelter." I never called it an obsession. People do what they need to do.

"Amy Strausshiem was the most recent girl to disappear," Richards started, setting her jaw, putting her game face on like she always did when she was determined not to show emotion. "Her mother came into the shelter. The woman had been to a dozen city police departments. She'd tried to talk the newspapers into running a story. She'd been to dozens of bars in the area, tacking up posters.

She'd been to drug clinics, homeless shelters and the goddamn morgue, Max."

Her eyes had moved on to a spot somewhere behind me, unfocused.

"All I could do was listen, no different than anybody else had done. I'm a detective but I've got no bodies, no ransom notes. These aren't children, or Alzheimer's patients or Saudi immigrants. Nobody gives a damn. They're just young women who are gone."

I knew that it was true of nearly any big metropolitan area. South Florida's missing girls were no different. Even the famous ones—Beth Kenyon, Colleen Parris, Rosario Gonzalez, Tiffany Sessions—were never found. Hell, in 1997 a man fishing in a canal spotted a rusted, overturned van in the water not far from the roadway. When the police wrecker pulled it out, they found the bones of five teenagers inside. They'd been missing for eighteen years.

Richards was on her own on this one, some kind of a mission to keep women safe on the planet, tilting at Cervantes' windmills I thought, but I wasn't going to say it to her face.

"OK," I said. "What makes O'Shea stand out in these disappearances?"

She again set her face.

"Two of the girls who've gone missing were definitely seen with him and a third one, maybe," she said.

I nodded.

"He's been in all of the bars where these girls worked just before they vanished and seems to have a circuit of places that he rolls through on a regular basis. Maybe trolling."

He's Irish, I thought, but didn't say it.

"He's had opportunity and he's an ex-cop who would know enough about how things work to get away with abducting these girls without leaving an obvious trail."

She stopped and was looking down at the table, maybe assessing how flimsy her evidence sounded when it was spoken out loud and left hanging out there. I stayed silent, knowing there had to be more.

"He's been involved in this kind of thing before, Max" she said, finally meeting my eyes.

Few people could surprise me the way Richards could.

"What? In serial abductions?" I said. "Jesus!"

"Not serial," she quickly corrected. "But the disappearance of a woman known to him and to other cops in your old city of brotherly love."

I must have been staring. Nothing in my memory even hinted at the kind of case she was talking about.

"I'm sorry, Max. I know you don't exactly keep up with news from home," she said, giving me a break. "A few years ago there was a hell of a dustup in your old division. Somebody sent in an anonymous letter accusing four local officers with having sexual relations with a young counter clerk at a local twenty-four-hour convenience shop. Faith Hamlin, an adult, physically, but the background on her was that she was working with a preadolescent IQ."

I shook my head, not sure I even wanted to hear.

"Faith worked the overnight shift at the store. Someone dropped a dime on the eleven to seven patrol crew that included O'Shea, said they were all getting sexual favors behind the counter or in the back room while on duty. Internal affairs probably would have deep-sixed the allegations, but the letter was full of names, times, dates."

"Was the girl the one who wrote the complaint?"

"No."

"But she substantiated it?"

"No," Richards said. "IA interviewed her but according to the reports, she denied everything. No sex, no inappropriate actions by the cops, all of whom she said she knew by name, but they'd only been nice to her and protected the place at night while she was working."

"OK," I said. "So they drop it, no complainant, no crime."

"Except a couple of days later, she disappears," Richards said. "Gone."

Richards caught me staring again while I tried to put the scenario together in my head. Preposterous? No. I'd heard the same kind of shit before. Cop groupies. Gangbangs. The tales got passed around in the locker rooms all the time. It was the victim and the disappearance that twisted this one.

"Don't tell me IA still dropped it?" I finally said.

"No. Actually I was quite impressed with the investigation that they did. Some woman is running the show up there and she's tough," Richards said. "They ground down all four guys, including O'Shea. Polygraphed three of them and got confessions on the sex acts but they all said they didn't know where Faith was and had no part in her disappearance."

"Three of them?" I said, knowing the answer. O'Shea refused the polygraph and quit. The investigation never turned up a body or signs of a crime. They had nothing to hold him on.

"He got a Florida driver's license eighteen months ago and gave an address down in Hollywood," Richards said. "He's been working security jobs on and off with Wachenhut and the Navarro Group, mostly pulling guard duty at marinas and car dealerships."

"Come to Florida. Shed your overcoat and your problems. Hell, cruise the beach and pluck oranges off the trees," I said.

I caught her watching me, a grin pulling at one corner of her freshly glossed mouth.

"Max, you sound like the CliffsNotes of *The Grapes of Wrath*."

"OK," I said. "I'll plead to intellectual plagiary. But what you've got is still circumstantial."

She went silent for several beats and again was looking beyond me.

"He's got this way about him," she said, shifting back to my eyes. "It's this quiet confidence. He's not one of those 'Hey, baby. Let's party' kind of guys. He's good-looking, smart and knows just the right things to say to these kinds of women to lure them, get them to let their guard down."

The quizzical thought running through my head must have been on my face because she answered before I could ask how she'd managed to get all her detailed observations.

"He tried to pick me up," she said and then seemed to wait for my reaction.

"In a bar?"

"Yeah. While I was working on the case."

"You went undercover?"

"Yes," she said.

"As a bartender to try and get someone to abduct you?"

"That's a blunt way to put it, but yes, basically to get a feel for what these girls were seeing and maybe get lucky enough to pull a suspect list together."

"Let me guess," I said. "O'Shea made you?"

"Yeah. Probably before he actually asked me out," she said. "Picked me up after work on our first date and when I got into his car he asked if we needed to stop at the P.D. so I could punch out my time card."

She was shaking her head at the memory.

"Hey, hard to pull that on a good cop. And the guy was a good cop when I knew him," I said.

She seemed to gather herself.

"But not when you didn't know him, Max. His department file showed three reprimands for undue use of force during arrests. He lost time while he was in an employee health services program, which probably meant he was drying out someplace even before the Faith Hamlin case."

The waitress came by. I nodded my head to another refill and took a long sip. I'd hate to see what my own department file would show. It had already made me a suspect once in South Florida.

I looked up at her and maybe she could see the doubt in my face, or maybe she thought she needed to put an exclamation on her motivation.

"His wife filed a domestic abuse charge against him, Max," she said, and her mouth went tight into a line. "He's not without some bit of a warm-up."

I let the words sit. I knew where her head was at, and there wasn't anything to say.

"You want me to talk to him," I said, more statement than question.

"Look, Max. God knows you don't owe me anything. But you've got a past with this guy. And you're good at reading people. Anything you could get might help."

I leaned forward.

"You got an address and number for my old comrade in blue?"

She pulled a business card and pen from her purse and wrote on the back. "He's been showing up at Archie's on Oakland Park on Thursday nights," she said.

I pinched the card between my fingers. She reached over and touched my hand with her fingertips as she slid out of the seat and then put two one-dollar bills on the table.

"It was great seeing you, Max. Thanks."

I sat and watched her walk away. This was a woman I'd swum naked with in the turquoise water of her backyard pool, who I'd made love to, with difficulty, in a rope hammock until dawn. Now I had no idea where we stood. No, I thought, maybe I'm not so good at reading people.

I was back at the Flamingo, tying on my running shoes. I was grinding at a case that wasn't mine, wasn't Billy's and that I wasn't sure I needed to be sticking my fingers in to begin with. My former fellow cop's face was becoming clearer to me every minute that I worried at the rough-edged stone of memory rolling around in my head. I wasn't sure I wanted to know his secrets.

I pulled on an old gray T-shirt and walked out to the beach to stretch out on the bulkhead. It was past noon, an insane time to run in the heat of an early September. The summertime highs of the low nineties wouldn't break for at least another few weeks. The sun was high and white and the only savior was the ocean breeze that had come up in the night and stayed, blowing the smell of salt and sargasso grass in from the southeast. I breathed deep while propping my heel up on the handrail to the wooden stairs. When my hamstrings stopped stinging, I walked the soft sand down to the lifeguard stand where a tall brown-skinned city employee name of Amsler was looking after a smattering of bathers. Weeks ago I'd introduced myself after spotting a setup under his stand where he had rigged a seven-foot-high chinning bar. I knew he saw me coming, but he never shifted his sunglasses from the sea.

"Hey, Bob," I said in greeting.

"Knock yourself out, Max," he said without turning.

I did twenty-five chin-ups with my palms turned in, blew out my breath, shook out my shoulders and did eighteen more with my palms out, touching the back of my neck on the bar until I failed at nineteen. I gave Amsler a wave off the bill of my cap and started jogging south against the wind.

I started slow, letting muscle and bone warm to the task. My knees had taken a pounding over the years and tissue had to swell a bit to cushion their ache. Real or imagined, I always felt a lump of pain high in my right thigh where a bullet had burrowed to the bone a couple of years ago. I rolled my head from side to side, stretching the tendons in my neck and picking up the twinge of long-term damage caused by another wound, a through-and-through in muscle near my throat that led me to take a disability payout and quit the Philadelphia department after ten years. I'd lived a violent life, had followed in my father's footsteps. The inevitability of it haunted and clung to me like an odor.

The sweat and swell and pulse of blood let me open up after a half a mile and I got into a rhythm. I worked a line down on the hard pack, trying to stay just above the surf wash, but still smacking through an occasional shallow film of water. I kept my eyes on the old lighthouse at the Hillsboro inlet and tried to convince myself I was twenty-five again. Though the more dedicated runners I've met say they try to get themselves into a mind-clearing state akin to yoga when they do long distance, I can never get that wall up and shut out my internal rambling. I've also never been in good enough shape to just run on endorphins and euphoria. It hurts too much. I checked my watch and at the twenty-five-minute mark I turned, waded in to my calves and scooped two hands full of ocean up and over my face and shoulders, and started back.

They tell you not to push so hard you can't carry on a conversation with a partner during a training run. By minute forty, I couldn't have had a grunting dialogue with a caveman. My lungs were burning and the blood was thumping in my ears. The wind was behind me but I could feel the push. Instead its direction only made the air I was trying to pull in taste warm and thick. I did the last half mile on guts and pulled up short of the lifeguard stand by a hundred yards. I walked the rest of the way, fingers laced on the top of my head like a prisoner on a forced march. As I passed his perch, my lifeguard buddy called out, "You're a glutton, Max," and he didn't have to say for what.

I stood under the outside shower for at least five minutes until a young boy whose parents must have been renting one of the bungalows came up with a bucket in hand and stared at me long enough to shame me into letting him have the spigot. I went inside, toweled off and made an overdue call to Billy's office. His assistant, Allie, answered on the second ring—a modern-day rarity in the new business world—and was her usual cheerful and professional self.

"Hi, Mr. Freeman. Mr. Manchester is back in town and left a request that you have dinner with him and Ms. McIntyre at the apartment this evening."

"Great. How was their trip?"

"They were both smiling this morning despite the jet lag," she said. "But Venice, who wouldn't," she said.

CHAPTER 4

I went to the kitchen, used the microwave to cook bacon, and put together two huge BLTs. I hooked a cold beer out of the fridge and had lunch on the porch in a chaise longue. Out on the horizon huge anvils of cloud were anchored several miles out, their flat bottoms a soot gray and tops bunched up like thick rolls of white smoke. There was weather out there, but I didn't know enough about the pattern to say what. I took a long pull of the beer and lay back, grinding on Richards's words, trying to pull her face into focus but instead coming up with Colin O'Shea's on the streets of Philly years ago.

I was out of my patrol car, walking the west end of my South Street beat like I'd been told not to do. The action on South was down by the riverfront where the street had recently taken on this hip revival. Artists and musicians and slackers pretending to be creatives had first moved in to low-rent apartments and storefronts that had been long ignored. And sure enough, the buzz that something different was happening brought more. People showed up to check it out. Capitalism followed the people. Now it was shops and clubs and restaurants and suburbanites with money and time on Saturday night. It wasn't a new phenomenon. People cluster together, commerce breaks out. The same thing had happened up on Market Street back in the 1680s when the city was first founded and look what came of it.

Of course the other element that followed commerce and people with money in their pockets were the predators. So my shift sergeant's orders were pretty clear: "Safeguard the tourists and business owners. Stay where the money is, Freeman, east of Eighth Street."

So I was west of Eighth, checking out rumors of a crack-cocaine stash house that was feeding the area addicts and newbies testing out the new high. I had parked the squad car next to a hydrant, took the portable radio with me and walked down past the "art garden." The garden was a funky strip of empty lots and old tenements that was festooned with painted designs, murals, gaudily decorated mobiles in the trees and collections of junk turned into baffling artworks. Even at night the collection of buffed aluminum and brushed tin would glitter in the street-lamp light. I ducked into a recessed entryway and frowned at the neon green color the door had been painted and peered around the brickwork. I was following my boy Hector the Collector who was dragging his cuffs a block away and didn't even bother to check behind himself.

I had pulled up on Hector's action in the crowds on the east side. For two weeks I'd spotted him making his surreptitious deliveries to the corner dealers and the bartender suppliers in the clubs. I'd even braced him in an alley one night, but my timing had been off and he was empty-handed but for a small wad of twenties that might have had some trace cocaine residue on them but hell, eight out of ten bills on South Street did.

"Yo, officer. What up, man?" he'd said when I spun him and pushed his face into the brick of the side wall of Mako's Bar and Grill.

"Spread 'em out, Hector," I said, rapping the inside of his knees with my baton and then going through his sweatshirt pockets and finding the cash. I stepped back and he snuck a look over his shoulder.

"Hey, it's the walkin' man," he said, smiling with his voice.

"Business a little light tonight, Hector?" I said, holding up the roll. "Or you change your hours of collections?"

He shook his head slowly and I knew there was a grin on the other side of it.

"No, sir, officer. You got me all wrong, walkin' man."

"You know I'm not wrong, Hector. I've been watching your game for weeks. And I told your salesmen, especially your man Sam down at the Palace, not on my shift," I said, poking the baton in his kidney for emphasis. "And not on my beat."

Now I knew the grin was gone. I saw the kid's scalp inch forward, pulled down by his frown. He didn't like me knowing the name of one of his main dealers who I'd caught passing rock in small plastic bags he tucked under the hollowed-out bottoms of beer schooners. The buyers were giving him huge tips and then always cupping the glasses with their opposite hand as they slid the drink off the bar, and then slipping that hand into their pockets. They thought it was stealthy. I picked up on it in ten minutes. It took less time to get Sam to flip on Hector.

"Hey, man. Chill," he said, trying to recover. "Why'n't you just stay in your damn car where it's nice and warm like the others, man?"

I didn't say anything, just took a step back, confusing him. He snuck another look but had to twist around to find me. His eyes were holding that I-don't-give-a-shit look and they were aimed at my hand where his roll was still in my palm.

"You can keep that, walkin' man."

I lifted my arm like I was shooting a free throw and bounced the wad off his head, and the bills separated and spilled down around his feet.

"No, Hector," I answered, using his own words. "You got me all wrong, man."

I'd left him alone for four days and now he was leading me to the stash house Mamma Blue had told me about. Four doors down from Mamma's Down South Country Kitchen, Hector checked the traffic and skipped across the street and disappeared into the alley between two boarded-up storefronts. I waited a couple of minutes in case he was smart enough to check for a tail and then continued down to Mamma Blue's.

A woman with a lot of hard years behind her eyes and a magical way with smothered pork chops and pan-fried chicken, Carline Dennis had opened her little restaurant years before the revival of South Street and had refused to move east to join the new current of money. She had built a clientele that cut across all racial and socio-economic lines because her place was friendly and courteous to everyone who walked across the threshold and her food was unmatched anywhere north of Savannah. The cars on the street in front included a BMW, two Mercedes, a sprung-bumper Cadillac and a sagging Corolla. I had been slipping in and out of her place since I was assigned to the district and twice had spotted the mayor inside having lunch.

When I stepped in tonight I was greeted by Big Earl, a man with mahogany-colored skin and hooded eyes who went about 320 pounds or more. It was Earl's job to deter any riffraff from entering or panhandlers from hitting on the patrons at the curb. He stuck out a ham-sized fist and we touched knuckles.

"What's up, boss?" he said in a burbling baritone.

"Mamma in back?" I said. "I need to use the phone."

Big Earl tilted his head straight back but the pupils in his yellowed eyes never moved, just rolled with the movement like buoy markers in water. With that permission I walked back through the full tables of diners, trying to be as unobtrusive as I could.

The kitchen was filled with the sound of crackling grease and the odor of seasoned steam. There was a high-rhythm dance going on between cooks and prep workers and busboys and dishwashers and in the middle of it all was Mamma Blue, sipping at a wooden ladle and looking like hurry-up was not a characteristic she ever wished to possess. The woman was as thin as a broomstick and her back was similarly straight. When I excused myself from the path of a waitress with a saucer of gumbo balanced on her palm, Mamma turned at the sound of my voice in her kitchen and gave me a full measure with her dark eyes.

"You ain't back here for no donation to the policeman's ball, baby," she said.

"No, Mamma. I need to use your phone, ma'am."

Her hair was steel gray and her pinched and leathery skin was so black it gave off a bluish hue just below the surface.

"You know where it at, Mr. Max," she said and turned back to the large pot of bubbling gravy she was doctoring.

As I slid past I touched her small crumpled ear with my cheek and whispered thank you and she smiled, but just as quickly a shadow of concern came across her face.

"You ain't doin' nothin' gone cause problems for my people in here now, Mr. Max?"

It was Mamma who had tipped me to the comings and goings of known crack dealers and runners from the building across the street. She had surmised that the suppliers had picked the location because of the block's eclectic mix of rich and poor diners. A fancy car here drew no second look, or a young man sporting a new Nike warm-up.

"Right under they nose," she'd said. "Lord, your own police commissioner eat here twice a week."

I had asked her why Big Earl hadn't told me. The man surely would have picked up on the action.

"Earl don't care 'bout nothin' cept me an his own self. What them boys doin' over there ain't his concern," she said.

Then why did she care? I thought.

Mamma seemed to recognize the question in my face and had said: "Earl is a man. He ain't never gave birth to no daughters who smoked they life away and they children's lives to ash with that crack. It's us women who carry that burden, Mr. Max. If you can stop it. Stop it."

That next day I'd started tracking Hector the Collector and tonight the trail was ending.

"I wouldn't put your people in harm's way, Mamma. I'll be

here," I said and went to the phone and called the narcotics squad. I'd been feeding them my surveillance for a week. Now I told them one of the main players was in the building. The sergeant on the other end asked a few questions, had a quick conversation with someone while cupping the mouthpiece of his phone, and told me they'd move on it with an entry team within the hour. I winked at Mamma Blue as I left her kitchen and she narrowed her dark eyes and turned back to her simmering pot.

I told Earl to stay inside for a while and the giant man either chuckled or belched and said: "Wasn't plannin' nothin' but."

I went out on the sidewalk and took up a spot in the shadows just east of the restaurant where I could watch Hector's stash house. The night was warm with the smell of alley trash mixed with exhaust fumes. If I smoked I would have lit a cigarette. I hated stakeouts. After twenty minutes my portable radio hummed with static and I stepped further back and answered.

"Just passed your squad, Freeman. You on foot again?" It was my narcotics friends.

"Affirmative."

"Switching to tack four," he said. I switched the channel on the radio to a less congested frequency where half the district wouldn't be listening in.

"We're calling in some patrol backup for a perimeter and we'll be going in through the back. You'll have some help when we go, Freeman. But you've got the front for now."

"I'm ten-thirteen."

A young couple came out of Mamma's and got in their car. When they pulled out, I saw their headlights slide over a dark figure across the street who was moving down the east side alley, the word POLICE stenciled onto his back in bold yellow letters. I walked back down to Mamma's entrance where Earl was standing, watching his customers drive away.

"Do me a favor, Earl," I said. "Keep everybody inside for the next few minutes."

He nodded his head, but his eyes stayed level, focused on something over my shoulder. I turned and saw Hector coming out of the west side alley, just starting to pull his sweatshirt hood up over his head, and he looked into my face.

"We're going in," the entry team's leader spat out from the radio at my side and the crackle was like a starter's pistol. Hector bolted.

"I got a runner," I barked into the radio and started sprinting.

Most foot pursuits are useless. Belts and radios and handguns and batons flailing on your hips. And most cops won't muster the kind of adrenaline it takes to outrun the fuel of fear that is jacking up the guy they're chasing. But Hector had become a special case for me, and he wasn't much of a track star. Within a block I was gaining on him. He made a stupid move no non-athlete should attempt by trying to hurdle and slide over the hood of a parked car to make the corner. He went down and I heard that ugly snap of leg bone when he hit the street. He'd gained one knee when I got a fistful of hood and hair and yanked him back down to the ground.

The kid reacted to the pain by squirming, but I put my own knee into the middle of his back and pushed his face into the asphalt with one hand while using the other on my radio.

"This is Freeman. My runner is in custody," I said, then had to catch my breath and look around. "Uh, corner of South and Thirteenth."

Hector had smartened up and quit struggling when the headlights of a car caught us from the north and stopped. I squinted into the brightness and heard the car door slam.

"Goddamn, Freeman. What kinda squirrelly animal you got there?"

When the uniform and the face stepped up I recognized Patrolman O'Shea. He was too handsome to be a real cop, and every time I saw him he had a bemused look on his Irish face.

"You on the perimeter, O'Shea?"

"Yeah. Heard on the tack that you had something going, Freeman."

I clipped my radio and took my handcuffs off my belt. O'Shea leaned in.

"Hey, it's good ole Hector down there. How you doin', boy?" he said, and then I felt and heard the patrolman kick the kid hard underneath me.

"Nasty-looking angle on that leg bone, Hector," O'Shea said. "Guess you won't be running too much in the yard over at Greaterford."

Hector sucked at his teeth in pain and whispered something about someone's *madre*. O'Shea cocked his boot.

"Hey, I got him, O'Shea," I said. "I got him under control here."

The words had barely cleared my mouth when the crack of gunfire sounded in the distance down South Street. O'Shea and I both looked up and stared out into the pools of shadow and light. Within seconds I caught a glimpse of spinning blue lights and heard the swell of sirens. I'd paid little attention to the movement of the kid below me and was just fumbling with the radio when I sensed O'Shea step forward and bark: "You little bastard!"

Hector cried out and I looked back to see a polished boot crushing the kid's hand into a small .38 caliber pistol he'd pulled from somewhere. I dug my knee harder into his back and heard the bones in his hand crack like a crab shell as O'Shea put all of his weight into it. He then reached down and I could smell the Dentyne on his breath as he wrestled the cheap gun from under the kid's hand and chucked it into the nearby gutter. He stood up with that smile and looked down at me.

"Now you're in control, Freeman," he said. "Now you're in control."

CHAPTER 5

When I woke up in the chaise, a pair of small blue eyes was staring into my face, topped by a mop of blond hair. I blinked and focused and when I raised my hand to wipe away whatever look I was holding on my face, the boy from the shower turned and ran.

I took a couple of minutes to orient myself, caught some bits of the dream still behind my eyes and then checked my watch. I'd been asleep two hours. I needed to get on to Billy's. I shaved and showered, dressed in khakis and a white un-ironed oxford shirt and slipped on my Docksides. The cab of my pickup truck still held the heat of the day so I kicked the A.C. up and pulled out, heading north on A1A. Though the trip to Billy's apartment building would be faster on I-95, I tried to avoid that craziness of high-speed tailgaters and opted for an occasional glimpse of ocean between the mansions and condos, even at the expense of hitting dozens of traffic lights.

When I got to the twelve-story Atlantic Towers, I pulled directly into the front visitor's lot. Twenty-four spaces, all of them filled. As I inched down the row, the burp in the pattern of parked Acuras,

Lexuses and high-end SUVs was a sedan that had backed into a spot. The driver was sitting behind the wheel. I stopped my truck and looked at the man, wondering if he was getting ready to leave. He pulled down his sunshade and waved me on. I could tell only that he was white, from the hands and thin arms. Maybe middle-aged, with a stubble-darkened chin. There was a long black telephoto lens attached to a camera body wedged on the dash and he turned his face away, searching the passenger seat for something, maybe a snack. I hated surveillance, too, I thought. By habit I filed a quick description of the car into my cop's head and moved on. I found a spot around the corner where the maintenance people parked and where my F-150 would not seem out of place.

The lobby of the Atlantic Towers was all polished marble and brass and the concierge/manager with the fake English accent was like part of the furnishing. He took a slight, barely perceptible bow when I approached his desk.

"Mr. Freeman."

I nodded.

"I shall call Mr. Manchester and announce you, sir." The phone was already in his hand. I again nodded and turned to the brushed stainless door of the elevator without comment. I didn't like the guy. Too damn frumpy. Plus, I knew he'd been born in Brooklyn and the accent was a put-on.

The inside of the elevator was paneled dark wood and the light on the penthouse button was already on. Seconds later the doors opened onto a private alcove with a handsome set of double oak doors at one end. I raised my knuckles to knock but a turn of the European-style brass handle beat me.

"Max, how wonderful to see you. Come in, come in," said Diane McIntyre, swinging open the door and then reaching up on her toes to kiss my cheek.

Billy's attorney friend, and now fiancée, was radiant. Her hair was a glossy and subtle auburn. She was dressed in a loose silk blouse oddly paired with sky blue sweatpants and was padding around in bare feet with a glass of wine in her hand. There was a smile on her pale but slightly flushed face. She was a happy woman.

Billy was on the other side of the huge single room, behind the kitchen counter, working some new magic at the stove.

"M-Max," he said, over his shoulder and then broke away from the steaming pot. "Y-You are l-looking healthy."

We shook hands and then he pulled me to him in an uncharacteristic embrace. "G-Good to see you."

While he got me a beer I sat on one of the stools at the counter and surveyed. I was familiar with Billy's penthouse, had lived here my first few weeks in Florida before getting settled into the river shack. I'd come and gone often as Billy slowly pulled me into his cases as his investigator. The big, fan-shaped living area was plush with thick carpeting and wide leather sofas. Billy's eclectic art collection adorned the textured walls and topped the blond wood tables. But I picked up some new, more colorful additions; a delicate ballerina sculpture, a large painting of a field of flowers. A woman's touch, I thought, as Diane pulled out the stool next to me, sat and took a sip of wine.

"So Max, let me tell you about our trip to Venice," she said, smiling and anxious like a little kid who can't hold an exciting tale any longer. I could see Billy grin and then while he cooked an incredible pan-seared snapper, we both listened, Billy only interrupting when he felt it was safe.

She was halfway through a description of a stroll through the Piazza San Marco when Billy said: "I w-was trying to f-find the similarities with Fort Lauderdale, the Venice of America, b-but just the water in the canals d-didn't do it."

Diane gave him a "get real" expression while he winked at me.

Billy is a supremely confident man. He is GQ handsome, athletically built, although I have never seen him do anything physically strenuous short of captaining his forty-two-foot sailboat. He is a brilliant attorney and had proven to me personally that he could manhandle the markets by investing my police disability buyout and making me comfortable if not rich. His only flaw is the stutter that embedded itself during childhood and has remained. On the phone or even from the other room his speech is flawless. But face-to-face he cannot control the staccato that jams his tongue. The stigma kept him out of the courtroom as a trial attorney, but sharpened his abilities to research and absorb through every other method of communication. And it hadn't seemed to slow him down when it came to beautiful women.

What Billy may have lacked in loquaciousness, Diane McIntyre made up for. The woman could talk. But I was always impressed by the intelligence and lack of bullshit that accompanied her discourse. She eschewed the typical small talk. Rarely gave opinions on something she wasn't knowledgeable about. And knowing that, you crossed her at your own peril.

Once, while working a stock fraud case for Billy, I'd been in the county courthouse when she was trying an elderly-abuse case. I'd ducked into the gallery seats just as she was ripping the skin off a state administrator in cross-examination. With a controlled passion she laid out damning statistics, entered photos of bedsores on her client, documented the phone logs from the seventy-eight-year-old woman's daughter showing calls to the administrator and the abuse hotline and recited, without notes, the state's own rules on oversight of their licensed nursing homes and how they'd broken them. Within minutes everyone in the courtroom, including the judge, was looking at the administrator, who could do little but hang his head. I still remembered her final line: "Would you put your own mother in such a place, Mr. Silas?"

She and Billy had been engaged since last spring. He had fallen hard, and it wasn't just because she was gorgeous.

Diane took us all the way through dinner and coffee with descriptions of the Basilica of Saint Mark and the Correr Museum and 2:00 A.M. wine tasting at L'Incontro. When the dishes were cleared, I thought she might continue but she gracefully excused herself with: "I'll leave you both to business while I go make some phone calls." Billy and I exchanged looks and took our coffee to the patio.

The dominating feature of Billy's apartment were the floor-to-ceiling glass doors that made up the entire eastern wall and opened onto the ocean. I stood at the railing and looked to the horizon where there was still a hint of blue.

"Anything n-new on Harris?"

"I've been watching him, but the press coverage must have pushed him under his rock for a while," I said.

Harris was a physician who'd been writing tons of prescriptions for pain pills to Medicare patients in return for kickbacks. Billy had been working the guy for a class action suit by a group of cancer victims. I was logging his movements and interviewing poor patients who had been or still were seeing him. We were doing well until a high-profile conservative radio talk-show personality got busted for feeding his pain pill addiction with illegal prescriptions. In the media frenzy Harris had significantly cut back his operation. But Billy had done his work and we probably had the guy nailed already. One of the radio host's lawyers had called Billy through the attorney grapevine, but Billy had refused to share any information.

"I'm more worried about the cruise ship guys," I said. "Rodrigo has been real twitchy the last couple of times I went up to talk with him. He's worried about his job and I think the others in his crew are telling him to back off getting any kind of legal representation because they'll all get blackballed from working."

Billy had me working a line on a dozen cruise ship workers who had been injured in a boiler explosion as their ship was coming in to the port of Palm Beach. The cruise ship business was huge in South Florida with tens of thousands of tourists packing the floating cities for luxury trips to the Caribbean. But the unknown population was the thousands of workers, almost every one a foreigner, who cleaned and catered and served and smiled for those vacationers for wages that those same Americans wouldn't let their teenagers work for. But the explosion had cast a light on their world belowdecks and Billy had been contacted to represent men who had been mangled and bloodied and burned during the accident. Rodrigo Colon was one of the burn victims willing to talk.

The cruise ship company had paid for their initial medical treatment and was putting them up at a second-rate hotel, but the workers all knew that once they left the U.S., any claims to treat their injuries or compensate them for their ruined bodies would be lost. Their contracts would be ripped up and they would lose all future opportunity to work in the industry. Billy knew he couldn't change the economics of the world, but he did think he could push the rich American cruise industry to do the right thing for those who had been disfigured and disabled in the explosion.

"It's w-worth it to k-keep trying, Max."

"Yeah, I'm bringing Rodrigo in to see you," I said. "Maybe you can convince him to recruit the others."

I was watching the blackening ocean. An uneven cloud cover blocked any early stars. Billy was waiting me out.

"Anything else g-going on out there?" he finally said.

I took a long sip of coffee and blew the heat out of my mouth into the sea air and told him about Richards's call and her request of me to interrogate an old Philly cop I'd worked with.

"That's w-what she said? Interrogate?"

"Maybe not that specific," I said. "She asked me to talk to him. Gave me the option. Didn't want me to think I owed her."

I was thinking of the dream, of O'Shea digging the gun out of Hector the Collector's hand. Did I owe him, too? Billy let the silence hang between us. It was not uncomfortable, but I could feel his eyes on the side of my face.

"I thought you t-two were through."

"Yeah," I answered. "I thought she was through with me."

Later I turned down the invitation to spend the night in the guest room. Things had changed in Billy's house. Diane came out of the den to kiss me good night and I was at the door when I stopped.

"Speaking of surveillance," I said, trying to be amusing, something I should have given up long ago, "I suspect you've got some paparazzi in the parking lot shooting film of your fellow residents or their guests."

They both looked at each other. Billy was first to shrug his shoulders. It was unlike him not to ask for details, but no questions were forthcoming. I backed out.

"Just be careful not to wear anything trashy out front," I said to Diane, pointing my finger from the blouse to the sweatpants.

"Good night, Max," she said and smiled, and I turned to the elevator and heard the oak doors lock behind me.

CHAPTER 6

He walked in, let his eyes adjust to the low light, and was pleased to see two open stools at the end of the bar—one for himself and the other for quiet. He'd been here before, a neighborhood place the way he liked. A single, twenty-foot real wood bar spanned one wall, its lacquered surface redone enough times to make the deep grain look like it was floating just below the surface. The lights rarely went to half strength, even during happy hour. Tonight there were two groups of drinkers along the bar: Three guys and a girl in the middle, all friendly and chatty. Three more men at the other end by the windows with shot glasses in front of them and colored liquor on ice at the side.

He sat on the stool at the other end and hooked a heel on the rung of the empty one next to him, staking claim on the space. He knew the bartender who was working the shift alone. She was in her mid-thirties and had lost her figure to the years but her face was still pretty. She came his way and stopped at the thigh-high cooler under the bar and pulled out a Rolling Rock, and uncapped it on her way.

"Hi, how are you tonight?" she said with a pleasant smile and put the bottle on a napkin in front of him. Her eyes were brown and clear and he'd determined when he'd met her before that he didn't like the intelligence he saw inside them.

"Fine, thanks," he answered, being pleasant himself. He took a long drink and looked into the mirror behind the liquor bottles on the shelves behind her. When he focused he could use the reflection of another wall of mirrors on the opposite side of the room and watch the drinkers all down the line. He liked that aspect of the place, being able to watch without being noticed. A television tuned to ESPN hung in the corner above him. The sound was off and one of the wry announcers was moving his mouth around while photos of boxer Mike Tyson flashed behind him.

Christ, he thought, there's your problem. If all your sports shows and media would just make a pact never to mention that asshole's name again, he'd disappear into the fucking alleys or the prison yard where he belonged. Why do they let an animal like that use them?

He tipped his empty at the bartender and then watched the reflection of the girl from the middle group walk behind him and load dollar bills into the jukebox in the corner. He took a drink of the fresh beer and tried to place the first tune, a thing from the past by Journey about a small-town girl livin' in a lonely world and a city boy born in south Detroit. He thought about Amy. On those late-night dates and long intimate conversations she had confided in him. Her parents in Ohio. Her father a drunk. She'd come to Florida to start fresh, had a girlfriend that was supposedly coming to visit but who had never shown up. She probably told him more about herself than she had any of her coworkers. He was a good listener. Women liked that about him. Christ, if she'd only kept her place instead of trying to run him. Hell, he could have loved her. Shit, she hadn't even raised her arm to ward him off when he'd shot her in the face.

He hadn't had to look around or wonder if anyone had heard the report of the .38. The Glades were like that, a few miles out and it was dark and alone. He'd taken a plastic yellow tarp from his trunk and rolled her body onto it and tossed her jeans and shoes on top. Then he'd pulled the load down through the trees and into the wet vegetation some forty yards from the dirt roadway. The moonlight had given him enough light to find a wet depression in the mangroves to leave her. He'd buried the first two and later he wondered why. All that forensics shit you saw on television was useless if they never find a body. And they never did. Other than that old woman running around with the posters of his second girlfriend, no one was even looking.

Christ, had it been a month? Two? He'd stayed out of the bars for a while, especially Hammermills. But he started back, had missed the air, the mix of cigarette smoke and perfume, the subtle sexual electricity—not like one of those strip places where the women were plastic and may as well have sticker prices on their asses. A place like this had real people, girls you could appreciate, women that you could fall for. He'd been growing anxious again, bored with work. The compulsion had come on faster than last time and he didn't fight it. He was lonely. He needed to own someone.

The song ended and he watched in the mirrors while the bartender greeted a new girl. They were changing shifts. The older one was being managerial, introducing her around to the regulars. She did the foursome at the other end, some of them shook her hand. The new girl was small and seemed slightly self-conscious but had worn a short skirt on her first night. She had good legs. She'd be popular in this place, he thought.

"And this is Lou and Tommy and Liz and, I'm sorry, Absolut on the rocks, what was your name again?" said the bartender, introducing the middle group now. The unknown customer reintroduced herself and actually reached out and kissed the new girl's hand.

"And down here at the end is Rolling Rock. Except when he's serious and then he's Maker's Mark," she said and smiled, pleased with herself.

The new girl nodded and smiled. She had blue eyes and curly blonde hair that didn't have to be streaked to be pretty but was. He gave her his polite smile and said hello. While the other bartender cashed out and gathered her tips he watched the new girl. She had two studs in her left ear. Three rings on her hands, one with a blue stone. Her breasts were not large, but on such a small frame they appeared voluptuous. After the other girl left, she busied herself with rinsing and wiping and setting things up her own way and motioned to the empty bottle in front of him. When she extended her hand, he noted that her nails were bitten to the quick.

"Another one?" she said, and her smile seemed easier.

"Yes, please," he said. "And a shot of Maker's Mark on the side."

I was up at the beach before sunrise and out on the edge of the Everglades by breakfast. Dan Griggs, the park ranger assigned to the five hundred acres designated by the state as a registered wild and scenic area at Thompson's Point, was cooking eggs.

"I think I got that lunker snook you've been trying to hook over to the west side down by the shade turn," he was saying from the back room.

"Like hell," I answered. I was pouring coffee from the ranger's electric maker in the office section of his dockside station.

"Yeah, I hate to say it. That crafty bastard been teasing you more'n a year now, right?"

He would not meet my eyes when he carried the pan of eggs in and pushed them onto two paper plates at his desk.

"Wasn't my fish," I said, setting his coffee in front of him and taking one plate. "He's too damn wise for you, Danny."

The ranger leaned back in his metal office chair and propped his heels on the corner of his state-issued desk. He was lean and blond and smiling when he dragged the plate of eggs onto his lap.

"He had to be twelve pounds."

"Liar."

He grinned and just looked at me over the rim of his cup.

"Catch and release?" I finally said.

"Of course, Mr. Freeman. I gotta leave you something to aspire to."

Griggs and I had gotten off to a shaky start when he'd taken the job several months ago. He was replacing an old and long-revered ranger who had been killed by a man whose presence on the river had been in part my responsibility. People who knew the story blamed me, and I had not argued the point. Then, government forces had been trying to evict me from the old research shack for which Billy had a ninety-nine-year lease. He was still in a paper fight with them by e-mail and Federal Express at my request. When someone tried to burn me out of the place I had put Griggs at the top of my suspect list, but the young man had spun my suspicion by helping to repair the damage with carpentry skills I sorely lacked. The camaraderie of the project and the guy's obvious love of the Florida wilds had led to a friendship and an admiration. That, and he liked a cold beer on occasion.

"Been pretty slow. Must be September," Griggs said, looking up at the clock. He didn't see me furrow my brow at the odd gesture.

"Some kayakers up your way last few days. A few fishermen out here on the wide. I suppose you've been in the city."

It had long been a practice of mine not to answer rhetorical questions so I stayed quiet at first. He knew that I did P.I. work for a living and romanticized it.

"I stayed at the beach," I finally said, giving in.

"Pretty girls?"

"Some."

We both were quiet for a few moments.

"Man. A vacation place at the beach and a residence in the swamp," he said. "You're a regular mogul, Mr. Freeman."

"Yeah, and I've got to get out to the mansion," I said and got up. "Thanks for breakfast, son."

Down at the dock I flipped my Voyager canoe and wiped out the webs that a golden-silk spider had put up between the struts. I loaded in containers of fresh water and a canvas bag of clean clothes and then floated the bow. Planting my left foot in the middle of the hull and gripping the gunnels on either side in a well practiced move, I pushed out onto the flat river water and glided out. When I'd settled into the stern seat with my paddle in hand, I turned to wave at

Griggs, who was standing on the dock with his thumbs in his belt loops, and I knew he was jealous.

The sun was high and white and flickering off the water and I took my first few strokes north and drifted. I moved my weight around on the seat to find the right balance and then put some shoulder into the paddling. The river was wide here and moved strong to the sea when the outgoing tide pulled at it. I kept my course close to the sand banks so I wouldn't have to fight the middle current, and found a rhythm.

The fumbling city boy who'd come here without a clue for the feel of the water and natural wind and wilderness had morphed into a competent riverman. The hours of hard paddling had earned me technique. I could dig into a purchase of water, pull through a stroke and kick the blade out at the end to send a spiral of water like a spinning teacup out behind me. And I could do it at sixty strokes a minute if I put my back into it. For a mile and a half I worked my way up past the sand pine terrain and then the low mangroves took over. The river narrowed and moved north and west for another mile until finally entering a cypress forest and tunneling into a shady greenness that was truly prehistoric.

My T-shirt was soaked through with sweat by the time I slid in under the canopy of trees. It was several degrees cooler here and I shivered with the change. I let the canoe drift in while I peeled off the shirt and pulled a dry one from my bag. The quiet here never failed to amaze, as if the lack of noise itself was something you could touch. Each time back from the city I could feel it cup over my ears like a changing of air pressure. I let the canoe come to a stop and listened for a full ten minutes before finally dipping the paddle and following the clearing water, which was now leading back to the South.

For a half mile I steered through the cypress knees that broke the surface and around fallen red maples. The hard sun was gone and the shafts that made it through the canopy speckled the ferns and pond apple leaves like luminescent streaks and drops of paint. Two bald cypress trees marked the entrance to my place and I paddled in on a shallow water spur off the main river. Fifty yards into the green my stilted shack stood hidden. I lashed the canoe to a small dock, gathered my things and after carefully checking for any footprints on the moist risers, I climbed the wooden stairs to, as Griggs had called it, my permanent residence.

Inside I stowed my supplies and started a pot of coffee with the fresh water on a small propane stove. The room held a mingled odor of mildew, still swamp air and fresh-cut wood from Griggs's and my repair work. The northeast corner showed the new honey-colored planks where we'd stopped and the blackened, soot-marked pine that was still structurally sound. Nothing inside was painted, so I'd left the scar. Along the opposite wall hung a row of mismatched cabinets above a butcher-block counter and a stainless slop sink. An old hand pump that might have been installed when the first owner built the place in the early 1900s as a hunting lodge still worked, with the help of some new rubber washers. With a half dozen pumps of the handle I raised water directly from the swamp below and rinsed out my coffee cup.

While the coffeepot burbled, I went to one of the two worn armoires that stood against another wall and searched the bottom drawer. I had not carried much to South Florida that would remind me of my Philadelphia days. There had already been plenty in my head. But I had a small, gray-metal lock box that I now pulled out and put on the big oak table that took up the middle space of the room. I poured a cup of coffee and sat in one of the two straight-backed chairs and slipped a key into the lock. Inside was an oilskin cloth wrapped tightly around my 9 mm handgun. I held the weight of the package in my hands and then set it aside. Underneath I'd tucked important papers: birth certificate, passport, a life insurance policy and three letters I had written to my ex-wife but had never sent.

Under them was an old photograph of my mother, taken when she was a shy Catholic nursing student. With it were her rosaries, which she asked me to keep as she lay on her deathbed. Snapped inside a plastic case was a medal of distinction from the Philadelphia P.D., awarded to my father back when both he and it were yet untarnished. I kept digging until I found the yellowed tearsheet from an old neighborhood tabloid.

It was a photograph of two dozen men, standing in uniform and looking self-conscious. My graduating class from the police academy. I was in the back row, among the tallest, face stern, hair short and swept to the side. I scanned the other rows but finally had to refer to the list printed in small letters below to find Colin O'Shea. He was in the second row, his hair curly and dark and seeming too long for standard requirements. His face was pale, his head slightly tilted as though he were about to whisper something out of the side of his mouth to the man next to him. The paper was faded, yet I thought I could detect a smirk on O'Shea's face. I took a sip of coffee and twenty-year-old memories came back.

He'd been good in class. One of the smart ones who would sit back and listen, watch the others offer up wrong or incomplete answers, and then just when he could tell the instructor was going to give in and enlighten us all, O'Shea's hand would fly up and he would have the answer down pat. He was a good athlete. Finished high in P.T. In team drills he would give a hand and encouragement to the stumblers and overweight guys, the ones who were no threat to him. But when it came to competition he would hang back just off the leaders, drafting, and then try to surprise and outsprint them at the end. It wasn't cheating. It was calculating. The better guys would still beat him, but he would still seem pleased with himself, like he'd pulled something off, had changed the finish and in his way won. I watched him, like I watched all the others, but stayed clear of his game. When he tried to use our connection to the South Philly neighborhood to buddy up, I just acknowledged him and moved away and stayed on my own path, whatever the hell I thought that path might have been.

I finally shoved the photo aside, got up and selected a book from the shuffled stack on the top rack of my bunk bed. They were mostly history and travel books—Billy's contribution to my derelict education. I spent the rest of the daylight reading a collection of stories by Ernie Pyle called *Home Country* out on the staircase landing, my back against the door. Between pages I looked out into the canopy when a quiver of leaves shook under the weight of a green heron.

While Pyle described the Drought Bowl of 1936 in the Dakotas, my ears listened to the low croak of a wood stork working the shallows to scissor a snake or baby gator in its long, drooping bill. After dark I warmed soup on the propane stove and ate it with the fresh bread I'd brought back from the coast. Later I sat in the pool of light from my kerosene lamp and listened to rain gather in the trees and then patter down on my tin roof. The irregular beat was not unpleasant. Finally I undressed and lay down on my bunk. It was just cool enough to use a thin cotton sheet as a cover. I left the lamp burning on the table. For some reason, lately, I did not want to sleep in the dark.

On Thursday I went back into the city. Billy and I had talked about work now that he was back. I knew from experience that his high energy level had him fidgeting to get plugged back in. I was bringing Rodrigo Colon into the office for a joint interview. I picked up the young Filipino down the street and around the corner from the hotel where he and the other injured workers were staying. The small man climbed into the passenger seat of my truck, pulling his right leg up after him.

"Hey, Rodrigo," I said. "*Kumusta ka?*"

"*Mabuti naman,* Mr. Freeman, *salamat,*" he said.

It was the extent of my Tagalog, but Rodrigo dipped his head at my effort. He was used to being spoken to in English on his job. He took my offered hand in greeting and then glanced nervously out the back window. When he turned I could see the wrinkled purple scar that covered the right side of his face. It was like a dark birthmark that spread from his now nonexistent eyebrow down over his cheek and disappeared into the collar of his shirt. Treatment of the burn from the escaping steam had left the skin the mottled color of a dark grape. Angry-looking stretch marks pulled at the corner of his mouth and eye when he smiled. I pulled away from the curb.

As I drove to Billy's office, Rodrigo watched the world roll by through his passenger window. Though he'd been a cruise ship worker for five years, his station as a maintenance-grade utility man kept him belowdecks most of the time. In the many ports of call, rarely did employees like him have the time to see the landscape. I asked if he'd heard from his wife in the Philippines. He nodded. Rodrigo and the others I'd interviewed through an interpreter said the company that signed workers up in Manila would pay for wives or husbands to visit, but only on the promise that they would both return home.

"Yes. She is sick for me," he said. "She is to come here, but has no money."

I pulled into a parking lot on Clematis Street and got a warm greeting from the operator who knew me. I took a ticket and we walked the four blocks through downtown West Palm Beach to Billy's office building. I caught our reflection in the plate glass of a clothing store: a tall and tanned white guy dressed like a weekend boat captain and a five-foot Southeast Asian with a limp and a tic that caused him to turn his face from each person he passed. It was South Florida. No one blinked. But when we reached the lobby, a familiar security man stopped us.

"Hello, Mr. Freeman," he said, talking to me but looking at Rodrigo.

"He's OK, Rich. One of Mr. Manchester's clients," I said.

"Sure, Mr. Freeman. But you're still going to have to go through the metal detectors."

"Yeah, we understand," I said.

It was a new world in America. One where no one simply vouched for another.

When we went through the security point, Rodrigo walked through without a beep but was still swept by a guard with a metal-detecting wand. It took me three passes, dumping everything I had in my pockets into a plastic box, until I finally found the offending foil chewing gum wrapper I'd stuck in my back pocket instead of tossing it out in the street. We rode the elevator to one of the top floors and entered a set of double doors that was unmarked. In the outer office we were greeted by Billy's assistant, whose usual charm and social ease seemed oddly strained.

"Hello, Mr. Freeman, so nice to see you."

"Allie," I said. "This is Mr. Colon."

They shook hands and Allie looked directly into Rodrigo's face without flinching or showing in any manner that she had noticed the burn pattern.

"I'm sorry, Mr. Freeman. He's running a bit late with an unexpected appointment," she said, looking back over her shoulder at Billy's closed door like she didn't know what might come out of it.

"I do have your coffee waiting, though," she said and asked Rodrigo if he would join me.

He declined and followed my lead and sat in one of the high-backed leather chairs, just on the front edge, his hands clasped in front of him as though he were afraid of getting something dirty. Allie brought the coffee and while I drank I watched Rodrigo cut his eyes at the paintings and artwork strategically spotlighted in the room.

In a low voice I asked him about his children at home to try to relax him and he turned and smiled, but before he had a chance to form a word the door handle to Billy's office snapped down and the door opened too quickly. A man marched out with a face like Rushmore, a stern look set in stone. He was white-haired and impeccably dressed in a blue business suit, stiff-collared white shirt and politically correct red-patterned tie. His shoes were freshly polished.

He did not acknowledge our presence or even offer a civilized response to Allie when she said: "May I call down for your car, Mr. Guswaite?" He walked directly out, leaving a silence and a slight movement of air behind.

"One moment," Allie said and slipped quietly into Billy's office. Rodrigo was studying his own shoe tops. He'd seen men of power pissed before. A few minutes passed and Allie returned with a professional face.

"Mr. Manchester is ready for you, gentlemen."

Billy was standing inside the door, his own impeccable suit jacket on, tie cinched up and his face showing nothing but amiability.

"M-Max. Mr. Colon, *Magandang hapon! Ikinagagalak kong makilala kayo*," Billy said, greeting Rodrigo in his own native language. The kid from the North Philly ghetto, I thought.

Billy steered us to the angled couches that faced the floor-to-ceiling windows. The view was extraordinary, looking east out over the lake and then the Spanish-tiled roofs of the mansions on the island of Palm Beach and the blue-gray Atlantic beyond.

"I kn-know you have t-talked with Mr. Freeman s-several times and answered m-many of these questions, Mr. Colon," Billy began, switching back to English. "But I n-need to hear them myself."

Rodrigo nodded, maybe understanding half of what Billy was saying. But his eyes were intent on the lawyer's face so I sat listening for a few minutes and then took my coffee to another part of the room, giving Billy the authority and control he needed to have.

While they talked I stepped around, reacquainting myself with the paintings Billy had hung in this, the space where he spent most of his time. All were originals done with such talent that you could not help but find a new angle or texture or blend of color that you had not noticed before. I roamed over to his bookcase, which was stacked only with Florida statues and lawyerly tomes that held no interest for me.

As I rounded his desk I saw a splayed-out collection of eight-by-ten photos of Diane McIntyre. They were cropped from the shoulders up and a warm but professional smile was fixed on her face. The white blouse under her blue business jacket was buttoned at the neck. Her hair was perfect. Among the shuffled papers were layout sheets I recognized as campaign posters and I recalled from Billy's discussion before leaving for Europe that Diane was considering a run for a county court judgeship. The stone-faced Mr. Guswaite, I thought, political animal of some sort.

Movement at the couches got my attention and I joined the others. Billy had put Rodrigo at ease and they were clasping hands, the lawyer saying something again in Tagalog and adding: "Please have Allie take down that phone number and Mr. Avino's contacts. *Ako'y nagpapsalamat*, Mr. Colon for your courage." When Rodrigo stepped out to Allie's desk Billy turned to me.

"Thanks for b-bringing him in, M-Max. I think w-we can work this without too much t-trouble. That part about the lower rung of workers getting p-paid by the cabin boys to handle some of their w-work so they can impress their supervisors by increasing their own n-numbers. It's amazing. The hungry ones work twenty-hour days just to g-get ahead. It's like an entire s-social crab pot on each sh-ship with race and color and p-payoffs all tossed into the mix and all invisible to the American customers around them."

"Nothing a good union couldn't fix," I said, only half joking.

"There's a p-political land mine," Billy said. "How about if we just try to get some of these m-men compensated for having their faces b-burned off?"

"Sounds fair to me. So how come the rest of them won't join up?"

"They're scared, M-Max. He says the Filipino job brokers have long arms. They make money by providing cheap labor, not on workers who have to get paid for injuries. He says the p-pipeline from Manila to Miami is short enough to send an enforcer to shut down dissent. They're all looking over their shoulders."

I told him I'd watch out. I'd already given Rodrigo my pager and cell number. We were already setting up prearranged sites off the street. But I didn't want to tell him that I couldn't afford to be the guy's twenty-four-hour bodyguard when we had other cases to work. My own acceptance of Richards's request had just put another pinch on time and I wasn't going to bring it up. I changed the subject.

"Speaking of politics," I said, motioning toward his desk and the photos and layouts.

Billy did not bother to look back.

"She w-wants to be a judge. I t-told her I would help in any way I could."

I stayed quiet. I knew Billy. His face said more was coming.

"But it s-seems that the good ole boy p-political cabal th-thought, when they heard her fiancée was a r-respected attorney, I'd be an asset."

"Let me guess," I said. "They didn't know you were black?"

"How w-would they? I'm never in the courtroom. N-not much for their f-fund-raisers or cocktail circuit."

"Jesus, Billy," I said. "You think that's going to make a big difference?"

He looked past me for a few moments. I could see something working behind his eyes, a twinge of pain he rarely ever showed. I wondered if he'd misconstrued my question, thought I'd pointed it at his and Diane's personal relationship.

"In love and politics, M-Max, everything m-makes a difference," he said, manufacturing a wry grin. "When you mentioned the paparazzi the other night, you weren't far off. We've caught people taking photographs of us together before, on the street, coming out of the courthouse, leaving one another's apartments."

"Campaign sludge?" I said. "I doubt an interracial marriage would cause a second look in South Florida."

Billy was still watching out over the skyline.

"State p-politics doesn't get run by the residents in South Florida, M-Max. The power is still in Tallahassee where the real South still runs d-deep."

His knowledge of law and languages aside, Billy had not left his ghetto beginnings and real-life taste of racism behind. I did not want to get into a discussion of his paranoia, or my naïveté, and left him at the window.

I drove Rodrigo to the block where he took treatments at a small walk-in medical clinic. Once again, around the corner and out of sight, we had lunch at a whitewashed lunch counter that opened out onto the street, with a row of worn swivel stools that sat on the sidewalk concrete. The place bragged on its original Cuban sandwiches and Colombian *arepas*. After my first mouthful I decided they were justified. If you can back it up, brag on.

While we ate, Rodrigo introduced me to three other cruise workers who had obviously come at his urging. One man wore a bandage from his wrist to his shoulder. Another covered his head with a large-brimmed hat, but I could make out the signs of singed hair and burn scars at the nape of his neck. I took down names and promised only to pass them along to Billy. I paid the bill and shook Rodrigo's hand and climbed back into my truck and headed south to the Flamingo where I might swim and sit in a sea breeze and forget about changing the world for a while.

*   *   *

I did ten blocks in the ocean, swimming parallel with the beach and looking up every twenty strokes to catch a familiar condo face or clump of palms or open street-end to mark my progress. Five blocks of freestyle south, against the current, five slow ones back, even with the push. Then I sat in my sand chair and let the sun and breeze dry the salt into a fine film on my skin, which seemed to crackle and pulled at the creases when I finally stood and went inside.

I tried to read, first the prerevolutionary Adams book and then the local newspaper: Palestinians and Israelis were killing each other. Madonna was, well, being a celebrity. Republicans were promising tax cuts. The front page could have been ten years old, or perhaps, sadly, ten years into the future. I thought of calling Richards to back out of my promise to meet with O'Shea, tell her I was too busy with work for Billy, tell her something important had come up. Instead I went out and sat on the porch until long after twilight when all the color had leaked out of the day.

CHAPTER 7

I got to Archie's Bar at nine and was instantly put off by the glass-fronted door that had never been changed from when the place was the coffee shop or H&R Block office or nail salon it had been in a previous life. Not exactly the Irish pub I was expecting. I'd found a parking spot around the corner on a side street that bordered the out-of-date shopping center. I plugged the meter with quarters and then walked all four sides of the square before going in. After leaving Billy's office I'd become paranoid myself about a tail. It wasn't anything specific, no matching headlamps or too familiar silhouette of a single driver. But it had been a feeling I'd learned over the years to pay attention to. My sidewalk sweep of the center and the parked cars hadn't pushed it away.

The lights in Archie's were too bright for my liking and once through the entry I slid immediately to the left to a spot with a wall and a view. The bar itself was a shallow horseshoe. A row of small tables barely big enough for two ran down the wall in front of the bar. Three bigger tables filled the space at the rear of the room. OK, I thought, maybe it had been a deli.

There were twelve seats at the bar, all of them taken. Two women in their fifties sat in front of me, drinking something dark in ice. A thick, cloying perfume made me step back and I watched the tip of one of the women's cigarettes dance with the movement of her lips as she spoke to her friend. Next to them were a couple of beer drinkers; polo shirts with printing over the left breast pockets, both of them wore mustaches that worked down into beards that just covered their chins, one red, the other dark. Their eyes kept flicking up to what had to be a television screen that must have been in the corner above me facing out. I skipped past the two younger girls, one who sat determinately with her back to the Fu Manchu brothers. Next to them was a gray-haired guy who appeared to be in his sixties who was bent into a video poker game bolted to the bar, his pale face changing color along with the glow of the screen.

There was a couple talking animatedly next to him and then my only possibility at the opposite end, sitting alone next to the opening where the bartenders would have to enter and exit. His hair was dark and curly, trimmed above the ears, and the overhead light caught his prominent cheekbones, which from where I stood made his face appear gaunt. His shoulders were broad, but sitting down it was hard to guess his weight. The sleeves of his denim shirt were rolled to the elbows and his hands were folded in front of a beer bottle, knuckles up.

I stayed against the wall. His eyes seemed to watch everything and nothing, moving from the TV to the tables just behind him, from the girl couple to the bartender's ass when she turned away from him, never lingering long and never coming close to locking on mine. It had been ten, maybe fifteen years. If it was O'Shea, I couldn't tell from here. I pushed off the wall and began to work my way toward his side. The room was smoky and a stereo was playing some kind of techno-country thing that was too loud for the space. I shuffled between the tables and the people standing. The place was at capacity, over if the fire marshal decided to come by.

The guy at the end never turned to watch a six-foot three-inch man move up next to him, but when I got to his elbow he turned before I could say a word.

"Hey, Max," he said, offering a newly opened Rolling Rock that I had not seen him buy. "How 'bout those Phillies?"

His eyes were clear and gray with only the creases at the corners to give away his age. The pull at one side of his mouth, the Irish grin, had not changed.

"Colin O'Shea," I said, accepting the bottle. "Wasn't sure it was you."

"Is that why you took fifteen minutes to get over here, Max? I thought maybe you were just casing the place for a quick robbery."

"Didn't think you'd noticed."

"I might be old and off the job, Max. But I haven't gone blind yet. I think I even saw you get a snootfull of Annette's perfume over there," he said without turning. "To be honest, it's why I sit way the hell over on this side."

No, I thought. You've still got your cop instincts, O'Shea. You're over here because you always sit with your back to the wall and your eyes on the front door to see who walks into the place.

"So, how the hell you been? It must be, what, a dozen years?"

"Might have been that night they had us all on that fire at Methodist Hospital when they had us doin' the evacuation," he said.

The memory was vague in my head, a winter night, people in wheelchairs, firemen with crusts of ice on their jackets.

"I think I remember you hauling some old bird down the stair-well and he was already yakking in your ear about suing some-body."

"Yeah, and you were probably escorting the nurses, O'Shea. Al-ways the ladies' man."

For the first time, he snapped his eyes on mine, just for an in-stant, trying to find something there.

"So, you on vacation, or what?" I said, looking away.

"Yeah, sure, Max. This is part of a special Disney package." He waved his bottle in a small circle.

I shrugged my shoulders. Let him tell it.

"Naw. I've been down here maybe three years now," he said. "Got sick of the cold. Needed something new."

I nodded again.

"I heard you were down here somewhere, though. Guys up in the district said you kinda wigged out after you took that .22 in the neck and dropped both of those skells in the Thirteenth Street robbery."

My fingers started to go instinctively to the soft, dime-sized circle of scar tissue the bullet had left just below my ear, but I stopped myself. One of the suspects I'd killed that night was a thirteen-year-old who was unarmed.

"Hey, that was a righteous shooting, man," he said, clicking the lip of his bottle against mine and raising his eyebrows in a conspiratorial expression. But he was stepping into a space where he had no right to enter and I felt a small sulfur flare of anger heat a spot between my shoulder blades.

I let it sit and O'Shea drained his beer and wiggled it at the bartender. He watched her walk to the cooler. When she bent to dig out a cold bottle from deep in the ice her short top slid up, exposing a tattoo of some kind low on her back and blooming up out of the waistband of her jeans. O'Shea watched without blinking, but so did I, and so did the mustache boys. She returned and put the beer in front of him.

"There you go, darlin'," she said and looked over at me with a question. I waved her off.

"Friendly place," I said. "Your regular stop?"

"Just one of many, Max. You know us Irish. But it is regular enough for me to know it's not one of your stops, old friend."

The tone had suddenly changed.

"Yeah, well, I was . . ."

"Asked to stop and check me out?" he said, interrupting. "By a long-legged blonde detective who doesn't give an old alcoholic cop enough respect to know an undercover sting when he sees it?"

I was surprised enough to stay quiet while considering an answer. O'Shea looked behind me and then signaled the bartender.

"Tracy. We're gonna take a table," he called out to her. She waved and he said: "Come on, Max, let's sit a bit."

He took the chair against the wall under the St. Paulie Girl poster, leaving me with my back to the crowd. The beer maven above him held six steins and a smile and he matched her grin.

"Good-looking woman that Detective Richards," he started. "Maybe the legs threw me the first two shifts she did over at the Parrot, but not much more."

"You knew why she was there?"

"At first, no. I figured the local narc squad was trying to hook into the over-the-counter trade. I'd been told that back in the day every bartender in South Florida had a connection. But that shit's over. Law enforcement isn't interested in the nickel-and-dime stuff anymore. And the dealers are way too careful now."

"She said you hit on her, Colin," I said, trying to catch something in his eyes.

"Yeah? She like that?"

I felt a warmth rise into my ears.

"I was trying to figure her game," he said, then took a long drink of his beer. "She was a lousy bar girl. Worked hard, but didn't work the customers very well. Acted too friendly too soon. Asked too many questions. I watched her do some other locals before she tried me. Bartenders don't interrogate. They remember the drink you order, not your hair and eye color and any distinguishing scars."

I could see Richards doing the rail of men at the bar like a lineup.

"Well, Colin, you've got the eye of experience to know a good barkeep when you see one."

"OK, I'll give you that one," he said without a hint of offense. "I've fucked up in the past. You probably already know about internal affairs in Philly, about my ex and the domestic violence charges. But I've never hit a woman in anger, even though I don't expect anyone to believe me."

He looked away, maybe with embarrassment, but then turned back.

"I was an ass and I'll admit it. But fucking disappearing women? Come on, Max."

His eyes were looking into mine now, and I couldn't turn away. He knew how cops hate to be stared at by perps. He was trying to show me he wasn't one of them.

"So you know what the detective's after. What's your assessment?" I said, appealing, maybe, to the cop still in him.

"On what? A serial abductor of barmaids? Shit, Max. It's a target-rich environment down here, but you're talking about sick. That's not some sex crime of opportunity. Some sex assault wants that, cruise the beach late at night. Hell, go after the chicks at the dance clubs, drop some Rohypnol in their drinks and voilà! Happens all the time."

I took another drink. He was right. I let him go on.

"Shit, these girls behind the bar are smart, Max. They got the assholes trying to play them every night and they can see 'em coming a mile away. I don't see them falling for some crazy fuck."

"So why don't you tell that to Richards? Help her out. Get her off your ass?" I said.

"No, no, no, Maxey boy. You must know that one. You wouldn't be here. What, you got a P.I. ticket and worked a case with her before? She pulled my Philly file and made a connection and sent you on a confidential informant mission?"

I stayed silent.

"No way," he said. "She's a man-eater. She wants somebody's balls on the wall and I'm not handing her mine."

He sat back then against the wall. Shania Twain was singing high and hard. O'Shea raised his hand to signal someone, then held his thumb and forefinger two inches apart and tipped the small, imaginary glass twice. I wasn't sure whether to push him or leave him. If I was going to feel guilty afterward, so be it. He hadn't blinked yet.

"Richards says you dated two women who are now missing, not a trace," I said. "What was the saying in the academy, Colin? Twice is a coincidence, three times is a felony?"

The bartender left her busy station and came and set down two shot glasses of honey-colored liquor and fresh beers. It was the first table service I'd seen in the place. She put her fingertips on O'Shea's shoulder before walking away.

"Look, Max. I date a lot of women. I go to a lot of bars. Hell, I dated Tracy a few times," he said, tipping his head to the bartender as she left. "And there she is, in the flesh."

"Yeah, how about Amy Strausshiem?" I said and the name made him turn his face away. He sipped at one of the whiskeys.

"So Amy's one that your new friend Richards is looking for. Who else?" he said.

I didn't answer and just shook my head. Even if Richards had given me the other names, you don't give information to suspects. Besides, it wasn't my case, I kept telling myself. All I did was agree to talk with the guy. O'Shea seemed to accept the silence.

"I heard Amy's mother was in town," he said and I almost believed the sound of sympathy in his voice. "I went out with her. Nice girl. Smart. But she was too much of a challenge for me if you know what I mean."

"No," I said. "Tell me what you mean."

"She liked excitement. Liked to get her adrenaline up, which is fine to a degree, but Amy was walking a wire. I don't need that challenge, Max," he said, finishing the shot and winking at me. "I don't date women for the challenge."

O'Shea had a reputation as a ladies' man back in the day. The dark curly hair and the smooth talk. But I remembered a time at McLaughlin's, a cop bar in Philly, when three of us watched him try to work a woman at the jukebox. No one warned him it was another cop's girl and when the guy got back from the men's room an anticipated confrontation went flat in a hurry when O'Shea tucked tail and slunk away.

"You ever date my ex-wife back home, Colin?" I said, surprising myself, but suddenly wanting to know. The question made him laugh.

"Christ, Max. Everybody dated your ex-wife," he said and then watched my face.

"Look, only time that woman took a break was the months she was married to you, Max. But once that conquest was done, she kept right on mowin' through 'em."

I tried to keep my face straight, just stared at the booze sitting in the tiny glass in front of me.

"Is that an answer, Colin?"

"OK. Yeah, I went out with Meagan. The girl was like a dominatrix without the whip, man. Goddamn control freak. Everything was about her. First sign of weakness—*Bam*!

"You know that television show, *Highlander?*, tough guy with the sword who lops some other guy's head off and then sucks the guy's power in to make himself stronger? That's your ex, Max. No way. I bailed quick on that one."

I was shaking my head, watching the ripple my own movement set up in the amber whiskey. Maybe I let a wry grin of my own move the corner of my mouth, remembering.

"Hey, Maker's Mark," O'Shea said, signaling the shot. "Have some good stuff with me, Max." But I was thinking and didn't respond.

"Hey," he said again. "I'm serious."

I left O'Shea at the table with the glass still full. I shook his hand, told him to stay out of trouble in a half jovial way, and made my way outside. On the sidewalk I took several deep breaths of night air to get the stink of cigarette out of my nose and looked up to find the moon. It was nowhere in sight and the city lights obscured even the brightest stars. I looked at my watch, almost eleven, and weighed the effort it would take to get back out to my river shack. The world seemed infinitely more complicated now than when I'd started my day.

I went down the street to my truck and for some reason noted the deep shadow cast by the intracoastal bridge. I flashed back on Fulton Street where we played summer basketball in South Philly in the shade of the I-95 overpass as kids and where we would then hang out and smoke stolen cigarettes in that same darkness. Simpler times, I was thinking, when I made the corner and came upon two men breaking into my truck. The sight deeply soured my mood.

The larger of the two was standing at my driver's door, his weight leaning into the panel, his attention on something inside. The other one was up in the truck bed, actually sitting on the far rail, elbows on his knees like he was waiting for something. They were either the laziest car thieves I'd ever seen or weren't car thieves at all. I glanced quickly behind me and then stepped out into the street.

The smaller one saw me first and hissed and nodded to his friend. When the big man turned I saw the baseball bat in his hand and I could feel the adrenaline start to simmer in my blood.

"You guys looking for a ride to the game?" I said.

The big one turned and squared up. The other stayed seated up top and sniggered, nonchalant, like it was no big deal, like the chickenshit backups always did. I wouldn't have to worry about him unless I went down, then he'd come in with the steel-toed boots for the cheap shots.

"They said you got a smart mouth," said the bat man.

I stepped up closer, within ten feet, about the size of a small boxing ring, where I felt more at home in a possible ass-kicking.

"They were right. Maybe you'd like to give me their names, I'll send them my apologies," I said, stepping two feet closer.

"Only message they need is that you're gonna lay off dealing with the cruise ship workers," Bat Man said.

I checked the one up in the truck bed. He was still seated.

"What? You two shit-heads make a left at Haymarket Square? Busting unions with a stick?" I said, taking one more step and rolling my weight onto the balls of my feet. The bigger one choked up on his bat at the 'shit-head' slur. "I'm impressed with your sense of history, boys."

A frown of stupidity barely flickered across the big man's face while I assessed his one-handed grip on the middle of the bat. He'd be quicker when he swung it, but the blow wouldn't have nearly the impact. From the corner of my eye I saw the other one stand up. He was looking down, but behind me, and then I heard O'Shea's voice.

"Yo, Max. You forgot your change ole buddy," he said, wading right in. "And boy, it looks like you need it. What, the meter run out, fellas?"

The smaller man fought his cowardice and started to jump down to even the odds but it was dark and he misjudged the distance to the street. When he landed it was on the side of his heeled boot and his ankle went over like a crushed aluminum beer can and he yelped in pain. When Bat Man turned to see his partner go to one knee, I charged him.

I went low, head into the sternum, my elbows out, legs driving. His big body gave for two feet and then slammed to a stop against the door of my truck. Immovable object. I heard him whoof when we hit, but he was solid and didn't go down. I tried to grab a fistful of shirt for leverage and that's when I felt the whip of the bat across my shoulder blades. If he found the back of my head I was done.

My face was still pushing into his chest and when he stretched his arm free for a better aim, I flexed my knees. He must have swung down at the same instant I drove my full six-three up. The top of my head hit something blunt and square that gave in with the crackling sound of someone chewing ice. The bat blow landed low on my back without consequence, but a shard of white pain shot down from my head into my spine. I almost lost consciousness, but there was no almost for Bat Man. He slid down the door of the truck into a heap with me on top of him.

When I blinked my eyes to clear the spinning flecks of light in them I heard the repeating sound of someone kicking a wet sack of leaves and breaking the sticks inside. After too many blows the noise stopped and someone took me under his arm and helped me stand.

"Whooo-wee, Max. Aren't you some trouble, man."

O'Shea was breathing hard, but the other man was curled into a pile, maybe not breathing at all.

"Shit, man. That was some rock 'n' roll," O'Shea was saying. "I haven't stretched those muscles since I left the street."

I staggered a couple of steps but wobbled and felt the pavement start to tilt.

"Whoa, big guy," O'Shea said and helped me to the curb behind my truck and set me down. The top of my head felt like it grew in pain and size with every pulse of my heart and I was still blinking spots out of my eyes.

"Got some blood coming off that scalp, Max," O'Shea said. "Old Sammy Sosa there get the bat on you?"

"Head-butted him," I said. I reached up and patted the wet hair over the throbbing spot and came away with a dark stain on my fingers. "Guy must have a glass jaw."

"Yeah, well, you might be right 'cause it's in pieces over there now," O'Shea said, rocking back on his heels and looking. "You didn't learn that at Jimmy O'Hara's boxing gym."

I held my eyes closed for a moment and when I opened them a red film faded and my vision started to clear.

"Yeah, and you didn't learn that, either," I said, looking out at the lump in the street. "Is that guy still breathing?"

"Shit, yeah. He won't be doing it easy for a while, but he's breathing. Whattya think, I'm a killer or something?"

I could not tell if that was a mocking tone in his voice, but I could hear the distant wail of sirens.

"Shit, somebody called it in, Maxey ole boy. Time to go," O'Shea said.

He got up and looked around for witnesses.

"Easy, Colin. They're a couple of leg breakers who were sent to scare me off a case," I said. I wasn't yet even close to being able to stand.

"Yeah, OK for you, Max. But in the current state of things with your local law, I ain't takin' the chance of a night in lockup. That detective bitch of yours gets me in, I'm stuck for the long ride."

The siren was louder. I thought I could actually feel it on the back of my eyes.

"You gotta get her off me," O'Shea said, backing away. "You know I'm stand-up from the neighborhood, Maxey. Get her off me."

The sound of him trotting away into the night was then overwhelmed by the siren that wouldn't quit and blue lights whirling onto the walls, and I had the sudden urge to wretch.

*   *   *

I was in an office at the Oakland Park P.D., sitting in a metal chair, holding an ice pack to my head. I had refused medical treatment at the scene while paramedics loaded Bat Man and his friend into the ambulance. The big man had been able to walk with help. The other one was put on a stretcher. Neither of them was able to talk so mine was a one-sided explanation: Two guys tried to mug me with a baseball bat. Things got a little crazy.

I showed the officer my license, gave them my keys so they could check out the truck and registration. I repeated my story three times: I had a couple of beers at Archie's. I came out to find two guys trying to break into my truck. I tried to chase them off and they turned on me.

I almost thought I was going to walk away with one of those "We'll be in touch" deals when a shift sergeant by the unlikely name of Dusty Rhodes showed up. He talked with the patrol guys and surveyed the scene.

"How 'bout we take a ride into the station Mr., uh, Freeman," he said, looking at my license. "Let the nurse take a look at that wound and see if maybe your head clears a little."

So now I was stuck in the sergeant's office, my head was somewhat cleared, but my story wasn't gaining any more credibility.

"So you take on both these boys, uh, one with an extensive record of aggravated assault, battery on a law enforcement officer and attempted manslaughter," Rhodes said, reading from a sheet of printouts, "and the other one with possession with intent to sell narcotics, simple assault and some damn thing here that looks like conspiracy to be an asshole."

He shook his big, block-shaped head.

"And all by your lonesome?"

He was a veteran, a grizzled and old Southern shit kicker who didn't like things that stepped out of their logical order. I wasn't going to walk without giving up something. I told him I was an ex-cop from Philadelphia.

"I see," he said. "So this wouldn't have nothin' to do with some drug deal gone squirrelly?"

I told him I was a private investigator and showed him my license.

"I see," he said. "So you maybe worked with someone locally who could speak for your good standing, Mr. Freeman?"

I told him to call Detective Richards with the Broward sheriff's office. He looked at his watch.

"And Sherry is gonna vouch for you?"

"Yes," I said.

"I see."

He left the room and I shifted the ice pack, wondering immediately if I'd suffered brain damage. Then I rationalized. Favor for favor. She wouldn't mind. I looked at my own watch. After two in the morning.

In a few minutes Rhodes came back in with a cell phone in his hand.

"The detective would like to speak with you," he said, but stayed where he was after handing over the phone.

"Yes, Detective," I said.

"Are you OK, Max?"

She sounded legitimately concerned.

"Yeah."

"The sergeant says this mugging was down by Archie's and he's not convinced you were alone."

"Yeah."

"You were meeting with O'Shea?"

"Yeah."

"Did that bastard have anything to do with this?"

The intense anger in her voice took me aback.

"No. They were breaking into my truck."

"So one guy is still spitting teeth and the other had his ribs kicked in. Doesn't sound like you, Max."

"OK, sure. Maybe we can meet up tomorrow," I said, looking up at Rhodes and trying to look positive.

"Max, if that son of a bitch was setting up another girl . . ."

"Yeah. He's right here. Thanks. Call me tomorrow, I'll be home," I said and handed the phone back to the sergeant.

He left the room again and when he returned he had copies of my driver's license and P.I. license in his hand and a young patrolman at his side.

"We will be in touch, Mr. Freeman. Even though I suspect them other boys ain't gonna say much more than you when they're able," he said, handing me back the originals.

"Officer Reyes will give you a ride back to your vehicle."

I thanked him and dumped the ice pack into his trash can before standing.

"To be honest, sir," Rhodes said before stepping out of the way, "I don't like a stink in my backyard that I don't know the source of. So I hope this one blows away 'fore I step in it."

"That's honest enough, Sergeant," I said, and left with my escort.

CHAPTER 8

The new bartender's name was Marci and once he learned her shift he started hitting it regularly. He always tried to get the seat at the end of the bar, so he could use the mirrors. By now she would notice him coming through the door and have an open beer waiting.

"I'm impressed," he said the first time she remembered his brand. She'd given him that quizzical look, like she wasn't sure what the compliment was for. They liked compliments, he knew, unless they were rude.

"That you'd remember," he said, tipping the bottle. She smiled and he liked the shape of her mouth.

There was a knot of people at the middle of the bar, voices already cranked up with liquor, the one guy telling stories, impressing the others. He sipped his beer, looking up at the television for a minute and then watching Marci's legs when she went to the far end to wait on one of the old farts down there nursing their shots. He made sure he didn't let her notice him staring at her when she bent over the bar to hear a customer better and gave them all a better look at her cleavage. She wasn't dumb, he thought. Girl knows where the power is.

She came back his way, noticing the empty he'd slid into the trough.

"So, how was your day?" she said.

"Good. Kept busy. Met some new people. Made some money. No complaints," he said, being pleasant. They liked upbeat.

"How about you?" he said. They liked it to be about them.

"I went to the beach," she said proudly. "I swore that when I left Minneapolis I'd hit the beach every day."

He filed Minnesota away in his head. Long way from home.

"You, uh, do something different?" he said, waving his fingers around his own head but looking into her eyes. She gave him the quizzical look again.

"No. Oh, the ponytail?" she said, pulling the blonde whip of hair over her shoulder. "You like it?

"Yeah, I think so," he said. "Shows off the new tan."

She smiled again and when someone motioned to her from down the bar she kind of bounced away, pleased.

He drank his beer, played it cool. An occasional customer would nod at him in recognition and he would nod back, but always turn away. He was only here to get to know one person. He wasn't here to make friends. He looked straight ahead, used the mirrors to watch the rest of the room. The storyteller down the bar had taken over, rooster in the house, he thought. The two women in the group were already a drink over their limit and he was working to impress them. That's when the brothers arrived.

He heard the motorcycle come rapping up outside, the driver giving the throttle an extra twist of rpm's to announce himself. The first one in entered with a grin, hair blown back, T-shirt and jeans, neither of them black. He worked his way past the group at the middle of the bar and took the stool next to the quiet man. The second one entered with an amphetamine smile. He went straight to the rail.

"Hey, little blondie, come on down here with a bottle of Jack," he said, loud enough to make sure everyone noticed.

Marci took a shot glass with her. The head of the middle group turned too quickly and took in the character: Big guy, hair ruffled up from the wind, wearing the requisite black vest over black T-shirt. No jewelry but the poorly done, single-color prison tattoo was a dead giveaway to the quiet man, but he sipped his beer, watched the smaller, calmer brother next to him in the mirror and listened.

The group turned back to their conversation while the speed-baller downed two shots of Jack Daniel's and pointed Marci down to where his brother was putting down the money. He then insinuated himself on the gathering in between.

"Well ain't this a boring party," he squawked and draped a meaty arm over one of the women's shoulders.

"Christ, this isn't gonna last long," said the brother, maybe to himself, maybe to the quiet man who was looking ahead into the mirror. The brother went to put money into the juke and the volume of some overplayed rock song obscured the conversation going on down in the group. The quiet man snuck a look at Marci, who caught his eye and rolled her own. When the music stopped the argument seemed to ratchet up, like it was trying to fill the void. Suddenly the speeder and the rooster were facing off.

"You're a fucking liar, man. You didn't do no three years in fucking Starke," the big brother was yapping.

The rooster had turned but was leaning back, both elbows still against the bar.

"I've been inside," he said. "And I don't give a shit if you don't believe it."

"And I'm calling you a lyin' bitch," said the speeder, lowering his voice and sneering the words. "I'm out three months and the only way you was inside was as somebody's bitch."

The quiet man was watching the speeder in the back mirror now, waiting to see if a blade was going to come out of a back pocket. Marci stepped up on a beer case behind the bar and said: "Come on guys, settle down, all right. Settle down, we'll have one on the house."

The rooster hadn't moved his elbows. Dumb ass, thought the quiet man.

"See!" yelped the speeder. "Proof's right there. Nobody inside gets called somebody's bitch and then just stands there."

The guy strutted away from the group, point made, and came over to his brother, who was keeping his head low. "Shit, Bobby. Thought that bitch was gonna bend over for me right there," Speeder said, sniggering and taking one of his brother's shots off the bar.

The quiet man could see him in the mirror and tell he was still excited by his low-life conquest. His shoulders twitching, eyes jumping.

"So, who we got here, brother Bob? This a friend of yours?"

"Yeah, he's a old friend. Drinkin' buddy, right?"

The brother's voice was nervous. He'd probably spent his whole life trying to avoid getting sucked into his shit-head sibling's trouble.

"Well, hell, drinkin' buddy. How bout linin' up some drinks, then?" the speeder said, leaning into the quiet man and putting a pale forearm on his shoulder.

The stench of dried sweat came off him, mixed with the sweet sting of gasoline and exhaust. When the speeder removed his arm to turn and ogle and insult another woman passing through the bar the quiet man caught Marci's eye and he ordered a single shot of Maker's Mark. When she set it in front of him, he reached into his pocket as if to pay but brought out his police badge folder instead. He turned the shield face up and put it next to the shot, the silver of the official department seal glinting in the overhead lights.

Brother Bobby saw it first and looked at the side of the quiet man's face. The quiet man was still staring straight ahead and in a low voice he said: "Tell your fucking convict brother if he touches me again he's going back in the slam and the trip won't be pretty."

Bobby found the quiet man's eyes in the mirror and got up from his stool.

"Come on, Davey. Let's get outta here, man. This place is a dive," he said to the speeder, putting his body in between his brother and the bar and moving him toward the door.

"Come on. This is dead, man. We'll go down to the Riptide and score some shit and some real women who want to party."

Bobby was working him fast, not giving his brother a chance to object or latch on to anything else to spit his bile on. When the rip of the motorcycle engine sounded and the screech of tire on asphalt faded, the entire bar seemed to exhale.

When Marci turned back to the quiet man the badge was gone and he was sipping his whiskey. She took the bottle off the back counter and said: "This one's on the house."

He finished the shot and set it down and she poured.

"Thanks," he said. "That's sweet of you."

She had that quizzical look on her face.

"You're a cop?" she said softly.

"Shhh," he answered, putting a finger to his lips.

She smiled and turned away, tossing that tail of golden curls over her shoulder. He sipped the new whiskey and smiled to himself and whispered: "Got her."

CHAPTER 9

I was on the beach with a borrowed straw hat on my head and sitting under a wide umbrella. The breeze had gone flat and the ocean surface was calm and rolling like the slow swelling hide of some big sleeping animal.

I'd brought two sand chairs down after calling Richards and arranging to meet her here. My skull was still throbbing. I'd washed the blood out of my hair in the shower and poured peroxide on the wound last night. My attempt at a bandage came off during a twisting, turning sleep so I elected to leave it open to the sea air. A sure cure for open cuts, according to all those grandmothers who never lived near the ocean.

I was reading more of Adams's years in France when I heard her sharp whistle. I turned and Richards was up on the bulkhead, two fingers pronged into her mouth, the other hand shading her eyes against the morning sun. She waved me up but I shook my head and waved her down. Then I watched all her body language of frustration as she took off her business pumps and made her way down the wooden stairs in her dark slacks. She'd be pissed. But I never liked being called to someone's side like a dog to its master. She knew that, didn't she?

"Good morning," I said. "Too nice out here to resist. Here, I brought you down a chair."

If she was angry, she swallowed it and sat down in the low chair in the shade, taking obvious care to brush away any sand.

"How's the head?"

"Only hurts when I laugh." I tapped the straw hat and smiled.

"Well. Your carjackers aren't laughing. Sergeant Rhodes tells me one guy had to have his jaw wired and the other has four broken ribs."

There was no question in the statement. So I didn't reply.

"He says he's doubtful that you would be able to cause such damage alone, despite your extensive law enforcement background."

It still wasn't a question.

"Neither one of these gentlemen wanted to bring charges against you and refused to give statements. I told Rhodes that you'd probably do the same."

She was quiet and might have been listening to the brush of water on sand but I doubted it.

"I already gave him a statement," I said.

"Right. That you surprised them while they were breaking into your truck and they attacked you. You alone."

This time she waited me out. I knew what she wanted.

"I talked with O'Shea in Archie's," I said.

"And?"

"He was hard to read. It's been a while," I said, avoiding her eyes. "He admits he hops a lot of local bars. He admits he knew Amy Strausshiem. He went out with her. And he has no idea where she is."

"He brought it up?"

"Sherry, he saw me coming a mile away," I said. "Just like he made you."

She looked out at the water, seeing some vision stuck in her head, thinking.

"I know you must have interviewed other bartenders, managers? Did they give you anything on O'Shea? Or anybody else you looked at?" I said

"Christ, Max. As soon as you put the idea of a serial abductor in their heads they start thinking gargoyle. Who's the ugliest, creepiest guy in the room," she said. "This generation doesn't even know who Ted Bundy was."

But they do know about the Gainesville Killer who slaughtered three University of Florida coeds and took out a boyfriend in the process. Give them some credit, I thought, but kept my mouth shut.

"The guy that looks like Freddie Kruger isn't going to get anywhere close to these women," she said.

I'd worked with detectives who focused on their convictions before, refused to back up and look wide.

"Look," I said. "O'Shea said he dated lots of women. You talk to any of them?"

"A few."

"He scare them?"

"No. They went out with him, had a good time on a date or two. Some he stayed friends with. Some he never called back."

I concentrated on not even moving my chin. She was watching for "I told you so."

"Maybe they weren't what he was after," she finally said.

"The missing girls have anything else in common?" I said. "Physically? Emotionally? Were they addicts?"

"No, goddammit! They were smart, lonely women who didn't have close families and were bartenders, Max."

I shut up and let her fume. She'd probably done this same dance with her supervisors half a dozen times. I could tell she was out there on her own on this one, obsessed. Maybe too much.

"The guy takes advantage of that loneliness, Max. The woman behind the bar is the one who runs the room and all the men who want a drink and a peek at her ass," she said and I was getting uncomfortable with the way she was staring out at the sea. "I see him as a guy who doesn't act like the others. He's smart. It's like a challenge to him. He's nonthreatening, likable even. He brings their guard down somehow. Just like O'Shea."

"And then what?" I said.

She didn't answer.

"Kills them for the thrill and disposes of their bodies without a trace? That's kind of Jekyll and Hyde," I said.

"Are you denying that O'Shea is a violent man, Max?" she said. "You saw him. You saw him boot stomp that guy last night. That was the two of you in the street, wasn't it?"

I didn't answer.

"You wouldn't cripple a man like that, Max."

"All right," I finally said, turning my face to the water. "The guy's got issues."

I knew it was a bad choice of words when I heard it come out of my mouth.

"Issues? He's got issues?" She stood up. "What? Are you defending him now? You guys have a few beers, relive old times and then go out and kick some ass together and become brothers in arms all of a sudden?"

I stayed in my chair, knew I hadn't played it well.

"He knows you're after him, Sherry," I said quietly.

"I *am* after him, Freeman. And whether you help or not, I'll still be after him."

It is hard to storm away from someone in soft sand. But Richards was a woman with talent and she did it effectively.

I stayed on the beach for an hour after she left, watching people walk the water's edge. The old shell hunter staring down into the sand who made a pouch for her collection in the folds of her long dress. The jogger with curls of gray hair on his chest and headphones clipped over his ears and his mouth moving to a song only he could hear. A young woman walking alone, her narrow shoulders down and her sunglasses pointed out at middle distance, not in a hurry, not with a purpose, her lips in a tight seam. See no evil, hear no evil, speak no evil.

I could sit here and let the blue drain out of the sky and the water. I could let Sherry Richards chase her obsession alone. I could let a man who had once saved me from a bullet twist in the wind. I could let the unknown fates of a number of innocent women remain just that, unknown. I could just listen, "no different than anybody else had done," Richards had said. Even though I couldn't change the world, "it's worth it to k-keep trying," Billy had said. But all the roads in this case led back to Philadelphia, a place I had run from long ago.

I sat and listened to the surf whisper and watched the light go out of the sky until the horizon disappeared. Then I got up and went into the bungalow and made some long-distance calls to voices I had not heard in years.

CHAPTER 10

I changed my plans the minute I walked out of the terminal of the Philadelphia International Airport. I'd have to stop somewhere to buy a coat and at least another pair of socks. I was freezing my ass.

The sky was solid gray and sat low over the city like a dirty tin bowl and I had to search to find the wiper knob on the rental car to clear the cold drizzle off the windshield. I got on Penrose Avenue and coming over the George Platt Bridge I could both see and smell the smoke and steam coming up out of the refineries below. I tuned the radio to KYW and listened to that familiar sound of a newswire machine chinking in the background and the patter of a deep-voiced announcer accompanying working folks through their day. I had spent my entire life in an intimate dance with this place. I should not have been surprised by the way I remembered the steps, both the easy ones and the moves that were ankle breakers, but I was.

I turned up Broad Street and saw both the day Tug McGraw led a World Series parade and the night I killed a maniac in an abandoned subway tunnel just below. Farther north I passed South Philly

High and in my head found the smell of fresh-cut grass on the football field and three blocks later the odor of chemotherapy drugs dripping into my mother's veins at St. Agnes Medical Center.

A horn blasted behind me and a taxi driver was tossing his hand up at the now green light. I ignored my instinct to flip him off and when I heard an advertisement for a coat sale at Krass Brothers I turned east and moved on into the old neighborhood. The years in Florida had thinned my blood if not my memories. February in Fort Lauderdale is eighty degrees and sun. I needed to get warm and I had work to do.

Before I'd left Florida I told Billy about my confrontation with Bat Man and his unfortunate sidekick and the warning about union organizing and the cruise ship workers. He didn't seem concerned. I told him I didn't have their names yet and he said he'd get them off the public records on the police run sheets and incident reports and then check them out.

When I'd told him I was going to Philadelphia the thought had silenced him in a way I'd never seen before. Billy is never stunned, by calamity or foolishness or the myriad whims of humans. He stared into my eyes as if he were looking for some truth in them and then quickly gathered himself.

"I w-will stay in closer contact with Mr. Colon," he said. "You will do, my friend, what you need to do."

He then helped me find a series of electronic clippings from the *Philadelphia Daily News* and the *Inquirer* databases on the disappearance of Faith Hamlin and the subsequent investigation of five police officers. Colin's name and suspicion were prominent, especially after the others confessed and supposedly came clean. I thought I recognized two of the other names but couldn't be sure.

Billy also found the present name and address of O'Shea's ex-wife, through the divorce records he got from an attorney contact in Philly. With a name and date of birth, we found her address in Cherry Hill, New Jersey, across the river from the city. Then I called my uncle Keith. He was still a sergeant in the Eighteenth District and he was understandably shocked to hear from me.

"Jesus Christ, Maxey. Is that you? Where the hell are you, boy? You in trouble? Christ, we thought you fell off the fuckin' edge of the world. You coming to town? You're coming over to the house then, right? No. No. Better you come over to McLaughlin's first. You know your aunt. We'll have a couple before that whole scene. You know she still goes to visit that church your mother turned to in those last years and she says feels her sister there. Damn, Maxey, it's good to hear your voice, boy."

I hadn't managed ten words. When he finally took a breath I told him I was coming in on business. I was working for a lawyer in Florida and did he know anyone in internal affairs that might help me out?

"IAD and lawyers, Maxey?" I could see him shaking his old Scottish head. "The devil and his henchmen. But for you, son, we can find someone maybe we can trust."

I had planned to go straight to my uncle's but on South Street I stopped at Krass Brothers. When I stepped out into a puddle of slush in my Docksides, I made a mental note to hit the Army/Navy on Tasker for some boots. In the store the terse, clipped speech— "Whattaya, forty-two long?"—caught me off guard at first. South Florida isn't exactly Southern, but I hadn't realized how much of my own whipcrack city-speak I'd lost. When I told the guy, "Something warm but I'm not going skiing," he tried to get me into a knee-length cashmere. When I told him I wasn't working for the stock exchange he pushed a three-quarter leather on me.

"Hey, I'm takin' my pops to the Flyers' game here!" I said, trying to regain a bit of Philly speak.

He found me a tan, goose down waist-length with cloth elastic cuffs. I thanked him very much.

"Yo, I thought you was just offen' your yacht or somethin'," he said, looking without shame at my shoes.

I got a pair of lace-up work boots on Tasker and then drove through the neighborhood.

The streets seemed too narrow, the stoplights too frequent. People on the sidewalks had their heads down in the sleet, not that I would recognize anyone. On Tenth I got caught behind some joker double-parked but I just sat there five doors down from the house I grew up in the next block past Snyder. I waited, looking at the old stoops and the front window of the house where a kid I knew named Fran Leary used to live. It was still ringed in Christmas lights. A young guy wearing the same leather coat I'd just turned down came out of a doorway and waved at me before he got in to the double-parked car and pulled away.

I moved up until I could see the cut-stone steps and the wrought iron rail that led up to the house I grew up in. The second-floor window that looked out on the street was to my room, where I had spent nights reading books and fantasizing about Annette the cheerleader and listening to the Allman Brothers Band on a tinny old record player. It was also the place where I cowered and tried to ignore the sound of my father's heavy, drunken steps and the sharp snap of a backhand and the muffled protests of my mother. I was one hundred feet away but did not want to see my front door and feel the ugly memories that I'd closed behind it. I had seen both of my parents die in that house. My father, a broken and shamed former cop, fell to a slow and deserved poisoning. My mother, who came home from the hospital to die, convinced that God had filled the hole left by her treachery with cancer.

I turned east instead and then up Fifth and past South Street to the Gaskill House, a bed and breakfast where I'd reserved a room. The place was a redone coach house built in 1828 just a block from Headhouse Square. The manager of the Gaskill had befriended me when I was walking a beat there by showing up with hot coffee at eleven o'clock each night at the corner of Third. His name was Guy and now, years later, he met me at the door with a handshake and what may have been the same huge ceramic-and-steel coffee cup.

He was envious of my winter tan and Florida address. I was, as always, envious of his collections of antiques and the stone and wood eat-in kitchen down on the basement level of the house.

"Your friend Mr. Manchester called and faxed three pages for you, Max," Guy said. "I put them in an envelope on your bed upstairs. We got a cancellation so I've given you the blue room at the top.

"Remember, breakfast eight to ten," he said as I climbed the stairs.

The room was done in Colonial-era furniture, poster bed, writing table, a small fireplace on the west wall. The thick comforter and window treatments were blue and muted yellows and dark burgundy, colors you rarely saw in Florida. I pulled out some paperwork and sat at the desk and called Colin O'Shea's ex-wife. I'd put off contacting her until I got here, not wanting to give her an easy excuse to dismiss me. She was now listed as Janice Mott. It was past five when I called and introduced myself as a private investigator from Florida, which at least keeps people on the line if only for the sake of curiosity.

"I was a Philadelphia officer with your ex-husband, Colin. We actually grew up close to each other in South Philly," I said, a dose of familiarity.

"If Colin has debts, Mr. Freeman, I have no idea where he is. I haven't seen him in years," she said.

I could hear kids in the background. I thought I was going to lose her.

"No, ma'am. I know where he is. I just saw him two days ago," I said quickly, taking a chance, a gamble, that she would care.

She lowered her voice.

"He's not dead, is he?"

"No, Mrs. Mott. He's all right. He kind of got jammed up down in Florida and I'm, uh, trying to find out more about his, uh, domestic background."

Once again, I knew I'd used the wrong wording.

"He never hit me, Mr. Freeman," she said, the words now almost a whisper.

"I'm sorry, Mrs. Mott, he . . ."

"Colin never physically abused me when we were married," she said.

The statement held both a sense of strength and apology.

"I know they called it domestic abuse, but it wasn't physical." She hesitated. "It was a way out."

A way out, I thought. She'd already left him by the time O'Shea got caught up in the disappearance of Faith Hamlin.

"I, uh, really don't know anything about the details of your past relationship, Mrs. Mott," I said. "But honestly, that is the area I'm trying to explore," I said.

"To help him or hurt him, Mr. Freeman?"

She was smart and blunt. And she would see right through any bullshit answer I might toss her.

"Honestly, I don't know, Mrs. Mott," I said, and waited.

"Colin does have that effect, doesn't he?" she said.

"Confusion," she answered her own question. "It's his stock-in-trade."

She agreed to meet with me, in a public place. Her son had an ice hockey game at three the next day. Meet her there, with identification, and we could talk. No promises.

I pulled around to the back of McLaughlin's at eight. It was already dark and I had missed the transition from daylight. There was no fade of color, no blue to disappear, no rose-tinged cloud of sunset. The gray had simply turned a deeper gray and then been overtaken by the dusty glow of city light. The sleet had turned to light snow and up in the high streetlights it drifted down and swirled in whatever wind current caught it off the buildings. It turned to slush on contact with the concrete and car tires slashed through it on the street. I was hatless and shivered and then heard the music in McLaughlin's buzz against the window and went inside.

The place was full and conversation was battling with an Irish melody on the speakers, neither winning. For someone used to the natural humidity of the subtropics, the hot, dry air was enough to make you want to drink just to dehydrate. It was a cop bar, dominated by clean-shaven faces, working men's clothing, the pre-game show to the 76ers' game, an appropriate locker room level of loud voices and the guffaws of a joke badly told. The few women present were older wives and the young ones' impressionable girlfriends.

I spotted my uncle at a table in the back. He was flanked by a couple of cronies his own age. As I worked my way back I saw his eyes pick me up halfway and make a decision before the smile started. He was out of his chair, rattling the pitcher and glasses on the table with his girth before I reached him.

"Christ in heaven, Maxey boy," he said, embracing me with his stovepipe arms and wrapping me in the smell of cigar smoke and Old Spice aftershave.

"You are as skinny as a fuckin' sapling, boy," he said, standing back at arm's length. "And dark as a goddamn field hand." A few heads turned, but not for more than a look. My uncle was an old-timer. Gray-haired and thirty years with the department, his language and his political incorrectness was grandfathered in. He introduced me to his friends, both with over twenty years themselves, and we sat. There was a pitcher of beer on the table with a frozen bag of ice floating in it. An open flask of what I knew was Uncle Keith's special blend of Scotch stood as its companion. He poured shots all around and raised his own for a toast.

"To the wayward son, what took the money and run," he announced with a wink.

"Aye," said the others, and we drank.

For the next three hours we drank and they told old stories. Carefully and with loyalty to my uncle no mention was made of my father, the legendary one whose death would always remain a secret of the brotherhood of the blue. We drank and I described only the beauties of Florida, and their eyes went glassy with reverence of a dream of golf and sun. We drank and my uncle exhorted me to show the bullet wound scar in my neck and they toasted Mother Mary for bad aim and mercy. We drank and they bitched about pensions and union stewards and the job in general and when I found an opening and asked Keith about an IAD contact they stopped drinking.

"We got a guy there, I called and gave him a heads-up, Maxey," my uncle said. "His name is Fried. He got attached over there a few years back after blowing out his hip in a pileup with a fire truck responding. He was with the detective squad up in East Kensington. He'll give you what he can."

I nodded my head and watched the others doing the same, avoiding my eyes. I could feel the vacuum at the table.

"IAD and lawyers, Max," he said, echoing his words on the phone from Florida. "Can I ask what it is you're into, son?"

We leaned our heads in together and the others tried unsuccessfully to pay no attention.

"I'm actually checking in on a former cop, a guy from my rookie class, Colin O'Shea, from the neighborhood," I said. "Any recollection?"

Since I was a pissant kid I'd known my uncle's brilliance for names and descriptions. He was the human equivalent to getting Googled. When he hesitated I knew it wasn't because he was stumped. He was considering his answer as he looked around the table and caught the glances of his crew.

"That would be the O'Shea of the Faith Hamlin situation?" he said, now watching my eyes.

"Yeah," I said. "I did some research."

Now he and the rest were looking down into their drinks, uncle Keith shaking his big head.

"Not a good time for the department or the district, Maxey," he said.

"Tell me."

He brought his eyes up and started in, his voice low but his mouth stiffening with the distaste of the telling.

"Had to be four years ago, after you left, word goes out on a missing persons' report out of the district. A woman, middle twenties, ya know, kind that elopes to Atlantic City or something. At first nobody pays much mind."

He stopped to sip his special blend. The other guys are straight-faced, like a poker game, but when they follow my uncle's lead, you know they're all listening and agreeing.

"But this girl, people know. She was a kid from the neighborhood who was kind of an outcast. Connellys down on Tasker had taken her in from a relation when she was young 'cause they couldn't handle her. She was, you know, not really retarded, but slow. Kids her age avoided her. But she did know how to, you know, ingratiate herself on people, trying to get them to, uh, accept her I guess."

"An' not bad-lookin', neither," said one of the crew, a veteran who'd been introduced as Sergeant Doug Haas.

"Not that I was going to add that detail," Uncle Keith said, narrowing his eyes at Haas.

"What?" his friend said. "I'm lying?"

Keith turned away.

"The family understood this, her physical attributes, and tried to keep her in someplace low profile," he continued. "They got her a counter job, working the register at this little corner store on Fifth Street near Sinai Med Center. She did the overnight, selling coffee and smokes to ambulance drivers and such who worked late."

"And cops on the beat," I said.

"Yeah," Keith said, and the heads went down and shook together.

"So somebody gets the word when she goes missing and tongues are waggin' because these cops on the Charlie shift are always in the place and they aren't offering up much in the way of information, like on the last time they seen her and such, being that she just disappeared off the face of the earth in the middle of her shift and nobody sees anything."

He took another sip, getting to it more slowly than Uncle Keith was used to getting to it.

"The rumor ain't rumor for long. Word gets around that these four cops were passing her around, each getting a piece of it back in the storage room while each partner was watching the front."

"They said she liked to pay them back for protecting her," Sergeant Haas broke in again.

This time my uncle just shook his head in agreement.

"And Colin O'Shea was a part of this?" I said.

"He was one of them," Keith said. "And once IAD got onto the case, he was the only one who didn't come out and finally own up to what they'd done."

"They cracked them?"

"Like fuckin' walnuts, Maxey. All of them were suspended and eventually fired for what they did to the girl even though she wasn't underage and she wasn't around to dispute that it was consensual. But to a man, they all said they didn't know where she'd gone or what happened to her."

"All except O'Shea," I said.

"He never admitted any part of it and was never seen in the city again."

"Christ, IAD must have done some knuckle pounding," I said. "Was this guy Fried the lead on the case?"

The table again went dead still. No one would look up from their whiskey. No sipping, no head shaking.

"And what else, Uncle Keith?" I finally said.

"Well, Maxey. You got somebody else over in that office that you have some recollection of from the past," he said, looking up through those damn bushy eyebrows that had scared me as a kid. I waited him out. "Meagan Montgomery is her name now."

"Meagan?" I said. "As in my ex-wife, Meagan?"

He nodded and said: "Yes. She would be the lieutenant for the unit now, after she caught the Faith Hamlin case and sent five cops down the slide."

I let the vision of my wife of two years sit in my head, as it had too many times on the plane trip back here. The one memory I thought I could escape was dead in the middle of my investigation.

"Well," I finally said. "I'll bet she can cut some balls off over there, eh?"

The old men in the crew sighed their relief, and then a bit boisterously I lifted a toast to women lieutenants and we drank, yet again.

At the end of the night I promised Keith I would stop by the house to see my aunt and shook hands all around. My head was swimming with the booze and music and smoke and faces. Outside, the sky had cleared and the temperature had dropped. The air felt like a slap. When I tried to breathe deeply through my nose to sober myself I caught that old familiar feeling of the air crystallizing in my nose and my eyes started watering. February in the Northeast, I thought and pushed my hands into the pockets of my new coat. I took a cab back to the Gaskill. Last thing I needed was a DUI. I'd get the rental in the morning on my way to the police roundhouse and my appointment with the IAD contact. As I sat in the back of the cab I tried not to think of Meagan Montgomery and the possibilities.

I woke at nine in the big four-poster bed of the blue room and panicked in fear. I had no idea where I was. The thick comforter around me, dark maple wardrobe, a fireplace on the opposite wall. Gaskill. Philadelphia, Scotch whiskey. In seconds it tumbled into focus but I was still unsettled that it had taken longer to right myself than it should have. When I stood I felt uncomfortably old.

Thirty minutes later I was downstairs in the kitchen drinking coffee, eating one of Guy's fabulous omelets and scanning the first few pages of the *Philadelphia Daily News*. Guy was devilishly accounting his own story of booking the entire house to a contingent in town for the Republican National Convention a few years earlier and their slow realization after they arrived that his was a gay-owned and -managed establishment.

"Of course when they left the next day I charged them for the full four days and they paid without a peep."

I got a cab to my rental and it took fifteen teeth-chattering minutes to get the heater up to speed. I was at the roundhouse near Franklin Square at eleven for an eleven-fifteen with Detective Fried and I parked in the visitors' lot.

On the third floor there were few uniforms. Shirts and ties. Suit jackets. Secretaries and doors with brass nameplates. Pure administration. I'd worn my collared shirt. Guy had read the extra-close shave and hint of cologne and had lent me an expensive sweater. The cuffs of my pleated chinos came down far enough to disguise the black work boots that still had a manufacturer's shine.

I checked in with the IAD assistant and waited uncomfortably in an anteroom for Fried. There was a large corner office that I knew would belong to the lieutenant. The door was shut. I didn't have to make out the name on the brass plate. I paced, fidgeting, and realized I was surreptitiously looking for a flash of blonde hair.

"Mr. Freeman?"

I turned on the male voice, wishing it quieter, questioning why I hadn't set this up as an outside meeting.

"Rick Fried," the man said, shaking my hand in a strong grip. "Good to meet you. Come on in."

I followed the back of Fried's suit into a small office and since he hadn't closed the door, I did. He slipped his coat off and hung it on the back of his chair before sitting.

"Your uncle speaks very highly of you, Mr. Freeman. And when Sergeant Keith speaks, the smart ones around here listen."

"He's a good man," I said.

"One of the best," Fried answered, unbuttoning his cuffs and rolling back his sleeves, just us working guys here. It was probably a technique for IAD interviews. He was younger than my uncle, older by ten years than me, at least that's what I was telling myself.

"He tells me you're a P.I. in Florida now."

I nodded.

"Nice tan."

I nodded again.

"OK. The sarge says you're working something on our former Mr. Colin O'Shea and I gather it's gotta be on the defense side, Mr. Freeman, 'cause I see that someone from the, uh, Broward sheriff's office has already made some inquiries on Mr. O'Shea."

"You handle them?" I said.

"Nope. The lieutenant does all outside agency contacts," he said.

Fried was reading from a lined check-out sheet stapled to the front of a file on his desktop. It was lying on top of a second folder.

"Well, I wouldn't say 'defense,' detective. I'm in a sort of neutral position," I said. "I was asked by a friend to offer an opinion because I knew O'Shea, years ago."

"Yeah, right, you two graduated academy together," Fried said, unconsciously, or maybe not, touching his fingers to the second file. "You two ever work the streets together?"

I knew the IAD game. Even if this guy was a friend of my uncle's, his whole existence in this job was give-and-take. Info for info.

"We ran across each other. He was from the neighborhood," I said. "Know what I mean?"

In South Philly, mention of the neighborhood still had a sense of being synonymous with a tribe of sorts. I was here on my uncle's honor. It snapped Fried back.

"Yeah, well, the file's pretty straight up on O'Shea," he said, handing it across his desk.

"Had some complaints. He was written up for excessive use of force. Then he and a couple others out at the Tenth got stopped on a drunk and disorderly, their sergeant handled it, kept it off the books, warned them to clean it up. But O'Shea stayed on the bottle. Another excessive a year later. Then his wife throws a domestic-abuse charge at him."

"Any of these excessive-force complaints involve women?" I said, looking through O'Shea's stats. High number of arrests. Most in districts I remembered as being high-crime spots.

"Naw. Lowlifes mostly. Drug collars on the street. One was a group thing where the bang squad went in on a house full of gang warrants and the hard boys started crying about being beaten afterwards. But I got the feeling that O'Shea didn't exactly shy away from a little extracurricular activity."

"You guys ever do any psych screens on him?" I said.

"Not if it isn't in there," Fried said.

I closed the file and put it back on the desk. As I did I glanced at what I was sure was my own file.

"I don't see anything in there about the Faith Hamlin case," I said, nodding at O'Shea's jacket folder, making the accusation that Fried was holding out on me as bluntly as I could.

The detective laced his fingers and sat back in his chair, like mention of the case had not surprised him.

"That's all part of an ongoing investigation, Mr. Freeman. "It's not public information."

I lowered my voice and leaned forward just as far as Fried had moved back.

"Oh, I thought my uncle's word carried more weight than that. There was once a brotherhood and even you guys were part of that," I said, watching his eyes, their movement, center to right, center to right, giving him away.

He finally leaned in.

"Your uncle doesn't have the power to hire and fire, Freeman," he said, showing his allegiance was with his paycheck. "My boss is where she is because of the Hamlin case. She took those guys down, and I'm not saying they didn't deserve it, but as far as she's concerned, the real perp got away."

"O'Shea," I said, without having to.

Fried nodded and leaned back again.

"Now, you got anything on him from Florida that's gonna help her nail his ass for the killing of Faith Hamlin, I'm more than happy to forward that information along, Mr. Freeman."

I sat back as well, more than happy to increase the personal space between us. Fried didn't know that I had once been married to his boss. Uncle Keith had been more circumspect than that.

I stood up and offered my hand.

"If I should come across anything that I think you can use, Detective, you'll be the first to know," I lied. "I appreciate the time."

"Hey, any friend of the sarge. Maybe I'll catch you out some night, buy me one," he said, just one of the boys again.

I grinned the guy grin while he showed me out. In the hallway I found myself shaking my head and thinking some line about six degrees of separation. My ex-wife and now my ex-lover had swapped notes on O'Shea and his connection with the disappearances of Faith Hamlin here, and about the disappearances of the women in Florida. They both had the guy's ass in their rifle sights. I figured I knew that Sherry Richards's motive was this hell-bent desire for justice for the victims. Meagan's I was equally sure of: a premier scalp on her already extensive collection, a step up her ambitious ladder to who the hell knew where, and yet another man-challenge to conquer. I didn't think either had mentioned my name or my intimate connection to both of them.

"Don't tell me that God has a plan, Mamma," I whispered to a pale empty wall. "Or he is one bizarre poet."

I was waiting for the elevator when I heard her call my name and there was no denying the voice.

"Max?"

I looked back down the hall toward IAD and she was standing in a cerulean-colored suit that I could only imagine her coming up with when the dress code said blue. Even from here I could tell the high cut of her skirt was not regulation. Her head was angled slightly with a questioning look and her honey blonde hair took advantage of the tilt to cascade down over one shoulder. She had called out my name once like that when we were married, late one night while she tried to sleep after a SWAT shooting she'd been in on. Her voice had sounded like she'd needed me, so I'd held her in our bed until she stopped shivering. But the next morning she had no recollection of it and I had been wrong about the needing.

"Max?"

I put my hands in my pockets and took a step toward her. The elevator bell rang and I ignored it. I watched her hand a load of files to a man in a suit next to her and wave him into the office, all without taking her eyes off me. As she approached she looked down once, then raised her eyes and reached up and took a strand of hair that had come loose and in one heartbreaking motion that burned in our past, she tucked it behind her ear. We met halfway.

"Max Freeman, holy shit, look at you!"

Her lips were sealed in a barely contained smile but her eyes were undeniably bright. She tossed her arms around my neck and I think I put one hand on her back. Her perfume was new. Her cheek soft and the same. I felt my weight anchor in my heels and the hug might have lasted a second too long for a divorced couple standing in a police headquarters who hadn't seen each other for more than five years. She stepped back, or I did, and she still held my shoulders.

"Jesus Christ, a beach bum? An oil rigger? A damn boat captain? What the hell have you done with yourself, Max?"

"Hi, Meagan. How have you been?" was all I could manage and my face felt stupid and flushed. She cocked her head. She was one of those women whose eyes told you she was smarter and wittier than you, but she was willing to let you try to catch up.

"It's the Florida sun," I said. "Plays hell with a guy's complexion."

I wanted to tell her that she hadn't changed a bit. But she did it for me.

"Did you come all this way just to see me?" she said with that teasing smile of hers.

The elevator pinged again and a group got off.

"Uh, yeah, Meg, in a way," I said, lying again. Home must have brought back that special talent in me. I guided her to a bench in the hall and sat.

"I'm actually working for an attorney in West Palm Beach on a case."

"You're a P.I., Max. How perfect for you and that independent streak of yours. Do I know the firm?"

"Uh, I doubt it. He's a one-man show. Kind of independent himself."

"It's just that my husband, Troy Montgomery of Montgomery and Wallace, does a lot of work with real estate attorneys in Florida," she said. She crossed her legs with the grainy *shoosh* of fine nylon and rested her left hand on her knee. The ring on her finger flashed, even in the poor fluorescent light.

"I, uh, congratulations," I said. "I didn't know you were married."

"Yes you did, Max," she said, fluttering the fingers of her left hand on which a rock the size of Gibraltar clung. "You've always been an observant cop."

"Anyway," I said, avoiding that trap. "I came up to talk with some folks about a former officer, Colin O'Shea. He was a few years younger than me. I think you might have met him."

She looked past me, spinning, I knew, the scenarios through her head. Meagan had been a sharpshooter on the SWAT team when we were married. She was tough, accurate and knew through training, and not just a little of her naturally conniving character, how to see a path in her head before taking it.

"Is this the O'Shea some agency in Florida is looking at as an abduction suspect?"

"Yeah."

Never underestimate a smart woman with skills.

"A detective down there called me. I gave her what we had in the file. You do know I'm heading IAD these days?"

I nodded.

"And I wouldn't be giving you credit, Max, if I didn't suppose that you also know about the Faith Hamlin case."

"Yeah, I do."

Without physically moving, space of some kind opened up between us on the bench. A step back, without one actually taking place.

"This detective, she was very persistent. Wanted to know more than what we had. Very aggressive."

I nodded again.

"You know her?"

"I've done a couple of overlapping cases."

"Overlapping?" she said, raising that eyebrow of hers. I'd determined years ago it was a skeptical twitch she must have been working on since childhood. I pretended to ignore it. "So, do you know more, Max? About O'Shea?"

Here came the info for info drill, I thought.

"I guess I know that he was your prime suspect in the Hamlin disappearance and that because he couldn't be charged he moved to Florida," I said.

Meagan did not flinch.

"And you also know that your overlapping detective friend is considering him as her main suspect in the disappearance of other victims."

I fell back on my refusal to answer rhetoric.

"How Republican of your local constable to farm out investigative work to a private contractor, Max," she said. "Or are you somehow working for Mr. O'Shea as a defensive player?"

Down the hall the suit Meagan had been with stuck his head out the door of her office and looked at us, briefly, no high sign, no clearing of the throat, before retreating.

"She asked me to talk with O'Shea, see what he might say to someone from the neighborhood. It was a favor," I said.

Meagan's eyes brightened, the sudden look of enthusiasm catching me, like it had the first time I'd met her.

"Then we've got to have dinner, Max," she said brightly as she stood. "You can tell me about this conversation with our Mr. O'Shea and what that perceptive mind of yours came up with."

"And you can bring along the investigative case file for me?" I said, playing the info game.

"All in my head, Max," she said, smiling and touching her hair with an index finger. "Yours for the asking."

"Tomorrow, eight o'clock at Moriarity's then?" I said, instinctively tossing out a place we'd gone to many times when we were together.

"Ah, a little slumming, Max," she said, and I'll be damned if her eyes didn't twinkle. "Perfect choice. See you tomorrow at eight."

When I stood, she leaned into my rising face and caught me with a kiss on the cheek and then turned on a heel and left me standing there wondering if I was an idiot or just a common fool. I gathered enough sense to turn my back to her before she reached her office door where I knew she would turn to see if I'd been watching her legs.

CHAPTER 11

I worked my way onto Race Street and headed east over the Ben Franklin and into New Jersey. The water in the Delaware River looked steel gray. The heater in the rental was still not caught up and I could imagine how cold the water was running below and the thought made me shiver.

Contrary to widely held and denigrating opinions of the depressed city of Camden, the sky does not grow instantly darker over there. It held the same shade of light shale, but without as many towers and skyscrapers to break up the monotony. I took the Admiral Wilson and spiraled through the next interchange to get on the Marlton Turnpike. From there I used the driving directions Mrs. Mott had read me over the phone. By the time I found the Majestic Ice Arena I was late for my appointment with Colin O'Shea's ex-wife.

It took another ten minutes to find a parking spot between all the SUVs and minivans. Inside the corrugated metal building the temperature difference was negligible. I could still see my breath as I walked the front aisle between the protective glass of the rink and the rising stands. On the ice was a haphazard spray of tiny hockey players shuffling in various directions and trying to keep their balance with their sticks. I worked my way toward a group of women who were only occasionally interrupting their conversations with a "Good job, Jimmy!" or "That's OK, Paul. Get up!"

I stood for a full minute in their view and was one step from going up to announce myself to the entire group when she stood and made her way down the stands.

"Mr. Freeman?"

"Janice?" I said, extending my hand. Hers was covered with a knit mitten and I shook it. "I'm sorry I didn't give you a description over the phone so you would know what I looked like."

"You look like a cop," she said, and I looked into her face to see if that agitated her.

"With a tan," she added and tried to smile.

I showed her my ID and P.I. license.

"Should we wait until your son is done?" I said, nodding out to the ice.

"Hell, no. They'll be out there another forty minutes," she said and pointed back toward the entrance. "Let's go have coffee."

I liked her already.

We sat at a table in a small snack bar area, both of us with our hands wrapped around large Styrofoam cups of steaming coffee. Kids were running in and out for pizza and sodas and candy and screeching and laughing and arguing. The chaos didn't seem to faze her. It was giving me a monumental headache.

"You said you were a friend of Colin's?" she started.

"We worked District Ten around the same time. He grew up near Eighth and Tasker and my parents were down around Snyder."

"Eighth and Mountain," she said.

"Excuse me?"

"Colin was Eighth and Mountain. My family lived a couple blocks away, on Cross."

"Ah, South Philly girl," I said, trying to soften her face. I was guessing mid-thirties. Her hair was still black and her dark eyes had a hardness that appeared to have been earned. She was wearing tasteful makeup in the middle of a school week and had on the reddest lipstick I think I've ever seen. It marked the edge of her cup with a heavy stain.

"Janice Carlucci," she said. "My maiden name. I met Colin when we were kids. I was told to stay away from the Irish so, go figure. I do exactly what my Italian parents say I can't do." She shrugged. "Shakespeare. Ya know?"

"I'm familiar," I said, sipping my coffee, letting her go.

"We got married after he passed the academy. If you're from the neighborhood, you know. Cop, fireman, your father's plumbing business. Job for life."

She was right, I just didn't like the condescension in her voice.

"It wasn't exactly what you wanted," I said.

She shook her head.

"I matured, Mr. Freeman. I saw something on the other side of the river." She raised her palm.

When she'd taken her mittens off I'd ranked the rock on her finger. It was practically up there with Meagan's. I'd already noted the expensive, fur-lined coat.

"Colin was stuck between proving himself in South Philly, being the tough Irish cop, or getting the hell out, go to college, be something more. Or, no offense, Mr. Freeman, be something different," she said

"He ever take that frustration out on you?" I asked, since bluntness seemed to be the order of the day. She held me with her dark eyes for a few moments.

"I'd heard he was an ass-kicker on the streets," she said. "You know, the guys sittin' around McLaughlin's or in the kitchen on poker night, braggin' an all.

"But never with me, Mr. Freeman. Yes, I filed the damn domestic charge. Because Colin wouldn't see anybody, not a counselor, not an AA group. He was letting his life rot and mine was going down with it. It was abuse."

I let her stare into her coffee. She didn't want to look up at me to reveal the moisture that was in her eyes. It was something I could never figure in women, that range of emotion, pissed and sympathetic, disarming and ruthless, heartbroken and heart-breaking, one to the other in a dumbfounding span of minutes.

"Then they used it against him," she said and left the statement sitting out there like the steam in the air. I waited until another pack of clomping skaters went by.

"When Faith Hamlin went missing?" I said, catching up to her. She nodded her head.

"They put it in the papers that Colin had already been accused of beating me when we were married, that he had a history. So of course he must have been in on what those guys did to that girl."

Out on the rink a horn sounded. A smattering of applause. My time was running out.

"Mrs. Mott, the authorities in Florida are linking Colin with the abduction and disappearance of at least a couple of women," I said.

As the words left my mouth she started shaking her head no.

"Do you think he's capable of something like that? Or could have become capable?"

When she looked up at me, the dry hardness was back in her dark eyes. Just like that, tough Philly girl coming right back.

"No way," she said. "Not the man I knew. Colin was never the kind who ever did something vicious without someone else to see it, to prove that he could do it to measure up, to prove he was as tough as the rest of you. He was always after that approval, from me, from his family. But on his own, push come to shove Mr. Freeman, he was a coward."

She drained her coffee like she meant it.

"You're a cop. You're talking about somebody with the balls to steal somebody's life, to kill them for some sick reason. That's what you're saying, right?"

"Yeah," I said, finding it hard to hold her look.

"I don't want to speak badly about Colin, but he is what he is. I lived with him, I know. A man like Colin just doesn't have what you're talking about in him."

"Did you tell that to the investigators on the Hamlin case?" I said.

"Who? IAD? Sure I told them, while they were interviewing me about any hideaways in the Poconos where Colin might be hiding or some shit. You think that made it into their report, Mr. Freeman?"

The horn sounded again and vibrated through the building. End of the period.

"I gotta get Michael," she said, hooking her thumb.

"I thank you for your time Mrs. Mott."

"Not a problem," she said, shrugging her shoulders like the South Philly girl she'd always be.

"One thing, though," she said, pulling on her mittens and raising her voice over the growing din of ice time switching. "If you see Colin again, Mr. Freeman, tell him I wish him the best, you know? He's got a lot to answer for. But this isn't one of them."

When I crossed back over the bridge into the city, lights were flickering on in the dusk. After dinner I walked from Gaskill a few blocks to the First Methodist Church and stood on the cold sidewalk outside looking at the weathered stone and mortar and the dull stained glass. Despite its old heavy architecture its spire still rose into the night with the majesty intended by its builders. It was in the basement of this church that Billy's and my mothers had met and formed an unlikely friendship and insidious plan. On pre-dawn Sunday mornings they prepared the early coffee and breakfast reception and shared their similar secrets. Then they conspired to kill my abusive father and my mother carried it out. After decades of shame and pain she gained her freedom. Then within a few years she herself was dead. Following her wishes she was cremated and her sisters-in-law still only whispered her name. She refused to lie next to the body of my father and carry the lie into eternity. But she had suppressed her own basic human need to have control over her life and took it in death, a measure of justice to keep her warm.

CHAPTER 12

I slept until noon. The gray light of day barely made it through the windows of the blue room. Judging by the outside, it could have been six in the morning or six at night. For several minutes I lay staring at the ornate molding of the ceiling wondering when it had been that I'd lost the sense that Philadelphia was my home. Without an answer I rolled out of the big bed and started searching through my bag for running shoes.

I coughed all the way down to Front Street. My mouth was still warm from Guy's coffee and each time I drew in a breath of chilled air it raked down my throat. I turned south and it took me till Alter Street and the Mummers Museum before my lungs and legs felt loose. I tried to get into a rhythm by staying on the macadam and off the curbs but any cadence I caught was quickly interrupted by double-parked cars, some delivery guy backing up a truck, somebody nosing out from an intersection. I was trying to grind off a sharp stone in my head. Two good cops, Sherry Richards and Meagan Turner (I couldn't bring myself to use her newly married name) were convinced that O'Shea was a predator. Somehow they could filter through what his life had been, his upbringing, his career, his wife's inside view of the man and still come up with a demon. And somehow, I couldn't.

I made it to Wolf Street before I finally gave up the run. The space under my oversized sweatshirt was warm and puffs of heat were rising up under my chin. My knees ached from the concrete pounding and the muscles in my thighs felt heavy and strained. An exercise in futility, I thought, and smiled at my own dull wit. I grabbed the ends of my sweatshirt cuffs in my palms, gathering the material around my cold hands, and started walking. The sun was still blotted out and I had to search to find it, a spot in the sky that barely glowed like a dull bulb behind a dirty sheet. I walked west without thinking and ended up turning back north. By the time I passed Mount Sinai Medical Center, a chill had set up in my sweat-soaked T-shirt and when I looked up to find a place to get some coffee I realized I had worked my way to the corner market where Faith Hamlin had worked her last night.

At the entrance two wide concrete steps led up to a wooden-framed screen door with a wide metal banner across its middle that said TASTYCAKES in lettering that was fading and chipped. The spring on the door yawned when I opened it and a trip bell jingled somewhere inside.

There was a blower the size of a stuffed suitcase mounted above and to the right that poured warm air down onto the threshold and kept the cold from infiltrating the place. I stepped in and stood in the airflow for a few seconds, rubbing my hands and resisting the urge to raise them up into the heater's hot face. To my right there was a thigh-high freezer chest with sliding, frosted-up glass doors that ran the length of one wall. *The Daily News*, the *Inquirer* and three different racing forms were stacked on its back edge. To the right were three rows of shelves with groceries and snacks and the kinds of cleaning products and paper goods you might run out of on an irregular basis at home. It was the kind of place your mom would send you for a gallon of milk or bag of sugar. I took a few steps in and spotted the stacked glassed coffeepots in the far left corner, warming on a stainless hot plate, and walked that way. There was no one behind the counter at the far end of the single room. No radio drone. No television hissing on a shelf under the rack of cigarettes.

I poured a twenty-ounce cup and the aroma of the steam was fresh. The top pot had been full. There was no decaf. I had no use for the open pint of half-and-half and packages of sugar. I took a careful sip and checked the rack of packaged treats beside me. Tastycakes, as advertised. I grinned and picked up a butterscotch package, my favorite as a kid, and tore the cellophane open and took a bite. I might have even closed my eyes because when I took another sip of coffee to wash down the flavor, a young man was standing behind the counter, staring at me.

I finished my swallow, tipped the cup and said: "How you doin'?"

He simply nodded and turned away. I guessed his age at somewhere in his early twenties. His shoulders were thin and his face angular and drawn under a mop of straight black hair that covered his eyes when he bent his head forward. He was shuffling something under the counter and did not look up so I shifted my weight from side to side while I finished my snack. Behind the clerk was a hanging roll of lottery tickets next to a Philadelphia Flyers calendar next to an eight-by-ten portrait of a dark-haired girl whose crooked smile and too wide eyes said that she had to be Faith Hamlin. She had been given a place of honor where everyone could see her, where everyone who bought a pack of cigarettes or loaf of bread could remember.

I tossed the rest of the cake and its wrapper into a small trash can and stepped over to the counter. The kid didn't look up.

"How, uh, much do I owe you?"

He finally met my eyes through a strand of hair. I raised the cup and gestured back toward the rack of snacks. "This and a Tastycake," I said.

"Two-oh-four," he said without moving to the register, just waiting while I dug into the pocket of my sweatpants.

"Who's the girl?" I said, nodding at the framed photo and trying to be nonchalant while I sorted some bills. "She's pretty."

The kid's brow wrinkled at the question and he actually started to turn around to see what I was talking about but stopped himself halfway. He turned back and I put three ones into his outstretched hand. His wrists were skinny and knotted. He stepped back and rang up the sale and was snaking out change with long, pale fingers.

"You a cop?" he suddenly said, and I may have mistaken the flat tone as an accusation. Maybe he was being a smart-ass because I was asking questions. Maybe it was something else. But I had an odd, sudden urge to reach over and snap his bony wrists.

"No," I said, trying to match his bluntness. "Why?"

"I dunno," he said pouring ninety-six cents into my palm. "You just look like a cop."

"No," I said again. "I'm not from around here."

"Yeah," he said, pulling a strand of black hair away from his eyes. "Have a nice day."

My coffee was cold by the time I hit Jefferson Square and I tossed the cup into a trash can. I jogged the rest of the way back to Gaskill with the thought of a hot shower motivating me and the same thought keeping at bay the proposition of having dinner with my ex-wife.

I got to Moriarity's by seven thirty and sat at the end of the bar by the door so I wouldn't miss her coming in. Billy had left a message for me to call him. When I reached him at his office he told me he'd gotten a call from Rodrigo Colon. One of the cruise workers had been roughed up outside the medical clinic by some muscle who had approached the group in an alley where they were smoking. It had been a warning and the only translation the workers came away with were shut up and go home to Manila or their injuries from the explosion would be minor in comparison.

"So he wasn't from the recruiters in the Philippines?" I'd asked.

"No, Rodrigo said he was American. White and bigger than you. Someone with an ugly or vulgar mouth," Billy said. "That was the best description he could give. He said he and the rest had decided to stay inside for a few days. Keep to themselves and lay low, but it definitely put a damper on his recruiting efforts."

I figured I already knew who Ugly Mouth was. Bat Man's jaw would still be wired from my head-butt. I told Billy I would wrap up here as soon as I could.

"So how's it going up there?" he'd asked.

"Thirty-six degrees and drizzle," I said. "And I'm having dinner with Meagan in about an hour." I had never heard Billy whistle before and he hung up before I had a chance to ask his meaning.

I was into my second beer and was eyeing the Schnapps when she finally arrived, fashionably fifteen minutes late. She was in a long cashmere coat and scarf and wasn't wearing a hat despite the drizzle. I had never seen her wear anything over her blonde hair unless a uniform demanded it. She opened the coat and put her shoulders back to shrug the coat off into the hands of a mildly surprised hostess. She had on a sweater and a dark skirt underneath. At least two guys at the bar subtly turned to admire the sweater.

She came over and as I started to slide off the stool she said: "Sit, Max. Let's have a drink at the bar first."

She positioned herself on the stool next to me and crossed her legs with that sound of nylon and surveyed the long room—bar running the length of one wall until a step up into a dining space at the very back. Small tables along the other wall. A few booths just to the left of the entrance. Dark wood, ferns and neon liquor signs throughout.

"My God, Max. The place hasn't changed in ten years." She smiled. "I feel like a college girl."

Just two blocks from Jefferson Hospital, Moriarity's was a favorite of the nursing and medical students and was mostly filled with a younger crowd.

"You never went to college, Meagan," I said.

She smiled and her eyes stayed bright.

"I feel like a college girl," she repeated and then ignored me for a few beats. "Get me a Merlot will you, Max?"

She waited until she'd had a taste and then asked: "So, how

often do you get back, Max? Keep in touch with any guys from the old days?"

"This is actually the first time I've been back to the city since I left, Meg. With my mom gone, there wasn't much reason."

She gave me a look of sympathy and then realized it was misspent on me.

"So this inquiry about Colin O'Shea is strong enough motivation to get you here?"

I have never been one to answer questions without thinking about my response first. I was even more careful with Meagan, who had always been a verbal chess player.

"It's a favor for a friend," I finally said.

To her credit, she saw the answer as a blocking move and let it pass.

"And what have you come up with so far?" she said, moving right to the business at hand.

"Since both your case and the one in Florida have to do with women, I'm kind of surprised by the opinions women have of O'Shea," I said.

"Ah, you talked to the ex?"

"Yeah."

"Same old Max," she said with that smarter-than-you smile. "You have to see their eyes, right? Tell if the truth is there?" I looked straight into hers.

"She doesn't think the guy that she was married to for what, six years, was capable," I said.

"Right. But she didn't mind filing a domestic abuse charge against the guy to justify divorcing him so she could run off to Cherry Hill with her boyfriend the pharmaceutical salesman."

"According to her, the abuse wasn't physical," I said and caught the flavor of defense in my own voice.

"No shit," Meagan said, flatly.

"What? You don't believe it?"

"Oh, I believe it," she said and then turned to face me again. The look felt like an assessment. I must have passed.

"I dated him a few times, years ago, when he was trying to make SWAT."

Maybe she thought it was a confession that was going to shock me. But even if O'Shea hadn't already told me, I'm not sure I would have reacted. I took a drink, like it had nothing to do with me.

"He never made the team?" I said.

"Too aggressive. Not enough patience. Thought it was all gung ho shit. He was one of those who could never find the balance."

"He ever get aggressive with you?" I said. "I mean in a personal way?"

She gave me one of those "Who, me?" looks.

"You of all people, Max" she said. "He got pissed off once and raised a hand."

"And?"

"I slapped him first when he hesitated."

"And his reaction?"

"He apologized. Said he would never have actually hit me," she said. "Like I would have let him."

"Christ, Meg," I said. "And now you think he's capable of whacking some poor grocery store clerk to cover up a sex scandal out on the beat?"

One of the sweater guys nearby looked over. Meagan smiled at him and raised her eyebrows. I signaled the hostess that we were ready to sit down for dinner and paid the bar bill.

Meagan was true to her word on answering any questions I had about the departments' and internal affairs' investigation into the Faith Hamlin case. While we ate she described how IA isolated the officers on the differing shifts and found discrepancies in the night crews' stories of how often they stopped at the market and who had actually been the last to see Hamlin. Although good cops usually have well tuned bullshit detectors when they're talking to mopes on the street, it doesn't mean they're good liars themselves. Despite the polygraphs that three of the cops had passed, Meagan's investigators had done searches of all the officers' homes and cars, looking for any sign of Hamlin or DNA that could have indicated she'd been transported, dead or alive, by any of them. Nothing. They also crunched the time lines down on each man, making them give details on their whereabouts during every minute that they weren't on duty from the time Hamlin was last seen. Two of the guys were married and took the biggest hit. The media was all over the story. No one escaped being flayed in public. But O'Shea took the brunt. He was the only one who refused to cooperate. He stonewalled. He'd told them to charge him or leave him the fuck alone. He demanded a search warrant be served on his home and vehicles. He knew enough about the law to argue to a judge that the department had no evidence of a crime, that Faith Hamlin could have done anything from simply walking away from the embarrassment of the situation to throwing herself off the Ben Franklin Bridge. There were no indications of a crime and no body. Though she might have had the mind of a thirteen-year-old, Hamlin was legally an adult.

"So what does your gut tell you, Meagan?" I said when I ran out of questions. "Colin killed her and dumped her over in the Jersey Pine Barrens?"

"I don't have the kind of instinct you always seem to think you have, Max. Hell, he could have chopped her up and stuck her in a barrel. It's been done before. And by guys a lot smarter than him. He might have had nothing to do with her. None of the other three ratted on each other. They just came clean," she said, not letting the conversation spoil her appetite for the veggie wrap she worked her way through.

"But you know the old saying: If you got nothing to hide, why not talk?"

"Shit," I said, shaking my head because she knew better and every cop worth a damn knew better. A lot of people went to jail for crimes they didn't commit because they talked when they should have shut up. The only thing that let some cops and prosecutors live with that was the belief that it made up for the crimes the guy did do.

"So, Max. Speaking of talking," Meagan said, folding her napkin and resting her chin on the backs of her hands. "What have you got for me?"

I didn't hold out on her. I gave her the details of my meeting with

O'Shea, including his admission that he'd dated a couple of the bartenders that had gone missing. I told her he'd been working private security and even detailed his participation in the alley fight.

She smiled at a thought, but didn't comment.

"Do you have an address for him?" she said.

"I'm sure detective Richards has an address, but I wasn't exactly tailing the guy, Meg."

"They have a trace on his phone or surveillance of some kind?"

"Not that I know of. As far as I know they're in the same bind you were in. No crime, no warrants, no taps or manpower."

"I don't know, Max," she said, folding her napkin on the table. "If that's all you have I'm not sure this was much of a trade."

I took my wallet out of my pocket without looking up at her, guessed at the bill total and put a few twenties on the table and slid my chair back.

"Yeah, it's not going to get you any captain bars," I said, getting petty by matching the dig.

"Oh, the jealous good ole boys' club got your ear already," she said.

"Hey, you've always been a multitasker, Meg. You find out what happened to your girl and get promoted for it, more power to you," I said, letting her lead the way out.

On the sidewalk the drizzle had stopped but it felt ten degrees colder. Meagan waved at a taxi that was parked across the alley in front of the Walnut Street Theatre. I opened the door for her and again she put her hand on mine.

"I was kidding with that trade comment, Max," she said.

"I know," I lied, knowing she had only been half kidding.

"It really was good to see you," she said and took a strand of her hair and carefully pulled it behind her ear and smiled. "Will you call if you get anything more from O'Shea that will help us, you know, with the girl?"

"You'll be the first," I said, and this time the kiss did not surprise me. It felt dry and perfunctory and did not even leave a warm spot on my chilled cheek. The next morning I flew back home to Florida.

CHAPTER 13

He was in her apartment, lying back on her bed, his work boots on the thin chemise bedspread, watching her get ready for work. Her face moved in and out of the mirror on top of her cheap dresser as she crimped her eyelashes and applied shadow and took particular care with liner. She caught him in the reflection and said: "What?"

"I'm just amazed at the work you put into all that when your eyes are already so beautiful."

"Yeah? How do you think we keep them so beautiful? We cheat," she said, smiling at him without turning around.

The few weeks they'd been together had been good. Sure he was kind of private, didn't like to stay and hang out with any of the other regulars at the bar when her shift was done. Didn't like to talk much with the other patrons and had pointedly asked her not to let anyone else know he was a cop. He said he had to be careful because it was like that situation with that prison asshole who scared the shit out of her that night in the bar when she saw him flash his badge. He said it should be a secret between them because he could get caught up in off-duty stuff like that and then he'd end up being liable and it made sense the way he explained it.

"If I let that other pencil dick get his ass whipped and then his fucking lawyer gets onto it and starts saying: You're a cop, why didn't you step in and stop it?

"Then the department attorneys get on me: Why are you getting involved when you're off duty? Was the guy a physical threat to you or others?"

Better to just scare the guy off, he said. He'd catch that idiot on the street someday and he'd be glad to do some ass-kicking when he was in uniform and it was his turf.

She liked that about him, too. He wasn't like the wimpy guys back home or the bar clowns who were all mouth. He told her some stories about suspects who fought him on the streets. He was aggressive in bed, too. But she wasn't complaining. They'd had sex here in her apartment the first time and she was a little frightened by how intense he was, but she'd had an orgasm like nothing she'd ever had in the past. He was strong and bold in the way he took her. It was exciting. After that they'd done it at night on the beach, once in the pool after he'd slipped the lock to the utility room and turned the underwater lights off. They'd even done it in the backseat of his car one night out somewhere in the Everglades where there weren't any houses or traffic.

She looked at him now, stretched out on her bed. She didn't like the boots on her spread but she knew better than to say anything. She found her perfume among the mess on the bureau and dabbed some on. She found him in the mirror. He had that way of kind of dominating a space when he was with her. Like the time he was getting beer from her fridge while she was letting the shower water warm and she heard him punch on her message machine and listen to the whole tape. Or the time he walked into the apartment before her and scooped the mail off the floor and went through each letter before putting it on the counter. Yeah, it was all junk, but she called him on it anyway.

"What? You afraid I'm going to see something from your boyfriend in Minneapolis?"

"That would be a trick since I don't have a boyfriend in Minneapolis," she'd said, and it was the truth.

"You'd better not," he'd said and then slipped his hands around her from behind and nuzzled her ear just like he was doing now.

She looked at him in the mirror. It did feel good to be wanted. Then he slipped his hands up from her waist and cupped her breast over her blouse.

"Come on, baby. You know I gotta get to work," she said.

"Yeah?"

He put his mouth on her neck and started unbuttoning her top button.

"If I'm late again Laurie's gonna kill me."

"No she won't," he said, working on the next button.

"No? She fired Roxy just last week. Though it was probably because she was always drunk by the time her shift ended."

"So let her fire you," he said, and now he had himself pressed up against her from behind and she could feel him getting hard against her. "You don't need to work there. I'll take care of you."

"Oh, you're gonna keep me barefoot and pregnant?"

He was unfastening the front snap on her bra and she put her hands on his to stop him and he did that cop thing where he suddenly spun his wrists and grabbed hers and in a split second he had her arms locked up behind her. With her shoulders pulled back, the bra snap gave way and when he pulled her elbows tighter together her breasts came out of the fabric. In the mirror both of them could see that she was now excited, too, and she thought: OK, I won't fight it. Just this once.

CHAPTER 14

My flight landed at Palm Beach International and I found my truck deep in long-term parking. When I opened the door, a wash of stale air spilled out. It was eighty degrees in the sun. Compared to Philly, the humidity felt like it was at ninety percent. Welcome back.

I tossed my travel bag into the passenger seat and then rolled up the new coat and stuffed it behind the seat where it might stay for another twenty years. I rolled down the windows and headed east, my cell phone in my ear and feeling anxious to talk with Billy. When I got to his office and he opened the door I realized that I looked like a slob, but then next to William Manchester, Esquire, most men fell to some level of slobdom.

Billy was dressed in a two-thousand-dollar Armani suit that was a dark, deeply woven color. The fabric contained shades of black and gray and held a textured shadow that could only be named subtle money, or unmistakable class. His short-collared shirt was such a brilliant white against his mahogany skin that the contrast was like a razor cut. I sat down on the leather couch in my blue jeans and crossed my legs like a gentleman, exposing the sweat socks tucked into the newly scuffed work boots I'd bought at the Army/Navy store in Philly. I balanced a saucer and cup of coffee on my knee and watched him move like I'd fallen into a damn magazine ad. My mouth may have been slightly open.

"D-don't stare, M-Max. I've seen you l-look that way at a b-blue heron out near the Glades and it's very discomforting."

"Ain't no bird got nothin' on you, partner," I said, almost whistling.

"We have b-been invited to a p-political fund-raiser downtown this evening," Billy said, snicking up the fabric of his trousers by the sharp creases as he sat across from me.

"Ah," I said. "If you can't beat them, join them?"

"No. As Diane would s-say: You beat them by joining them."

"The woman's got smarts," I said.

"We shall see."

Billy picked up a file and opened it in his lap. He was done explaining himself.

"OK, M-Max. While you were away, I ran the t-two individuals who attacked you in the alley," he said, clipped and businesslike. "A David and Robert Hix. S-Small-time thugs and n-not very g-good at being criminals."

"Brothers?" I said.

"Yes. David just g-got out of Glades Correctional on a r-robbery jolt that looks like it was probably a drug rip-off. He's on six years p-probation after d-doing three. Brother Robert has done c-county time in b-both Palm Beach and Broward. Check k-kiting, burglary and identity theft. W-with all these cross references, it l-looks like they travel as a t-team, but Davey does the h-heavier work."

Billy passed me the folder and I scanned the booking photos that he had downloaded off the Department of Corrections Web site.

"Did you show these to Rodrigo yet?"

"I've called him twice. B-Both times he's been short, almost whispering and asked for you. He says he's all right, but I could hear

A KILLING NIGHT

the fear in his voice," Billy said. "Hard to see how a Filipino mid-
dleman gets these two as leg breakers."

"It's a global village, Billy. We learned the hard way that the
criminals have cell phones and Internet sites, too. If their job re-
cruiter in Manila gets squeezed because his people are making noise
about legal representation on work problems, he makes a call to a
fellow shit-heel in Miami, who farms it out," I said. "I'll talk to
Rodrigo. Can I take these mug shots?"

Billy flipped the backs of his fingers and stood up.

"While I w-was asking around, I also t-talked with a prosecutor
friend in Broward about your Mr. O'Shea."

He walked over to the wall of windows and looked out toward
the ocean. Though we were twelve stories up, he never looked down
over the edge and into the streets. Billy never looked down.

"He tells me he's had to t-turn Sherry down on filing a probable
cause on O'Shea t-twice. He t-told her all she has is circumstantial
evidence, even with the Philadelphia incident. No b-body. No forensics. Just a couple of witnesses willing to say they saw him with two
women who m-may be missing."

"As far as I know, he's right," I said.

"She's also all alone on th-this according to him. Her p-pursuit
of these cases in general and O'Shea in p-particular is causing hard
feelings with her b-bosses and at the state attorney's office."

"Your friend say what they're going to do?"

"G-give her some slack for now b-because of her past record.
Nobody's telling her she's wrong. They all know the kind of investigator she is. B-But she needs some substance."

"I wish I could help her."

"Nothing fr-from Philadelphia?"

"Nothing of substance," I said, thinking of the portrait of Faith
Hamlin on the wall of the store, of tears in O'Shea's ex-wife's eyes,
the smell of whiskey and the guffaw of old cops and their younger,
too confident brethren. "I doubt you'd like the changes, or the lack
of them."

"I have n-no intention of ever experiencing them, my friend."

135

Billy looked at his watch.

"I need to m-meet Diane."

"Good luck with the Romans," I said.

"Et tu, b-brother," Billy said. "Et tu."

I spent most of the next day on the beach, letting the sun seep into my bones where the twenty-three-degree Philadelphia gray had chilled the marrow. Your blood does get thinner down here. It has to be a proven, scientific fact. Somewhere there's a university study working on a government grant to tell us all a fact that we all know.

I ate breakfast in the bungalow and then called Richards. When I got her answering machine I hung up before the beep. I spent an hour out on the sand and then stretched out and took an easy two-mile run. The sun was hard and white in a blue sky. The salt cream of big breakers caught my shoes. The wind was still blowing out of the east and the tallest palms along the shore leaned into it, their fronds blown back like the long hair of women with their faces into the breeze.

Back at my chair, with my heart still thrumming, I pulled off my running shoes and shirt and hurdled into the waves. When I was thigh deep I dove into and under an oncoming crest, dug my fingers into the ocean floor and then pulled while bringing my feet up under me, and then drove forward and up. With my arms spread in a butterfly stroke I burst to the surface, grabbed a lungful of air and immediately dove forward and down to the bottom to repeat the motion. It was a technique I'd learned from the summer lifeguards in Ocean City, New Jersey, where we escaped as teenagers from the hot asphalt streets of South Philly. It was called dolphining and it was exhausting but twice as fast as swimming to get through the shallow surf. Once out past the breakers I turned inland and bodysurfed a wave to the beach, and then dolphined back out. After five trips I was done, arms heavy and lungs aching from gulping and holding air. I sat heavily down into my beach chair. When my breathing returned to normal I reached into my small cooler and uncapped a bottle of Rock, took a long drink and turned my face into the sun.

I came awake when a shadow changed the light on the back of my eyelids and I fluttered them open. In front of me was the passive round face of the same small boy who had caught me unawares on my porch. Again he was staring down at the longneck bottle I'd unconsciously wedged in my lap and the notion flashed into my head that I was breaking the law by consuming alcohol on the beach. Maybe a look of consternation came into my face because the boy looked into my eyes, turned and ran. When I turned to see who the kid would run to, to report me, my cell phone rang.

"Yeah?"

"Freeman?"

"Hey, Sherry," I said, not quite out of the blur of sleep. "What's up?"

"You tell me."

Ahh. The beauty of caller ID. Even if I hadn't left a message on her machine, the detective's calls would all be digitally recorded, giving her the option to at least know who had tried to reach her.

"I thought we could get together again on this O'Shea deal," I said. "I took a side trip to Philly, maybe something you should hear."

I heard her hesitate and wasn't sure how she was going to take the word of my nosing around in Philadelphia without her knowing.

"Is this information that's going to help me, or hurt my investigation, Max? Because right now I've got another girl missing and I'm about this close to locking up your friend."

"Another one?"

"Susan Martin, Suzy. The missing persons unit is funneling anything they get with earmarks of my guy's M.O. to me. I have another frantic mother who's been everywhere, talked to a dozen friends of her daughter's, the girl's landlord down here and nobody's helping."

"Bartender?"

"Yes."

"When did she quit showing up?"

"Six weeks ago."

"Knew O'Shea?"

"I don't know yet. I'm going to question the bar manager now."

"I'll meet you," I said, taking a chance.

"Kim's Alley Bar during the eight o'clock shift change. You know where it is?"

"Yeah," I said. "I've been there before."

Kim's is an oddity in the present-day city of Fort Lauderdale. It's a neighborhood bar tucked in one corner of a landmark shopping center. The land was once occupied by Clyde Beatty's Jungle Zoo. In the 1930s the site was a training and birthing facility for the big cats of the circus; lions and tigers, predators all.

The present-day center holds restaurants and antique stores, a funky bookstore and a Laundromat. Across the street to the west is the Gateway Theatre which in 1960 held the premiere of *Where the Boys Are* and changed the atmosphere of Fort Lauderdale for the next twenty years.

But only half of Kim's changed since it was established in 1948. Once a true alley bar with a small entrance obscured in the shadows, it was later split into two separate rooms by its layout. On one side is a modern place with pool and Ping-Pong tables and dartboards and a small uninspired bar top. But down a narrow, dim hallway, on the parking lot side of the shopping center, is a treasure. In this room is an ancient bar-back crafted in rich African mahogany by artisans from a different century who knew intricate scrollwork and woodcraft. The cabinetry is old school, built in Baltimore in 1820 and then dismantled and moved to New Orleans. Kim's owner purchased it there and moved it to Fort Lauderdale in 1952. Without knowing its final destination, the proud head of a lion had been carved high in the center of the scrollwork, somehow a testament to the land's history. I had been inside a few times and never once drank a drop in the gamer's side.

I arrived just before seven and half the stools at the bar were taken. I took an open one at the close end near the windows and the door. A Steve Winwood CD was playing on the juke and the manager, a pretty woman with shoulder-length brown hair who I knew as Laurie was gathering receipts while a younger woman was refilling ice. Laurie looked over first.

"Hey, stranger. Haven't seen you in a while."

I nodded my hello.

"Rolling Rock, right?"

"Perfect."

Laurie turned to the other girl who pulled a cold bottle from the cooler and set it on a napkin in front of me.

"Hi," she said. "Run a tab?"

"Hi. No. Thanks," I answered, putting twenty on the bar top. "I'll pay as I go."

She had a clean, pretty face. Wisconsin, Michigan, Minnesota came to mind. She was bringing my change back when Richards came through the door. Determined.

She was wearing jeans and a collared blouse and her hair was pulled back and twisted into a severe bun. I turned away once she spotted me and looked down the length of the bar and my eye caught movement. A man at the opposite end got up faster than most comfortable drinkers would and started for the dim hallway. Guy just recognized a cop walk in the room, I thought, a grin pulling at my mouth. I marked him at about six feet tall, lean, clean trimmed dark hair from the back, and I would have let his image slip right through my head but for the look that the young bartender had on her face when she did a double take. First on the man, then back on Richards as she made it to my elbow and then back to the man disappearing into the hallway. There was a touch of confusion in her eyes that had melted into suspicion when she turned back to us. Richards said something to me but I was watching the girl as she walked down to the vacated place at the other end, picked up the money the man had left and the half-drunk bottle of beer. It was my brand.

"Max?"

Richards was repeating my name.

"Sorry," I said, turning to her. Her eye color was a definite gray and the eyes themselves were tightened down from lack of sleep.

"This is the manager?" she asked, nodding at Laurie.

"Yeah."

Laurie looked up from her receipts and Richards bobbed her chin up in a beckoning motion. Laurie raised an index finger, one minute please, calculating something in her head before coming over. Richards didn't like the finger, I could see it in the flex of her jaw muscle. But she let it ride.

"Sherry Richards, we talked on the phone?" she said when Laurie made it over.

"Oh, hi, yeah. Just let me get my things. We can sit back there if that's OK?"

The three of us took a table in the far corner. I brought my bottle with me.

"You two obviously know each other," Laurie said, and I apologized.

"Max Freeman," I said, reaching across the table to shake her hand.

"Rolling Rock," she said, smiling.

"You're very good at that. Remembering, I mean."

She shrugged.

"Part of the business. Half the people who come in here I know by their drinks. Half I know by their first names."

"Any full names?" Richards said.

"A handful," she said, looking Richards in the eye. "You know, it's informal. It's just the way it is."

"You ever see this guy in here?" Richards asked, taking out a shot of O'Shea and handing it across the table. She wasn't wasting any time worrying about tainting an eyewitness with a single suspect photo.

"Yeah. Not a real regular and not recently, but yeah, he's been in here. Uh, bottle of Bud and Irish whiskey, I think."

"Do you know if he knew Suzy? Dated her? Took her home some night?"

Laurie brought out a manila file folder and opened it on the table. Now she was all business, too.

"Like I told you on the phone, Detective, Suzy only worked here four months, till the end of the year. September eight, to, uh, just after New Years, the third," she said, looking at the dates on the top sheet in the file. "Biggest paydays of the year, then she splits."

She looked over at me like I'd be sympathetic.

"I never had a complaint, but she mostly worked the later shifts when I wasn't around. She worked that last weekend and left."

"Disappeared," Richards said. "No forwarding address. No calls back to you for references. Didn't pick up her last check."

Laurie was answering each question with a shake of her head.

"I hadn't even heard her name mentioned until last week when her mom called all upset and then I reported it like she asked.

"I wish I had more for her mom, and you, but I don't," she said and pushed the folder an inch closer to Richards and crossed her arms. The manager was getting defensive.

"Laurie," I jumped in, pulling her eyes to me. "How unusual is that? I mean for an employee to just walk away?"

"It happens a lot. Not as much in a place like this, but in the big, high-traffic clubs, a lot. The girls can make good money, but they move around from place to place. Sometimes they'll work in three different bars at the same time. Different shifts, different days. If they decide to drop one, they just do it. Sometimes without telling anyone."

"What do you mean by not so much in a place like this?" I said.

"This is more of a neighborhood place. Quieter. You don't have to yell over the bass music just to take an order. The girls actually like to work here to take a break from those places. At least you can talk to the customers here."

"Was Suzy friendly with any specific customers?" Richards asked, pulling the conversation back on line.

"Not that I know of. A couple of guys asked where she went but they're our regulars. They get uncomfortable if things change. It's like a routine for them."

"So you don't know if anyone tried to pick her up?"

Laurie smiled.

"Honey, they're always trying. But Suzy was pretty shy. Kinda quiet. Some of the bartenders get into the girl talk thing. Even know each other's last names. But mostly they hang out with each other and do the other bars together, but they don't get that personal.

"They'll say 'whoa, check out gin and tonic down at the end' or they'll describe some date they had with the big tipper who went dutch over at Coyote's. You know, typical stuff. You were there."

This last comment was directed at Richards, who tried to look surprised.

"Yeah. I heard about you working some shifts over at Runyon's and Guppy's," Laurie said. "Gossip like that gets around."

"Not that it did any good," Richards said, looking away, the first time I'd seen her lose that hard edge of hers in public.

"Well, it did scare the shit out of everybody," Laurie said. "The girls started being more careful. They did this little half-serious game of picking out the killer in each shift."

"Yeah? And did they come up with any consensus?" Richards asked, digging right back in.

"Sure. Carmine. That creepy little delivery boy from the Italian place who is under age and is always trying to schmooze a drink."

She laughed at some mental image of Carmine. Richards was not amused.

"So, what? It's a joke and everything goes back to normal?"

"Almost," Laurie said, tightening her mouth back up. "But not until Josie, this girl who worked three different places and then dropped out of sight and nobody knew where."

Richards got out a notebook from her jeans pocket to write something down.

"Three weeks later she comes waltzing back in here one night with a big rock on her finger telling everybody how the Chivas Regal guy and her eloped to Vegas," Laurie said, again looking straight at Richards. "Then everything went back to normal."

The table went quiet for a couple of moments.

"Anyone else here close to Suzy we could talk to?" I said, making an obvious motion to the girl working behind the bar who I had been watching in the mirrored wall next to us. It may have just been her curiosity, but somebody she had more than a customer relationship with had bolted out of here when Richards came in and the bartender noticed it, and now she was way too twitchy watching her boss talk to us.

"No. Not really. Marci only worked weekends and didn't come on full until a few weeks ago. They never even met," Laurie said. "Carla worked with her. I think she tried to get Suzy to share rent on an apartment. But like I said, she was kinda shy. Had a place of her own.

"Carla's got the Sunday shift this week. But you're not going to get the girls all scared again, are you?"

Richards put her notebook away and pushed the folder one inch back to the other side of the table.

"I'm sorry," she said as she stood. "But maybe they ought to be scared."

I followed Richards outside and stayed a step behind as she walked down the sidewalk toward the street that ran behind the shopping plaza. She didn't turn or say a word and I was just about to say fuck it and reverse myself and head back to my truck when she stopped at the trunk of a two-door convertible and leaned her butt against the back fender and looked up at me.

"New ride?" I said, trying to cut the tension.

"What do you have for me, Max?" she said, folding her arms in front of her. The paring lights high above put an unnatural shine to her tight blonde hair and a slick paleness to the planes of her face. She looked years older than I knew her to be.

"You're taking this too personal, Sherry."

I put my hands in my pockets. Neutral. Unthreatening. You learn body language when you are a cop.

"Somebody has to, Max. You haven't talked to the mothers of these last two girls, who haven't seen their daughters or heard from them for weeks or even months. They read me their last letters. They send pictures that are years old. High school portraits you get in those same envelopes with the gummy flaps and the sizes and package deals printed all over them. They want to show me Mother's Day cards they got from a completely different state three years ago. They tell me their daughter's hobbies. 'Oh, she loves the beach and horseback riding.'

"They're desperate, Max. And every goddamn agency that they get passed to next tells them until there's evidence of a crime . . ."

She lowered her head and I took a step toward her and she put up a palm to stop me.

"I'm sorry, Max." She looked up. "What do you have for me?"

I put my hands back in my pockets. I told her about the trip to Philly and the meeting with O'Shea's ex-wife. Without getting into my background with Meagan, I gave her a rundown on my conversations with IAD.

"Christ, you'd at least think that hard-ass lieutenant up there would want to throw some help into this," she said, and I had to work to sustain a poker face.

"The ex-wife says O'Shea never got threatening. Never physical. In fact, she of all people was sure he wouldn't have the guts to carry something off like this and I gotta tell you, Sherry, I get the same vibe."

She turned her face away and looked down the shadowed street and her lips were pressed into a whitening crease.

"Be objective, Sherry. You've got an ex-cop who liked to bounce from bar to bar, dates some bartenders, has a couple of failed trips with women and the capacity for violence with assholes on the street," I said. "That's a profile that could fit me and another two dozen guys in the business we're in. Maybe he's carrying some kind of guilty stink from what happened up in Philly, but you've got nothing on him."

"We'll see," she said and pushed herself off the car with a flex of her thighs.

"What does that mean?"

"I've got a warrant to search his place," she said, walking

around to open the driver's door. "One of your muggers from the other night is filing charges saying your buddy tried to kick him to death. He was bleeding and we think we might get some forensics from O'Shea's boots to match it."

I hoped my face didn't look as stunned and stupid as it felt.

"What the hell does that have to do with missing women?" I said.

"You know the game, Max. Maybe we can squeeze him. You never know what a little pressure will bring out once you have somebody inside."

She got in her car and started the engine and I stepped back as she pulled away. Maybe my former girlfriend hadn't just used me. But that's what it felt like.

After Richards left I walked back to my truck and sat in the parking lot watching the door to Kim's, grinding, nowhere to be and not feeling like going back inside. At eleven I walked over to Big Louie's, the Italian restaurant and pizzeria at the front corner of the strip mall. I got some manicotti and coffee to go. I may have even seen Carmine the delivery boy, an angular kid with coat hanger shoulders and a definite acne problem. He had a horselike face and a patch of peroxide blonde hair. He actually had some kind of tattoo on his calf that was impossible to decipher as it wrapped around a leg the diameter of a garden hose. If he tried to abduct one of the bartenders they would have slapped him silly.

Back in the truck I lowered the window to let the gathering odor of red sauce and garlic escape and had my dinner off the passenger seat. On occasion a lone man would approach the door of Kim's and I would focus my small field glasses from the glove box on him. What the hell was I on surveillance for? Had walking around on my old beat for a couple of days put me back in the zone?

I took another bite of pasta and watched a couple bend their heads together at the corner, instantly thought drug deal, and then chastised myself when I saw the flare of the man's lighter as they shared the flame to light their cigarettes. It was then that I realized the new fissure I was grinding was the man I'd seen slip away from the bar in Kim's when Richards had walked in. I'd caught the white glow of his skin between his hairline and collar as he disappeared into the dark and the smooth, athletic grace that got him to the hallway without a stumble or hesitation. There would of course be lots of reasons for someone to bail out of the back of a bar when a detective walked in the front, even if she was plainclothes, even if she just looked the part, and we both probably looked the part to someone paying attention. But the bartender had added to the feel that it wasn't right. If young Marci had some kind of drug dealing going on under the bar, even small-time stuff, they'd be careful. But there had been something in her eyes that lit my suspicion. Whether it was a carryover from my walk down South Street or not, here I was and it didn't necessarily feel wrong. Nice warm night. Box of manicotti. Hot coffee. Shit. I used to hate surveillance.

At one in the morning I decided to move. The lot was clearing and I had counted three times that a city patrol car had cruised through the center and now he was back. I watched the cop pull into a darkened spot almost in a direct line between me and the windows of Kim's, obstructing the view I'd had of Marci's bobbing blonde ponytail. It looked like he was going to stay awhile. Maybe he was there purposely to look after employees of the restaurants and the bar who were getting off work. Maybe some shift sergeant was paying attention to Richards's concerns after all. I did know that if this cop was smart he was going to notice me before long—single male in a pickup truck parked for hours and up to no good.

I started the engine and pulled out of the lot through the back street exit and swung west. There was another parking area used by movie patrons of the multiplex next door. With the right angle, I could still see Kim's front door and would hopefully see when Marci left and if she was picked up by a six-foot athletic man who shied away from the smell of cops.

An hour later my coffee was long dead and cold. The movie

had let out and I'd watched couples stroll to their cars and head home, chatting about the merits of plot and pyrotechnics and performances. The last movie I'd been to was with Sherry and the damn thing was out on DVD and could have been having its broadcast debut by now. The night had settled into that long after-hours feel when the city drops in decibels and the streetlights take on a more noticeable presence and the cut of headlights across a brick facade sends shadows moving that you would not have seen at ten o'clock.

At 2:20 Marci walked out through the wide wooden door. An older man was behind her and had his fist up against the deadbolt on the inside. We both watched the girl go to a late model, light blue two-door parked right in front and unlock the driver's side. She waved at the old guy who stepped back and pulled the bar door shut. Marci backed out of her spot and came my way, her lights flashing off my truck windows as she bounced over a speed bump and then turned onto the street. All right, I thought. It was an old cop's hunch. Sometimes that's all they are. I sure as hell wasn't going to follow the girl home. I pulled out of my own parking space and as I approached the street another set of headlights met mine. They jounced over the speed bump and I caught the opaque blue tint of the light bar on top. It was the patrol car. Done for the night. Everybody out safe.

He turned left, without a signal, in the direction Marci had gone. My headlights caught the outline of a dark-haired male officer, clean-cut, and then I turned north toward the beach house.

The annoying trill of the cell phone woke me the next day, snapping a dream that had me somewhere in the Everglades, someplace other than my river, someplace where I was unfamiliar and lost in a wooded hammock of gumbo limbo and poisonwood trees. It was night and I was crouched in a cover of fern, watching the glowing red spots of a gator's eyes that were becoming larger, though for some reason I felt no fear of them and as I tracked their movement through the trees they took on the shape of a car's taillights and I suddenly heard the sound of a horn in traffic which became the ring of my phone.

I swung my legs off the bed and blinked away the odd smell of the exhaust and marsh grass and picked up the cell.

"Yeah?"

"Freeman?"

It was a man's voice.

"Who's this?"

"It's O'Shea, Freeman."

I registered the Philly accent and recalled I'd given O'Shea my card at Archie's.

"Yeah, Colin. What's up?"

"I don't want to say you dropped a dime on me, Freeman. So tell me it isn't true," he said, biting off the ends of accusatory sentences.

"Well, you just said it, O'Shea," I answered, my head quickly clearing. "So tell me what the hell you're talking about."

"The sheriff's office just executed a search warrant on my apartment."

I was recalling Richards's squeeze plan.

"Did they arrest you?"

"Not yet. But I would like to know how the fuck they put me with you when your two muggers tried to take you off the other night and I saved your ass, again, brother."

I felt my anger mix with an unexpected whiff of guilt which tempered my response.

"I didn't tell them you were with me, O'Shea. But you're also not dealing with some dumb-ass detective with Richards," I said. "She was the one who put me onto you at your local hangout and a description by those two assholes and your patented boot work wouldn't be hard to put together. Your IAD file back home isn't exactly vague on the excessive-force complaints, either."

There was nothing but an empty electronic buzz on the other end of the line for several long beats.

"I'm gonna need a lawyer if this goes any further, Max," he finally said. "How's this guy Manchester you work for?"

Billy was brilliant, but the idea of him acting as a criminal defense attorney for a guy like O'Shea gave me more than a few seconds of doubt. I still couldn't say why I was walking a line with him. But guilty or not, he was going to need a good lawyer.

"Give me a number where I can reach you," I said.

CHAPTER 15

He followed her home, shaking his head and exhaling a little shot of disgust each time she put on a correct blinker or came to a full stop at an intersection. Marci and her proper driving etiquette. This girl gotta loosen up, he thought. But then, maybe she was doing everything correctly in her little blue Honda because he was behind her, toeing the line in front of the cop like all the other lemmings on the road. He liked that idea. Maybe some night he would pull her over. They could do it in her backseat with the lights flashing. She'd love it. But shit, wouldn't that just be asking to get caught? The thought flashed his mind back on the topic of the night. What the fuck was that BSO detective bitch Richards doing in Kim's earlier? He'd seen her come struttin' in all tight-assed like she owned the place. He split and was sure she never got a look at him. When he called Marci later behind the bar she said the woman and that big rangy-looking guy were together, that they were talking with her boss. He called her again an hour later and she said the manager, Laurie, told her they were community-watch cops just checking in to make sure the girls were safe at night and that there hadn't been any incidents.

My ass, he thought. He knew Richards. He'd had one of his friends point her out at a crime scene once. The grapevine had it that she was still rattling the cages about missing girls, even when nobody paid any attention. It's what happened when you let these broads get a little power, twist you with their fucking rank. He didn't know who Mr. Tan Man was. He'd watched him come in, take a sniff of Laurie and then checked out Marci's ass for a while. He had the look of a cop, too. But even an off-duty guy wouldn't dress like that and who has time to work the job and get out in the sun like that guy? At least the guy had good taste in beer. He'd be worth watching out for.

Marci pulled into the lot of her apartment building and he parked the cruiser across the street. Best thing about this department was that they let you take your patrol car home when you were off. They said it bolstered the perception of more cops on the streets. He liked it fine. It kept people out of his way and made them nervous when he was around. Marci waited at her car door until he joined her.

"Hi."

"Hi? That's it? Hi?" she said, pissed. He liked her pissed sometimes.

"Hi. How are you?" he said, playing with it.

"Jesus, Kyle. What was that all about today? You go flying out of the bar without a word and those people are there and you tell me Laurie's lying to me. What's going on?"

"Whoa, whoa. Easy, babe," he said and put his hand on her shoulder and rubbed her back. These girls get so emotional. You gotta calm them down a little. They're like wild fillies when you're trying to break them.

"Come on, let's go upstairs and I'll explain. I'm sorry I was so vague, babe. I didn't mean to scare you," he said.

"I'm not fucking scared. I just don't like not knowing what's going on," she said, stepping away from him. He let her lead the way to her second-floor apartment. When she got to her door he watched her unlock it and walk in, tossing the ring of keys in that little basket on top of the stereo speaker.

He watched her kick off her shoes and go into the kitchen and stand in the light of the open refrigerator staring while she pulled the tie out of her hair and shook her curls loose like she always did. Then she reached in for her bottled water and brought him a beer like she always did. She flopped into the corner of the couch and he joined her.

"All right," she said. "I'm taking it easy. Give."

It sounded like an order, but he let it pass.

"You know that I don't like people in the bar to know I'm a cop. That's all it was."

"Laurie said they were just community watch," she said. "But that big guy didn't look like community watch to me."

"Well, Laurie was right," he said. "But you meet these people when you're a real cop. You give them instruction and show them around the beat so if they see anything that needs to be checked out, they can call an officer to take care of it."

He watched her take a drink of the water, knew she was thinking.

"So you knew the blonde?"

"Yeah. I've seen her around. And I didn't want to take the chance she'd see me and spoil it. My privacy, you know, my place."

"Oh, so now it's your place," she said, and the grin was sneaking back onto her face.

"Ours," he said. "Our place, our secret."

He knew they liked that sharing shit. She was quiet a few moments, watching his eyes with that look like she knew him better than she really did.

"Let's go for a ride," he said, the thought coming on to him, bringing it up just like that, surprising even himself. He saw the winch in her face, like, pained, not scared, not like she knew.

"Come on," he said, putting his hand on her leg. "Mix up some whiskey sours that you like and we'll burn out to alligator alley, see how fast the cruiser can really cruise." He made his voice sound excited. Hell, it was excited, the thought of doing it again.

"Kyle," she whined, but that smile was again behind her eyes.

"You scared the shit out of me last time with that. God, when you turned the headlights off I was freaking." She couldn't hide that glimmer of the wild girl. He did that Groucho Marx thing with his eyebrows.

"Yeah? Come on."

He moved and the leather of the couch squeaked. But she resisted.

"No, come on, Kyle. I'm really tired, babe. That shift was really long. My feet are aching. Can't we just stay here and watch a movie?"

She put her hand over his on her thigh. He didn't like to let her win. But this time, maybe. Shit, wasn't it always this way? You're nice to them, take 'em out, give 'em all this attention, but you just can't ever trust them. They're finally going to turn on you and try to dominate your ass. They're gonna push and push and push the line until, fuck it, they go over it. Then you gotta end it. Can't just let 'em walk off thinking they won.

Afterward, after they'd had sex with the blue glow of one of his favorite movies flashing and shimmering off her skin, she lay quiet with her head on his chest. This was all he wanted, so why did they always have to go and screw it up by trying to take over?

"So the tall blonde is kind of attractive," she said. "Ever have to follow up with her as the real cop?"

She was running her fingers through his hair, letting her nails lightly scratch his scalp. He took a quick pull from the beer that was still on the coffee table. Jealousy, he thought. What a lever, man.

"Never," he said and then moved his mouth, cold from the beer, to her stomach and down and she squealed and giggled but did not try to get away.

CHAPTER 16

I met Billy at his apartment. Diane was there, cooking pasta and warming up a red sauce that I knew Billy had put together in advance. I recognized the smell of his special seasonings escaping from each snapping bubble of thick sauce as it simmered. I kissed Diane on the cheek as I helped myself to a beer.

"Counselor," I said in greeting. "You sure you want to sit behind the bench instead of opening your own boutique restaurant on Atlantic Boulevard?"

"I could do that, Max. But your lawyer would have to quit also and be my chef. And where would that leave you?" she said, stopping to have a taste of wine from the glass beside her.

"I'll be the dishwasher, of course. Work for meals only."

I joined Billy out on the patio where the breeze was coming in off the ocean. It was in the low seventies, same temperature, I knew, as the water. Billy had rolled back his sliding windows, but I knew that he also had the A.C. working inside, if for nothing else than to keep the humidity level down to protect his paintings. Sometimes he did this in midsummer, unruffled by the expense and waste of energy. I knew the kind of oppressive and foul air he'd grown up with in the row houses of north Philly. This was Billy's way of pushing that past back, of exerting his power, even over the weather itself. A few boat lights blinked out on the horizon. One hundred thirty feet below, the surf made the sound of a drummer's slow brushes on a snare head.

"So how was it, rubbing shoulders with the movers and shakers the other night?" I asked.

He smiled, looking out into the night, and shook his head.

"I d-didn't know why I was anxious, Max. Maybe because of b-being linked with Diane. On m-my own, I frankly don't give a damn. It's one of the beauties of l-lonely success."

He stopped, took a drink from his wine and cut a look at me. If we had reached out and clinked bottle to glass it would not have been any more obvious. We punched at each other's psyches like this often. We knew each other well.

"I've b-been in that company before, of course. And d-deep down, they're just capitalists. You m-mention the name of a stock that you know everyone is hearing rumblings about. You sp-speak knowledgeably about real estate movements. You agree, even slightly, with a brokerage firm's st-stand on the Republican governor's tax relief on capital gains. Hell, when it c-comes to money, every one in that circle is green, Max."

"So I take it that suit you were wearing made enough of a statement that you didn't have to?" I said.

"The women were entranced and only a handful of the men knew what they were looking at, other than a high price tag," Diane said as she stepped onto the patio and slipped her arm through Billy's. "He was the talk of the town."

"Without having to t-talk m-myself."

I could not tell whether the slight glow of the moment was balanced between them, or whether hers was spilling onto my friend, enveloping him in the bubble of her optimism. It was like stepping closer to someone else's campfire. Even if the warmth wasn't of your making it made you feel better and a cold man would find it impossible to resist. Diane had that way about her and I was both happy for Billy and a little jealous.

"If you gentlemen are ready," she said, breaking the moment. "Dinner is served."

We ate at the dining room table again, which had always been Billy's habit. He liked being surrounded by his paintings and sculptures and always served on china and crystal. I had even learned to eat in his home without bringing a beer bottle to the table.

Yet Billy was also not one for dinnertime small talk. And as usual he had sensed my reluctance to ask what I'd come to ask.

"So what's up w-with Sherry and this O'Shea?" he said, never shy of cutting straight to it.

"She's still got a bead on him. He's still hanging around, worried that she's going to grab him up."

"So why doesn't he skip the country?" Diane suddenly said, causing both of us to look at her. "I mean, come on, he knows the system and is paranoid enough about your friend Richards picking him up, I would think he'd take the chance to get out of the country before they find a body someplace and connect him."

If no nonsense was an attractive character trait, no wonder these two were together.

"Money?" Billy offered.

"Hell, an ex-cop from the States could find work in South America without much trouble," I said.

"Family?"

"I didn't get that sense from his ex-wife. They never had kids."

"Has to be somebody he cares about?"

"Richards says he lives alone and the way he's playing the bar scene, I don't think so."

Diane was watching us with a bemused look on her face until Billy noticed it.

"What?" he said.

"Maybe this man is innocent," she said.

Billy slipped his hand over and touched his fingertips on the back of his fiancée's wrist.

"An interesting position, coming from a future judge," he said and smiled at her. "And I b-believe Max was finally getting to that part."

He looked, expectantly, at me. Billy was good at watching my internal arguments. Sometimes he was even better at recognizing when I'd come to a decision than I was.

"I think O'Shea needs a lawyer," I said, throwing it straight out there.

Billy cut his eyes to Diane, she to him.

Then I told them both of Richards's plan to arrest O'Shea on the assault charge, about the tactic she used to get inside his apartment with the hope of finding something to connect him with the missing girls.

"Was she successful?" Diane asked.

"I don't know. O'Shea called me and said they'd confiscated his boots. Richards was figuring on bloodstain to connect him with the assault, but he didn't say what else they might have taken."

"It would be easy enough to get a copy of the warrant, see what they took out of the place," Diane said, the lawyer in her, working it even as an unconscious reaction.

"If he g-gets arrested, you just sh-show up at magistrate's court as an eyewitness and squelch the p-prosecutor's p-probable cause by entering an affidavit that you two were the ones who were attacked."

"Through who, Billy?" I said. "The public defender who's just going through the morning cattle call? You know how that works in front of a judge who's probably on rotation for three weeks because everyone hates that duty."

Billy and Diane again looked at each other. They knew I was right.

"The guy needs a lawyer," I repeated.

I knew what I was asking of my friend, who had not spoken in open court since his days in college when his law degree required him to display his stutter in front of fellow students. I knew he loathed the idea of revealing his flaw and giving others a reason to think they had some advantage over him.

"Can I get anyone coffee?" Diane said, standing to clear the table and then going to the kitchen without an answer which she knew she already had.

"I'd just hate to see the guy standing up there with no one to throw another possibility across the judge's bench," I said.

"The magistrate judge isn't likely to listen any more to Billy than she would the public defender, Max," Diane said from the kitchen. "Unless they try something outrageous like asking for no bond."

This time I knew she was right. But I also knew that if they were holding O'Shea on assault charges it would just bolster any argument the prosecutor made to a grand jury on filing an abduction and homicide rap on the guy later. I could hear it clearly in my head: "I know the evidence is circumstantial, ladies and gentlemen, but our suspect was also recently arrested for a violent act which shows his penchant for aggression."

Billy was quiet. Even as a behind-the-scenes litigator, he knew the workings and the working flaws in the system. He also knew that a lawyer can get a leg caught in the machinery and get pulled in, just as a suspect can. I was asking him to risk that chance that he might be pulled into an arena that he had avoided his entire career.

"O'Shea says he has nothing to do with these disappearances, Billy. And he asked me to help him."

"D-Do you trust him?"

I hesitated, something a good attorney would never do, whether they were convinced or not. People familiar with the working of courtrooms know that truth and justice are only in the eye of the beholder. The best lawyers know that their job is only to convince that beholder of their version.

I knew I could never accept that role and I knew Billy well enough to know how he disdained it.

"My gut tells me he's not involved," I said. "But I could be giving him more benefit than he deserves. The guy did save me from a hole in the back ten years ago."

Diane brought over the coffee, put mine in front of me and then sat next to Billy.

"Do you want to t-tell me that part?"

Even if he did phrase it as such, I knew it wasn't really a question. While I told the story, I went through the entire pot of strong Colombian blend. Diane got up twice to refill her wineglass. I reconstructed the drug bust on South Street and how O'Shea must have been listening in on the tack channel that night and horning in on the action. But there was also no doubt that he'd kept the drug runner from using the handgun I neglected to frisk him for. I could have been dead in the street, another cop funeral in the family.

I told them of my interviews with O'Shea's ex-wife and my trip to the IAD office. When I mentioned Meagan's name, Billy looked up into my eyes. He would let me gloss over it, but I was using truth to base my assumption of O'Shea's innocence on. When Diane heard that I had been married to an aggressive, type-A personality who was always bent on being the alpha-male of her block, she kept her eyes on the rim of her glass. But I could see the twitch at the corners of her mouth.

I stopped talking and she finally looked up.

"What?"

"It only lasted two years," I said defensively.

"I'm surprised."

"At what?"

"That it went that long."

She waited a beat.

"Any children?"

"No. Thank God," I said. "She would have eaten her young."

Diane coughed into her glass. Billy patted her back.

"Sorry," she finally said.

I smiled and shook my head. Billy brought us back on line.

"OK. If I was his lawyer. If," he said. "I would obviously argue f-for no crime to begin with. No body. No evidence. But say it m-moves to indictment anyway. Then as an attorney I try to sh-show that someone else could be responsible. Who? What kind of man abducts grown, s-smart single women whose only similarity is their chosen work?"

"Someone who's a psycho, but a different one," said Diane, re-joining us. She had switched her drink to ice water in a crystal tumbler.

"If I put myself behind that bar, I see the same group of guys every night waving their dicks around trying to show who can snag the attention of the good-looking bartender. So to be successful, this one's got to have a different schtick."

"Your honor!" Billy said in mock horror. "Waving their . . ."

"And at the risk of sounding shallow," I interrupted, "he's good-looking himself. She's probably got a target-rich environment, if you know what I mean. She knows she's onstage and can pick from the audience."

"Someone in their age r-range, I would suspect. M-Maybe a little older."

"But not Daddy," Diane said. "You said your friend Richards profiled these girls as being far from home, not necessarily close to family, independent-minded. I see that as a girl running away from Daddy, not to one."

"Someone who appears stable. Has a job. Isn't in there scraping change together or begging off a tab. These girls have seen enough of that."

"Someone s-safe. Or p-perceived to be safe," said Billy. "They see a lot of quick hit hustle going on b-between pickup and bar stool relationships every night."

"All right," said Diane. "We've got a good-looking guy with an aura of something out of the ordinary who appears stable, self-sufficient, not boring, smart and makes you feel safe."

The table went quiet for too long. I was staring into my coffee cup and when I raised my eyes they were both looking at me.

"Where were you on the night of January third?" Diane said with that mischievous look in her eyes.

"It fits you, M-Max. And your friend, O'Shea," Billy said.

"Who doesn't trust a cop, off-duty, in a bar?" Diane said. "Especially a blue-collar girl from a blue-collar neighborhood."

"I'm not a cop anymore, and neither is O'Shea," I said, going on the defensive.

"The problem with all this dime-store psychoanalysis is that none of us knows what the women were looking for to let themselves fall into this trap. And that's if they fell at all and aren't tending bar in Cancún or Freeport or Houston for Christ's sake," I said. "And what's the killer's motive in all this if they were abducted?"

This time I got up myself and poured the final cup from the coffeemaker.

"They're lonely, Max," Diane said, answering the first question. "You don't use logic to explain what one person sees in another to save them from loneliness."

She slipped her hand under Billy's.

"Just like m-most abusers, rapists, it's not about sex," Billy said. "The guy is trying to control something and can't, not even himself."

"Colin O'Shea doesn't want control that bad," I said. "Hell. He never wanted it when he did have it."

"I agree," said Billy.

"Yeah?"

"Yes. If he gets arrested, Max. Tell him t-to call m-me."

"I appreciate it, Billy," I said, and looked at Diane, who was now squeezing Billy's hand.

"And let's all pray for Cancún," Diane said.

CHAPTER 17

Marci woke Sunday morning thinking: "How did I do this to myself again?"

She could feel it hardening in the back of her head, that uncomfortable guilt and self-admonishment like she'd put off studying for a midterm until the date of the test or once again forgotten to check the oil in her car and knew that her father would back it out to move it from blocking his truck and see the light on and say "Didn't I tell you? That engine is going to seize up on you, young lady, and that's it. You're walking."

But this was worse. She was in too deep again with a man and shit, she was starting to tell it wasn't going to work. She was lying in bed, naked under just a sheet and watching the lines of sunlight streak through the blinds and crawl across the wall. It had to be eleven. He'd been gone since seven because he was working that daytime alpha shift or whatever they called it. She pressed a pillow tighter in between her legs and felt the bruise on the outside of her thigh. It was still that high, purple color of an underripe plum and was just getting a thin ring of yellow around its edge. He'd punched her a good one when she grabbed the cell phone out of his hand and kept right on bitching about him checking all her call-back log numbers.

OK, maybe she was overreacting. It was just his nature, wanting to know everything about her and who she was talking to all the time. It's what cops do, right? Born investigators and always need to know what's going on, he said. Christ knows she'd been with guys who didn't want to know a damn thing about her except whether she'd put out on the first half-drunken date. And so what if he called her at work a dozen times a night? He just wanted to hear her voice, he said. He was always asking if she could get out early because he missed her. Shit, when was the last time she had a boyfriend who showed her that much attention?

She rolled over to her nightstand and took a drink from the bottle of spring water. There was an empty tumbler next to it that he'd filled with Maker's Mark. The man could drink. Her daddy would be pissed off about that, pull that holier-than-thou on her even if he was the one who got her that first bartending job at the VFW in Eagleton. But the police officer part, he'd be proud of that. A law-abiding, respected man who would protect you when I'm gone. And he'd been gone, what, four years now?

She could still see him sometimes in her worst dreams at night, coming through the mudroom door, stumbling, and her father never stumbled. The frigid air from outside seemed to have ushered him in, the white vapor billowing off his overalls and jacket and coming with short, erratic puffs from the misshapen hole of a mouth. His big jaw was lopsided and hanging like a flour box tilted and about to fall off the edge of a counter.

"Daddy?" She could hear herself say the word and the brittle sound of it usually jerked her out of her sleep before she had to endure the sight of him falling, helplessly, against gravity and death to the linoleum floor. One eye was dropped and already sightless, but the other was clear and blue and wide like he was trying to record as much of his daughter's image as he could in the seconds he had left.

She had stood alone next to an uncle at her father's burial. The marble marker that held her mother's name, the one she had been taught to pray at from the time of her first memories, was replaced by a single headstone bearing both her parents' names. For some reason when she recalled that day, she remembered the clods of earth piled up on the grave, misshapen hunks yanked out of the frozen ground and too ice-hardened to smooth out. And she also remembered swearing to herself, "To hell with the rules. I'm leaving this place before it kills me."

Yes, Daddy would like the idea of her dating a cop. But he wouldn't like the rule breaking. And man could Kyle break the rules. That thing with the patrol car on the expressway. She thought she was going to pee! Then the drinking, while he was driving! "So what's to worry? They're not exactly going to pull me over."

And that time he was picking her up and before she could get to the curb those punks with the leather and nose-buttons started wolfing on her? She'd never seen anyone move so fast. She had ignored the two and went to open Kyle's passenger door and all she could figure later was that he had popped open his own side at the same time. When she sat down and her eyes cleared the roofline, he was gone, like a magic trick. A yelp from the sidewalk snapped her head around and there he was. One of the rivet boys was up against the wall of Nadine's Nail Design, hands up flat on the brick, legs spread and shaky. Kyle had the other one hooked by a fistful of black T-shirt and she heard the splat of that police billy club thing against the slick leather of his pant leg. When Kyle had them both against the wall she could tell he was talking but keeping his tone low, like he did sometimes with her when he got pissed and all she could hear was that low bass rumbling that came from his chest. She stayed in her seat, knew, even that early in their relationship, not to enter that bristling zone of electric air that surrounded him.

He was up close to the guys, in between them, his jaws working and both of them seemed like they didn't even want to turn their heads to look at him. She could tell what he was doing with the club that was now in front of him. She thought he was going to step down when the one on the left bobbed his head, saying something, and suddenly Kyle had a piece of the guy's ear, ring and all, in his grip, stretching it like the guy was some kinda Gumby toy and she could hear the dude whining: "OK, OK, man. OK."

Only then, after he made the guy cry, did he back away and come around and get back in the car as cool and unruffled as though he'd just checked on a locked door during some night patrol.

"Jesus, Kyle," she'd said as he started the car. "What was that about?"

"I don't let street turds like that insult my girl," he said, looking over at her, giving her that closed-mouth smile.

They had sex that afternoon at her apartment in a straight-backed kitchen chair and when he'd dropped his belt and the butt of that gun hit the floor she'd felt it thump in her heart and Christ, there was that guilt thing again. But she couldn't help herself for getting off on the excitement and twinge of danger that the guy carried around with him. What girl didn't like that page of fantasy that had her man standing up for her honor?

So why was she still lying in bed knowing, not just thinking, but knowing, that it wasn't going to work out and she was going to have to go through that whole high school–like breakup thing that never changed no matter how old you got. She watched the lines of sunlight hit the corner of her room like bars of paint and with each minute shear off at a new angle. Scared to tell him? Yeah, maybe. That whole thing with him disappearing out of Kim's when those other cops came in. The punch he'd bruised her with last night. Did he hit her high on the thigh because he knew it wouldn't show? That people wouldn't ask her what happened? They learn about that, cops did, didn't they? Sure, he'd snapped at her before, but he always apologized, always told her how sorry he was and how much he really, really cared about her. But what had once been flattering and endearing was starting to make her feel wary, like one of

Daddy's stewing rabbits out in the pens in the barn. They'd get petted and fed and cooed at for being so cute and fluffy but every older kid knew what happened to stewing rabbits when it was time. Kyle was waiting for something. And there was no way she was going to wait and see what it was.

CHAPTER 18

I was up in north West Palm Beach, three blocks from the hotel where Rodrigo was staying, waiting for him to meet me under the huge poinciana near the corner of Twelfth and Wright streets. The "flame tree" Rodrigo called it, because it was the time of year when the poincianas bloomed and the trees' blossoms were thick and the color of fire feeding off an unlimited supply of clean, dry wood.

I parked my truck in the shade of the tree's canopy and watched as the earliest blossoms, already leached of their life, fell on my hood like splotches of paint. The soiled orange color made me think of the scar on Rodrigo's face and then there he was across the street. He was walking with his eyes down, hands in his pockets in the unobtrusive but wary manner that people other than beat cops will never notice.

"Mr. Max," he said, climbing into the cab.

"Rodrigo, *Kumusta ka?*"

"OK," he said and immediately, wanting to please, pulled a sheet of ruled notebook paper from his jacket pocket and smoothed it on his thigh before handing it to me.

"For Mr. Manchester. Names of others hurt in the fire," he said and his eyes looked up through the windshield into the blossoms and he blew a short whoof of air from his nose at the irony of meeting under an umbrella of flame to discuss the matter at hand.

"But they are afraid," he said. "For the jobs they are afraid to talk to you, Mr. Max."

"Has anyone been scaring them, Rodrigo? Has there been anyone talking about organizing some kind of labor union or threatening you not to?"

The small man averted his eyes and his short, thick fingers went nervous.

"There is always talk. But only in whispers, Mr. Max. And we are only a few here now and we know it takes numbers, this union."

I reached into the space behind his seat and took the manila folder Billy had given me and showed him the DOC photos of the Hix brothers.

"Have you seen these men? Talking with the workers or just hanging around?"

He studied the faces, holding them side by side.

"This is the one," he finally said, fluttering the picture of David Hix, whose jaw I had broken with the top of my head.

"He is big, like you. Yes, Mr. Max?"

"Yeah, he's big. Where?"

"He big here." The little Filipino patted his stomach with both hands. "Fat, here."

"No, no," I said, unable to keep from smiling. "Where did you see him?"

"I see him at the food stand. Not talk to nobody. Sit and watch. Just watch."

I wondered if Hix had seen me with Rodrigo and his friend the week before, if that had been enough to put him on to me by someone who had hired him to look big and ugly in front of the workers.

"I watch him follow the, the, what you say?" Rodrigo said, putting his fingers to his thumb and finger to his mouth.

"Smokers," I said. "He followed the guys when they went for a smoke?"

"Yes, to the alley."

Bat Man liked the alleys.

"And he hit someone?"

"No hit. Push and threaten. With *huh*! *Huh*! Mouth not work."

My cell phone rang and I took the folder and replaced it while answering.

"Yeah?"

"Freeman? It's O'Shea."

"Don't tell me you're already in jail."

"No. Not yet. I took a few days off work and I'm trying to lay low. Did you ask your man Manchester about me? I mean, I don't have a lot of cash Freeman, but I'd feel a hell of a lot better if I had some back-up on this."

Rodrigo was staring out at the tree shade, trying to be invisible. Unlike in the new American cell phone society, conversations between individuals were still considered private events in his world.

"I talked to him. You can call his number if they arrest you," I said to O'Shea.

"Yeah?"

"Yeah. But he doesn't do this thing often, O'Shea. So it's a favor to me and since you've got some time, you might be able to help me to help you."

"Name it."

"Meet me in the parking lot in front of Big Louie's in the Gateway Shopping Center at eight," I said.

"All right. You, ah, need me to be carrying?"

"Not that kind of help," I said.

"I've got a carry permit, for the security job," he said, getting defensive.

"You really think it's a good idea to be carrying a gun when you're waiting for the sheriff's office to pick you up on an arrest warrant?"

He didn't answer and Rodrigo was cutting an occasional look at me. He knew enough English to be uncomfortable with what he was overhearing.

"Just meet me, Colin. I'll give you what you need to carry."

I punched off the phone and apologized to Rodrigo, who now had his hands folded on his thighs, holding his nervous fingers down as if he were trying to keep a small bird from fluttering off his lap.

"OK. If you see the big man again, stay away," I said. "And try to call me or Mr. Manchester. All right?"

He was nodding like a bobble-head doll.

"OK, Mr. Max. OK."

I smiled at him and told him to be careful and he nearly sprung out of the seat when he popped the door. I watched him walk away with the same gait, but using a different route. I sat staring out at the empty lot in front of me and two more spent blossoms of flame hit with a wet smack on my hood and I wondered if I was doing O'Shea or anyone else any favors with the next plan I'd concocted.

I took US Highway 1 to Fort Lauderdale. In South Florida US 1 is boringly homogeneous. Driving south you can pass through a dozen municipalities and never tell when the string of car dealerships, strip shopping centers, pastel business buildings and gas stations fall into another jurisdiction. It matters little to anyone except maybe a speeder whose city P.D. pursuers will actually give up the chase when he crosses into another town's turf. The sameness of the landscape and the parochial attitudes of the cops are a dichotomy for a road named US 1, which Billy the historian points out stands for Unified System 1 and not United States 1.

I'd called ahead and stopped at Billy's office and Allie had one of the firm's cell phones with a digital camera on it waiting. I then went on to Fort Lauderdale and swung down to the beach and parked near the Parrot Lounge and walked out to the sand. In the salt air and purpling sky I sat on the low beachfront wall and tried to figure out the cell phone camera. I took a shot of the Holiday Inn by mistake. I got a nice shot of a couple walking their pit bull on a silver chain leash. A young woman came off the sand and propped one foot on the wall near me and bent to wipe the grains from her ankles and calves. While faking a call I covertly took a photo of her. She looked up once at me and smiled politely and I said something about refinancing a mortgage to my nonexistent phone caller. Hey, it was a test.

By sundown I had the camera figured out. I attempted a couple of low-light shots that were adequate. When the darkness deepened I tried to capture "the disappearing blue." But even the digital quality couldn't do justice to the mystery of the melding colors and at seven thirty I walked back to my truck and drove back across the intracoastal bridge. At the shopping center I parked in the lot, facing Kim's, and did a quick eyeball. Plenty of cars. Busy over at the Thai restaurant across the way. Pickup orders coming out of Big Louie's. And a patrol car parked nearly in the same spot as last time. My angle was better, but still I could only see a silhouette of the officer's head. He appeared to have a phone to one ear and he was facing the other way. A knuckle to metal rap on my truck bed fender made me jump. O'Shea was in my side mirror and then at my window.

"How's it hangin,' Freeman?"

"Take a seat, O'Shea," I told him, reaching over to pop the lock on the passenger door.

I had not seen him pull in. Maybe he had walked. I realized I still didn't know where he lived or what kind of vehicle he drove. And still I was taking his side in a possible string of homicides. Maybe I was the one who wasn't being a very thorough cop.

O'Shea got in and settled. He had a three-day beard and was wearing jeans and a dark windbreaker. He had on a Phillies baseball cap and black soft-soled shoes, like an umpire would wear. I reached back behind the seat and brought out a thermos. He looked through the windows.

"What, you're on surveillance?" he said, trying to guess ahead.

"Yeah, in a way," I said, pouring him a cup. He blew across the top before taking a sip. I was matching his unfocused look outside, waiting, like I was at the edge of some cliff, unsure how deep the water was if I jumped.

"I was up in Philly for a couple of days," I finally said, still not looking at him. "I talked with your ex. She wanted me to tell you she wished you the best and didn't think you had anything to do with this or with the Faith Hamlin deal."

He didn't react, just kept looking forward, but I could see blue veins at the side of his forehead starting to bulge. He was holding something in. But after a few beats of silence, I knew it was going to stay there.

"You going to give me any kind of inside on the grocery store clerk missing up there?"

"No. I'm not," he said, and the veins pulsed back down.

"Christ, Colin. You can carry the old loyalty to the blue brotherhood a little too far, you know," I said.

"It's not loyalty to them," was all he said and then put the cup to his mouth and went quiet again.

"Look, Colin. I don't think you're in on these disappearances. Maybe I'm missing something, because IA in Philly and Richards down here are on you like stink. But I'm on your side on this, man. For some reason, I'm trusting you."

He stayed quiet but then turned and faced me.

"You said you needed me to help you help me," O'Shea said. "That kinda gave it away, Freeman. So let's get to it."

"Right."

I took out the cell phone and handed it to him.

"You know how to use the camera in one of these?"

He flipped the set open, looked at the face and turned it over once.

"Yeah."

"Yeah?" I said, thinking of my hour-long self-lesson.

"Yeah. What? You think I've been living in a fuckin' cave down here, Freeman?" Or a swamp, I thought, but didn't respond.

"But they don't have any range to 'em," he said. "Pretty useless for covert work."

"This is close-up," I said. "That's why I need you to do it."

I told him about my visit to Kim's and as much detail as I could about the man I'd seen slipping out the back way. I didn't mention Richards's presence.

"I'm thinking drug dealer," I said. "He and the new girl have something going. If he's got women bartenders selling over the counter for him, maybe they get caught up in the action, try to skim him or some shit. If he's ruthless enough, maybe he gets rid of the ones that he's partnering up with."

"I don't know, Freeman. I been in and out of these places for a couple of years now and never saw it," O'Shea said.

"Right. And you never told any of those bartenders you were an ex-cop?"

"Well, it does have a ring to it, you know."

"And they don't pass that around to their coworkers who might avoid doing business when you're in the place?"

"OK. OK. I get the point," he said and slipped the camera phone into his pocket.

"Like I said, six-foot, dark hair, clean-cut. Probably likes the same seat at the bar, down at the far end and he's probably alone."

"Down under the TV?" O'Shea said.

I looked at him.

"I know the layout."

"I figured," I said, still watching him. "Just hang at that end and leave the seat open. See if he comes in," I said.

"You want me to hit him up for some coke or ecstasy or what?"

"Like someone's going to buy first time from you, O'Shea."

"Hey, I could have been all right undercover," he said defensively.

I let that comment sit.

"Just the photo, all right?" I said and took fifty dollars out of my shirt pocket. "Stay till eleven or so and meet me back out here." He took the cash without a word, got out and walked, unhurried, toward Kim's.

I refilled my cup from the thermos, took a sip and when I looked over the rim I realized that all during our conversation I had been unconsciously staring out at a patrol car. The guy hadn't moved for nearly an hour. Nice work if you can get it, I thought. But I had to admit there had been some slow rainy nights on the Charlie shift when I'd huddled in the dry stairwell of the First Pennsylvania Bank entrance to the Broad Street Subway and lost myself in a paperback when I was supposed to be walking a downtown beat. But this guy's head had never even turned around to scan the rest of the lot. He was awake. I watched him put what now I was sure was a cell phone to his ear several times. But he seemed to only be focused on the side window of Kim's. For a paranoid minute I thought maybe I'd sent O'Shea into the middle of some kind of sting operation. Then I saw the cop snap his hand away from his ear. His brake lights flashed as he started the engine and he jerked the patrol car out of the space in reverse. His headlights popped on but not the blue light bar and he dropped the transmission into drive and pulled a screeching hole shot out of the lot. He gunned it past Kim's and a couple coming out of the Thai place had to jump back between two cars to keep from getting hit.

"Christ," I said out loud to myself. "I hope that B&E is real important, pal." And I reflexively memorized the number of his car that was stenciled on the left rear corner of the trunk.

I took another sip of coffee and checked my rear mirrors all around. It could be the only excitement of the night.

This time the rap of O'Shea's knuckles on my truck woke me out of a half-sleep. My eyes may even have been open, but I could not recall what I was looking at other than the pale glow of neon and lamplight out in front of me. I unlocked the door and checked my watch as he got in. Twelve fifteen.

"Sleeping on the job will get you a write-up, Freeman."

I let the comment pass. O'Shea settled into the seat, letting his body relax and deflate as if he had just done a hard shift down on the docks of the Delaware. He'd dragged in the odor of cigarette smoke and the sweet smell of whiskey came off his breath when he spoke. But his eyes were still clear and he would have convinced a highway patrolman that he was just tired. Some guys just had that capacity.

"Nobody that fits your mark in there tonight," he said, taking the cell phone out of his pocket. "Few old regulars, a couple I recognized from before. Some kids that I eavesdropped on who were from some alternative newspaper staff and your typical football experts blattin' on about how they would run the Dolphins' offense like they were on fuckin' talk radio. Bartender is new, though."

"Yeah," I said. "Marci."

"Good-looking little blonde. Marci," he said, looking away from me out into the night.

"But if she's running drugs, it's over the phone, 'cause she was on the damn thing every fifteen. Speaking of."

He held the cell out to me.

"Keep it," I said. "I want you to go back in tomorrow. Maybe stay till closing. It's a Saturday night and maybe something will be different."

He shrugged and pocketed the phone.

"You say so, boss," he said and sat silent, making no move to get out.

"You want me to drop you someplace?"

"No, I'm good. I'm just wondering, Freeman, if it's such a great idea for me to be hanging out in one place night after night, you know. Considering the circumstances."

Both of us were looking straight out over the lot now, showing no interest in each other's faces.

"You thinking about running, Colin?" I said.

"Shit, no."

"If Richards is going to grab you up, she'll find you anyway. You know the drill."

"Too fucking well," he said, popping the handle and stepping out.

"And if she gets you here, I'm your alibi," I said. "I'm trusting you."

"Yeah."

He closed the door and I watched him walk in the direction of the movie theater and disappear around the corner.

CHAPTER 19

That was it. She'd hung up on him and that was just over the fucking line.

Damn it, he thought. He'd had hopes for this one. He might even have been in love with her. Of course, he thought, he could have been in love with the others, too. But, shit. Why couldn't they just do what he asked them to do instead of turning on him? He knew Marci needed him. He could see it in her eyes when he told her how beautiful she was and when he had to protect her like that time with the jerk boys, Thing One and Thing Two, on the street that day. She was a little freaked out by that, he could tell when he got back into the car and her mouth was hanging open: "Jesus, Kyle. What did you do to those guys?"

What did I do? You stand up for your girl when a couple of ring-nosed, fake-leather twerps insult her on the street and you get questions? Shit, they were lucky it hadn't been dark. It had been hard enough for him to hold back from ripping that little shit's earring out. But he knew that might have sent the twerp to the hospital and he would have called his mommy and she'd have filed a complaint.

But Marci had settled down after he told her she was too special to him to let anyone diss her. Later she even laughed when he gave them the Dr. Suess monikers. "You're crazy" she said and he agreed and they had crazy sex that night. So why the hell couldn't it just be good like that all the time? No. They always had to start bitching. You give and give and they take and take and then they start telling you what to do. They always gotta try to run you.

He was driving out west. It always made him feel better when he was in the car when he was pissed. He made a rolling stop at the Hillsborough light onto 441 and punched it north. The car in front of him pulled to the shoulder when the driver saw him flying up in the rearview. Fucking right, he thought, rushing past, checking it in his mirror. Some people did the right thing. They recognized their place in the world.

He had known his place since he was a kid growing up in Oak Park in Chicago. He could still remember that day in fifth grade, that pasty-faced teacher with the flowery, down-to-the-ankles dresses and the perfume that smelled like the thick, hot summer lilac bush outside his mother's bedroom window. But that day was winter because they were inside in the gym and the time for P.E. was running out and they were trying to get one shuttle run in before the bell rang. Just one. He'd been ready for at least five minutes when the other idiot kids tried to figure out what three straight lines were, Christ! He'd spit in his hands and wiped the dust off the bottom of his sneakers so they'd grip on the tile floor and he knew he'd have the fastest time. But there she stood explaining for the third time that you had to pick up the first eraser and bring it back to the line and set it down, not throw it down, and then run back and get the second one and then race back to the starting line. OK, OK, Jesus! Let's go. But there was always some shit-head talking or pushing in line or asking if they had to set the second eraser down, too. So she started into the explanation again and he could see they weren't going to have enough time and "Come on! Let's just go!" he'd yelled and Christ you'd have thought he'd smacked her in her old, powdery face.

"Well! Since Mr. Morrison thinks he's in charge, we can all line up and follow him back to class. And you can all thank him for missing your chance to run the race."

Just like some wack job to blame her ineptitude on someone else. Put it on him because she was too weak to just get the lames to shut up and run.

Now the patrol car was blowing up on the taillights of another car on the two-lane. He reached over and hit the switch for the light bar and sent swirls of blue strobes out into the dark. The beams swept the open tree lines back off the edge of the highway and then exploded in blobs of color when they hit the white front wall of the feed store past Boynton Beach Boulevard. The car in front tapped its brake lights and started to slow and he moved out over the double yellow and punched it past. He caught a glimpse of the woman driver's face, tinted blue in his lights, eyes big and startled and helpless. Just like the old teacher. Just like his mother. The same face she wore that night when he was fourteen.

The old man had been making it a habit of coming home late in the night, drunk with the thick tissue of his eyes swollen with drink and his jowls flaccid. He woke up the house with the noise of the aluminum screen door slamming and everyone knew the routine was on. Upstairs he would hear the clumping of his father's greasy work boots, blackened from the oil and metal shavings of the tool and die shop, on the kitchen floor. His mother was anal about keeping that floor clean, always making everyone take their shoes off in the mudroom, scrubbing and even waxing the cheap linoleum on her hands and knees. And he wondered if the old man recognized that and tracked across it on purpose or was just too drunk to realize it. Then the thumping would start. The grunting, guttural barking of one voice against the high whine that started off demanding and brave but would lose that battle against a meaty hand smacking against thin skin and light bone. Before that final night he'd dealt with it by cowering. Pull the cover over your head. Stick your fingers in your ears. But that night he was tired of rules being repeated over and over. He went to the gun rack that hung on the basement wall. The .22 rifle was for rabbits. The big British .303 was for larger animals.

He took the gun down and was surprised that the weight did not overwhelm him as it had in the past. He loaded the receiver with ammunition from the small wooden drawers on the rack. He'd never really been taught, he'd just learned by watching his father and other men from the shop prepare for deer hunting season up north. The only thing he had been taught was never to point a gun at anything you weren't prepared to kill. He slid a round into the chamber with the bolt action, locked it down and went upstairs.

In the hallway he heard the command and the sharp wet slap and went into their bedroom unannounced. The barrel of the .303 came up and centered on his father's chest. The old man's hooded eyes went almost comically wide. His mother's were pleading.

He slowly circled the room where his mother had been slapped to the bed and held the gun amazingly steady and weightless. He put himself between them, giving his back to his mother so he would not have to see her weakness. Each time his father tried to slur some useless attempt at apology, he could remember his own steady, mechanical response: "Shut up!" and took another step forward, raising the rifle site to his father's face. If the old man still thought he had any dominance over him, it leaked away, replaced by the knowledge that his son was capable of blowing his brain matter all over his own bedroom wall.

He backed his father out of the room, down the stairs and over the once pristine kitchen floor. Through the screen door he forced him, stumbling, down the steps and out into the night and it was the last he saw of him, and from that time on, he, Kyle, was the man of the house.

He'd crossed Forest Hill Boulevard and was coming up to Southern by now and had lost track of time. He was not on duty and had turned off all the radios in the patrol car that would have been updating the hours in military time. He looked at his watch and it was past two so he turned around in a construction area at the roadside. He killed the headlights and sat there in the dark with the engine running.

Why couldn't she just do what he asked her to do? He shook his head, now looking back south. And then she'd gone and hung up on him in the bar and that was just over the fucking line. He'd give her one more chance, but it was becoming all too familiar. Don't test me, Marci. Nobody's going to love you out in those cold dark weeds with the rest of them. You'll be out there all alone.

CHAPTER 20

The moon was high and dusty white, mottled by its features, but still its reflected light put a pale sheen on the acres of Everglades sawgrass that lay out before me.

I was on the berm that formed the northern back of the L-10 canal. I'd come back to my shack and spent my time reading in silence and pretending to fish and paddling my river. I was still grinding the rocks of O'Shea's innocence, Richards's vendetta against him and the possibility of a stalker still working the bars. I was pissed that O'Shea refused to talk about the Faith Hamlin case, even while I was sticking my neck and Billy's out for him. What the hell was he hiding? He didn't owe those other three cops. Was I way off base on the bartender drug theory? Was there really someone stalking the girls, or were they just working the trade and then moving on while a drug pimp recruited his next one. Richards said she'd done backgrounds on all the girls without a sign of drug use or involvement. But if that was all it was, she was going to be kicking herself around worse than her superiors. I was turning the ideas in my head, trying to rub them smooth with logic and the sandpaper of "What if?" But

I knew I was waiting for someone else to act, make a mistake, uncover a body, wound instead of kill. The anxious feeling that crawled just under the muscles in my back and shoulders, had sent me out in my canoe paddling hard up the river in the middle of the night.

I'd pushed myself all the way to the culvert that the water management district had opened to divert canal water into the river. The natural slough of hundreds of wet acres that spread north and west had been the river's water source for thousands of years before men had started re-plumbing the Glades to fit their needs. Thirsty cities along the coast, a desire—no, a need—to lower the naturally high water table to create dry farmland for the sugarcane and winter vegetables and dry plots for yet more suburban housing. It was *homo erectus* in control of something as natural as the flow of rainwater.

At the berm I pulled the canoe up into a clump of marsh fern and climbed eight feet to the top. My night vision had returned to me after too long a dose of electric light in the city. In the moonlight I could even pick up the tiny white nodes of snail pods clinging to the razor-sharp strands of sawgrass like short strings of pearls. To the east I could see the false dawn of the city lights, but to the west only the shimmer of moving grass when the wind picked up and blew a pattern over the Glades. That's the direction I was facing when the chattering of my cell phone sounded in such a foreign way out here that it nearly made me duck. My reaction puzzled me and I let the phone ring again and then realized how on edge I had been waiting for someone else to pull the trigger on this case. On the third ring I punched the talk button.

"Yeah."

"Max."

"Billy. You're keeping late hours."

"Your Mr. O'Shea has just awakened me. He has been arrested at his apartment in Fort Lauderdale," Billy said. "As you predicted, Detective Richards has put together a probable cause statement charging him with the aggravated assault of Robert Hix.

"Mr. O'Shea informs that the primary evidence is a DNA match of a blood sample found on the boots that were obtained during the search of his residence."

Billy sounded professional, but not pleased.

"No surprise there," I said.

"He will be in magistrate's court at nine in the morning."

"You're still willing to do this?"

"I made you a promise, Max."

"I'll see you there, Billy," I said.

"Two other matters, Max."

"Yeah?"

"I am presently at the hospital in West Palm."

"What?"

"Rodrigo was beaten early this evening near the Cuban grill where he said you two have met on occasion."

"Jesus, Billy. Is he OK?"

"Cuts and abrasions. But nothing too serious," Billy said. He was using the clean, efficient diction he always fell into when pressed. Don't waste time on emotion or early supposition.

"It appears that the Hix brother you warned him about made a visit. Rodrigo tried to avoid him, but was cornered. The others backed away when Rodrigo was singled out."

"What was the message this time?" I said, trying to swallow back an anger that was souring the back of my throat. I could see David Hix's flat face in front of me. The sneer and the cocky way he'd wielded the bat.

"All he could make out was 'Go home' and an indication that he tell the others the same," Billy said. "He seemed to be blaming Rodrigo for costing him money."

"If Hix is working for cruise worker contractors and his handlers don't see progress, he doesn't get paid," I said.

Billy was silent on the other end of the phone for a moment.

"He may be in for a payday then, Max. Rodrigo is telling me no one will speak to us now. He's contacted his wife. He wants to leave and return to the Philippines."

This brother act was getting old, I thought.

"You said you had two other matters, Billy."

"When O'Shea called he also downloaded a photo of some man that appears to be sitting in a bar somewhere. He said you had asked him to take it."

"Yeah," I said. "Any felon that you recognize? Maybe of the drug distribution species?"

"No. I'll bring a copy with me in the morning," he said, and I could hear the question in his voice.

"It's just a hunch, Billy," I said. "I'll see you outside the courthouse at eight thirty."

I put the cell phone in my pocket and stood staring out over the Glades, the wind still moving the sawgrass, rippling through it like giant snakes below were bending the stalks in long curved patterns. I worked my way back down the berm, digging my heels into the soft dirt to fight against the angle. I was knee deep in the water when I got the canoe floated and then climbed over the gunwale and pushed out onto the river. I would have time to stop at the shack for a change of clothes and then get to the landing to clean up. I might get a nap in my truck if I got to the county jail in Fort Lauderdale early enough. It would be a long night but not as long as O'Shea's. He'd be in with a bunch of drunks and punks and scofflaws and perhaps even a few innocents who got swept up by a justice system that would take its time separating the merely tarnished from true bad boys.

The troubling stones I'd been grinding had, in the span of a phone call, taken on sharp new edges. I stroked the canoe downriver feeling their jagged rub, and the moon followed with me.

At eight in the morning I was outside of the jail, sitting on a concrete bench, watching men moving on a construction site across the New River in the morning sun. They were working the kind of miracle that people like me unfamiliar with the building trades always find unfathomable.

Their project was already some thirty stories high. You could watch the damn thing go up day by day as an observer, from poured foundation to concrete columns to prefabricated steel floor stacks and still find yourself stunned at the end of a month to see what men could raise. As I sat sipping a large Styrofoam cup of coffee I'd watched the distant small figure of a tower crane operator climb hand-over-hand like an insect up a ladder enclosed in a tall column of crisscrossed steel. When he got to the glass box at the top, he disappeared inside. I was too far away to hear him start the electric motors that powered the crane, but I saw it begin to move, swinging its balanced, perpendicular arm to the west and silently dropping its hook three hundred feet to pluck yet another load of materials needed at the top. A project manager in Philly had once told me that a good tower crane operator controlled nearly everything that went on at such a site. He had a bird's-eye view of all that was below him and as the building went up he was the one bringing the world up to join him. At thirty bucks an hour he was the master each and every day. Not a bad feeling, I thought, for a working man to hold.

At eight thirty I saw Billy walking up the wide stairway of the jail. He was dressed in a dark business suit. Conservative, not showy. Professional, not overly so.

"M-Max. You l-look tired," he said, shaking my hand.

"Sleep deprivation therapy," I said. "Does wonders for the soul."

"Yes. Those b-bags under your eyes certainly do m-make you look wiser, and older."

"Thanks."

He opened his leather briefcase and took out a photograph and handed it to me. Even though the lighting was dim and the shot too close, the detail was sufficient. The man was handsome. A strong cleft chin. Cheekbones high but perhaps that was from the shadows. The bridge of his nose was as straight as a rule. Never been broken, I thought. He wasn't a close-in fighter. The eyes were dark and even though they were focused off in another direction, one had the feeling that they were very aware of the photographer if not the actual lens of the phone camera. In the background I could make out the front of the jukebox at Kim's and the reflection of mirrors.

"F-From our client," Billy said. "You can explain later w-why you are farming out surveillance. R-Right now, we are due in c-court."

Inside, the lobby of the county jail was done in all government design. The floor was that easy-to-clean polished stone. The walls an institutional bone white. Floor-to-ceiling windows, double pane, made up the wall to the east and, since the entrance was actually two floors above ground level, there was a view of the river and the condo building going up on the other side. The preconstruction prices across the way were starting at $375,000 to $1.2 million for the top floors. The future residents would have a wonderful unobstructed view of the seven-story jailhouse. Real estate in Florida, I thought. Some gang of government officials had approved the building of a house for criminals on waterfront property. Location, location, location.

On the other side of the lobby were three lines queuing up to Plexiglas-covered windows as if they were selling tickets. There were women in work clothes, two toting small children. A man wearing navy, grease-stained pants and a light blue shirt with his name over the pocket was arguing with a young woman whose tear-stained face held a look of worry, heartbreak and befuddlement all at once. Both of them were comparing the content of their wallets, searching, I figured, for some way to make bail for a family member inside.

Down a wide corridor a security checkpoint was set up and beyond it a single wood-veneered door. It was topped with the sign MAGISTRATES COURT. We passed through the metal detectors with all the requisite emptying of pockets, removal of pagers and cell phones. Billy went through with smiles and nods. I had to stop for a wand check of belt buckle, sunglasses and the metal buttons on my canvas shirt.

"Clothes m-make the man, Max," Billy said.

"And the terrorist?" I answered.

He grinned but then went all business when we entered the courtroom.

There was nothing ornate about the place. The judge was already sitting up behind the large raised desk, his reading glasses down on his nose, his hands shuffling paper to a woman clerk standing beside him. There were less than a dozen people in the gallery, which was made up of rows of plastic chairs instead of the usual wooden pews. There was a freestanding half-wall that separated those chairs from another row. Two tables, left and right, that acted as a buffer between those empty seats and the judge.

I sat behind the wall while Billy went around to the table on the left and introduced himself to a harried, middle-aged man in a suit who seemed mildly surprised as he shook Billy's hand. He then sorted quickly through a sheaf of papers and handed Billy two pages. He almost looked relieved. Billy sat at the defense table to read and I watched the judge take a moment to look up over his glasses to access the new presence in his court. At the table on the right, an equally busy and equally suited younger man was going through his own stack of files. He would be some low-on-the-seniority-scale attorney for the prosecutor's office. He too stole a look at Billy.

At exactly nine, a barrel-chested officer who had been standing near the bench, apparently flirting with the judge's clerk, became serious and opened an adjoining door. Twenty men filed in, handcuffed in twos, a left wrist to a right wrist.

They were instructed to sit in the row of chairs in front of the short wall. They came in with the sound of shuffling feet and the soft clinking of loose stainless steel. Some were still wearing the street clothes they had on when they were arrested. Others were dressed in orange jumpsuits. They all had tired eyes and unshaven faces. A few looked tentatively around the room, into the gallery to find a family member or a friend. There were twenty of them and eight of us.

O'Shea was the twelfth man in, attached to a huge black man in a jumpsuit. His face was a stoic mask. He would not have said a word all night. He would have stared at a spot on the wall with the smell of gang sweat and alcohol puke and the single open toilet for ten men in the holding cell without comment or expression. His reaction to any attempt at conversation or query would have been that same hard stare that held his face now. I could not measure the anger or frustration behind his eyes as he came in and looked around the room, finally finding me and raising his stubbled chin in acknowledgment.

There was no formal call to order. When the men were seated the judge simply nodded his head and the clerk began to call out names. Each man would stand with his handcuffed partner, who was forced to rise with him. After the first few calls the named arrestee learned to raise his unshackled hand when the judge repeated, "Which of you is Mr. Whomever."

The charges against the man were then read. He was asked if he was represented by counsel or wanted the judge to appoint the public defender to act on his behalf. Again, it took only a few examples before the next man repeated: "Public defender, sir."

The P.D. would then walk over to his newest client with paperwork and have a quick and far from private discussion, and then return to his table.

"Status, Mr. Marsh?" the judge would repeat.

Marsh would then request bail, in the standard amount that he no doubt had memorized: $10,000 for a DUI or battery charge to $1,000 for loitering. The judge would ask the prosecutor for an opinion, which was a standard: "The state has no objection, your honor," and the rhythm moved on.

They were halfway through the alphabet when I picked up on movement near the entrance to the room and turned to see detective Richards enter. She too was in a dark suit. Her hair was pulled back. She was with a man who had the look of a supervisor. I looked away for a few moments and by the time I did a double take, she had spotted me, and probably Billy, too. Her eyes met mine and they were as cold as O'Shea's and I wondered why the hell I'd even gotten myself involved in this duel. Richards and her companion sat somewhere behind me and I did not turn around again. Billy continued his reading, though he could have memorized the few pages by now. If it was his protection against nervousness, it was a good one.

The clerk called out "Oglethorpe, Richard," and the black man next to O'Shea stood, bringing his partner the ex-cop up with him.

"Mr. Oglethorpe?" the judge said.

"Yes, sir." The man raised his free hand. He was as tall as O'Shea but outweighed him by a good sixty pounds and I could tell by the way the orange fabric stretched across his back that most of it was muscle. His skin was the dark brown color of a water tupelo trunk and from the back it appeared that the man was not in possession of a neck.

"Mr. Oglethorpe," said the judge, shuffling the papers and rereading for the first time this morning. "Mr. Oglethorpe you have been arrested on charges of two counts of murder in the first degree, two counts of aggravated sexual assault of a minor child under the age of twelve, battery of a law enforcement officer and attempted escape."

Although they had endured the earlier exchanges without reaction, the rest of the arrested men all leaned forward or back to catch a look at Oglethorpe like rubberneckers at a car wreck along the road. O'Shea maintained his stoic composure, though I could see the muscle rippling in his jaw at the effort.

The judge had removed his reading glasses and looked out, no doubt, at the two men.

"Do you understand these charges against you, Mr. Oglethorpe?"

"Yes, sir," the big man said. "Public defender please, sir."

The judge looked over at the left table.

"Have at it, Mr. Marsh."

The lawyer spoke briefly with Oglethorpe while O'Shea stood alongside, looking back to me. He picked up on someone behind me and for the first time he let a look of hatred slip momentarily into his eyes. I did not turn. I knew the target of that look.

The public defender returned to his table and made a monotone and professionally required request of bail for Oglethorpe. The prosecutor stood, shrugged his shoulders and the judge ordered the suspect remanded to jail without bond until a future court date without discussion.

O'Shea and his cuffmate sat for sixty seconds until the clerk called: "O'Shea, Colin."

"The charge, Mr. O'Shea, is aggravated assault," the judge said, looking down at the paperwork.

I watched Billy as he stood and buttoned his suit coat. Professional. Back straight. Chin up. Only I would notice the twitch in his Adam's apple, the flaw that I knew he was fighting, the voice that both he and I knew would fail him.

"William Manchester r-representing M-Mr. O'Shea," Billy said.

The judge again looked up over his glasses at Billy, taking him in.

"Yes, well. Your reputation precedes you, Mr. Manchester. Welcome to magistrate's court," the judge said. "No need to be nervous, son."

Billy did not move his eyes from the judge's face. The twitch in his neck went quiet.

"With all due r-respect, Your Honor," he said, "I am not nervous."

They both paused; something was being said between their eyes. Then Billy continued.

"Your Honor, we are requesting that M-Mr. O'Shea be released on his own recognizance at th-this time.

"Mr. O'Shea is employed, Your Honor, as a s-security officer for the Navarro Group, sir. A steady job he has held for nearly three years. He is n-not a flight risk."

Billy was fighting the stutter, commendably, I thought. But my ear was as a friend.

"Mr. Cornheiser?" the judge said, looking to the prosecutor.

"Your Honor, uh, the suspect's victim, Mr. Robert Hix, sir, was brutally beaten. He is still hospitalized with several broken ribs and as yet undetermined internal injuries. He has identified Mr. O'Shea in a photo array as his attacker. The victim's blood, Your Honor, was found on the suspect's boots, which were confiscated at the defendant's apartment during the execution of a search warrant signed by Judge Lewis, sir."

Both lawyers were playing the game, dropping names in an attempt to influence. Navarro was a respected former sheriff who ran a large security firm. Judge Lewis was probably a golfing partner of the sitting judge.

"The state asks that the suspect be held in remand, Your Honor," the prosecutor said, stealing a glance toward the back of the room. "Evidence of a capital crime involving Mr. O'Shea is continuing to be collected by detectives, Your Honor, and the state is convinced that he may be an extreme danger to the public."

Billy jumped on the prosecutor's move.

"Your honor, I see n-no reference to another, m-more serious charge in this arrest document. Mr. O'Shea in fact has n-never been arrested. In Florida nor in any other j-jurisdiction," he said. "In addition, the st-state knows that the mere possibility of an additional charge has n-no bearing on this proceeding and has no legal justification in even being raised."

The judge nodded, as if saying "I knew that," and looked over to the prosecutor, who was stalling by shuffling through paper.

"Furthermore, sir," Billy continued, "I have in court this m-morning a witness to the assault charge now in question, a licensed private investigator, Your Honor, whose presence at the time of the alleged c-crime is documented by police reports and who has signed an affidavit stating that both he and Mr. O'Shea were the ones attacked by the alleged victim and his brother and thus forced to defend themselves."

The prosecutor followed the direction of Billy's pointed hand and when he looked at me I could see the flicker of an unexpected twitch in his eyes. This was obviously supposed to have been a slam-dunk lockdown of O'Shea with little objection by the overworked and uninvolved public defender.

"Mr. Cornheiser?" the judge said, maybe even enjoying the elevated banter in his otherwise dull morning.

"I, uh, again, Your Honor," the prosecutor stumbled. "This was, sir, a brutal attack and the hospitalized victim, sir . . ."

"You're repeating yourself, Mr. Cornheiser. Bail in the amount of ten thousand cash or bond," the judge said, interrupting. He had been around long enough to know that when an attorney only had one leg to stand on, his only resort was to hop up and down on it.

"Thank you, Your Honor," Billy said, gathering his things.

"Thank you, Mr. Manchester," the judge responded. "And I apologize, sir, for my earlier assumption, counselor."

Billy bowed his head gracefully and walked across to where O'Shea was now sitting.

"We sh-shall have you out by noon," he said, and I heard O'Shea thank him. As Billy turned to go the big man cuffed to O'Shea stopped him with his voice.

"You got a card, Mr. Attorney?" he said, holding out a hand the size of a dinner plate.

Billy looked down into the man's face.

"I don't do this kind of work," he said dismissively and walked on.

Richards was waiting outside. She'd left after the judge announced bail. Her companion was gone. Her arms were crossed, lips pressed together. She was looking at the floor as we walked up and Billy excused himself before we reached her.

"I'm going to p-post O'Shea's bail," he said, heading for the lines. I went to face Richards alone.

"So, Max," she said when I got within hearing distance. Her eyes were the color of steel.

"I really didn't expect the two of you to double-team me in there. You must have done an exceptional sales job to convince Billy to stand up in front of a judge in person."

She and Billy had been friendly when we were dating. She shared his love of sailing. She respected his genius and had never asked me once about his stutter. She was pissed. Still, I knew that my explanation was weak. How do you tell someone you think they're wrong based on a gut feeling, a half-assed dealer theory and maybe a misplaced loyalty to a fellow cop?

"I hope you two can guarantee that he's not going to put another woman at risk while he's out roaming free," she said.

I looked away from her eyes, then back.

"Look, Sherry. I respect what you're doing," I said. "I just think you're wrong on this one."

"No shit."

I let her anger sit a few silent moments and maybe my own, too.

"Sherry," I tried again. "You've shot and killed two men in the last couple of years, men who were abusing women. You were fully justified in both."

"And saved your ass in one, Freeman," she said, her arms still crossed.

"And saved my ass," I agreed. "You're also a solid investigator and I know you haven't forgotten the rule to keep an open mind and consider all possibilities."

She looked down and I could see she was holding her tongue, taking my words like an unwanted and condescending lecture. I took my chance and pressed on.

"Can you honestly say this mission you're on hasn't gotten in the way of your eye for other suspects?"

I'd meant to appeal to her professionalism and now I was questioning it.

"Freeman, I've been working this for months. I've dealt out the other possibilities. Christ, I even posed as a bartender to run a living, breathing lineup past myself every night. Your friend is the one that sticks out. He fits the profile, and yeah, it's the profile I put together, but he's right there. If he hadn't made me as undercover, I might have gotten him to make a move or give up a piece of evidence. That didn't happen, but I saw him in action."

"OK," I said. "How about someone you never saw in action? Someone who might fit your profile, but who would have bailed at the first sign or recognition of a cop?"

She finally looked me in the eyes.

"What the hell are you talking about, Max?"

"Suppose you've got over-the-counter drug dealing going on in a bar? The supplier is smart, he recruits the girls working as bartenders."

I saw the head tilt start, the draw of exasperated breath.

"Just hear me out. OK?" I said. She relented and chewed on a corner of her lip.

"Suppose the supplier is smart enough to move these girls around, to different cities or states, or just sends them packing when he thinks they might compromise his action?"

I reached into my pocket and took out the photo that O'Shea had taken and offered it to her.

"Ever seen this guy before?"

She looked, brow scrunching, studying longer than necessary.

"I've seen him before," she finally said. "But I've never seen him here. This is Kim's, right?"

She was a good investigator, strong in the details. She probably recognized the jukebox just as I had.

"You have a name?" I said.

"No, I'm not that familiar."

"He snuck out of Kim's the other night as soon as you walked in."

The corner of her mouth turned up.

"Lot of people wouldn't want to be seen sitting at a bar by a detective."

"Yeah, I know," I said and waited.

"Why else did you single him out, Max?"

"He seemed to have some kind of connection to the new bartender, the one who was watching us that day when we were interviewing Laurie."

"Connection?"

"Yeah. When he bolted, she kept looking from us to the spot he left, very nervous."

She was still looking at the photo, her eyes narrowed. There was something else there, I was sure of it. And she was trying to decide whether she was going to share it with me.

"He's a cop. Works patrol. Maybe even in that sector," she said, looking up into my face.

"No shit," I said, mostly to myself.

"Easy, Freeman," she started. "Lots of cops wouldn't want to be caught at a bar by a superior officer, even if they're off hours. Who knows, maybe he doesn't want word getting back to the wife?"

"Can you get a name and run a history, get a look at his record?" I said, my head working the possibilities.

"Jesus, Freeman. You're ballsy," she said. "Trying to blow my case on the main suspect, and asking me to help you line up another officer for the fall guy? A defense attorney would have a field day with that. 'I understand, Detective Richards, you were also investigating another possible suspect? Doesn't that mean you aren't sure who may have done this?' " she said, making her voice deep and smarmy.

Maybe I should have just let it sit. She would think about what she'd said without my holier-than-thou response. But I didn't.

"Come on, Sherry," I said, stepping closer to her. "We're not like them, the lawyers trying to argue through who wins and who loses and to hell with what's right or just. We're cops. We're here to stop it. If there's even an outside chance with this guy, you can't just kick it to the curb."

"I'm a cop, Freeman. You used to be," she said. "Maybe your old cronies up in Philadelphia forgot some of the basics of homicide investigation while they were covering themselves for getting laid on the job." She started to say something else, then held it.

"I've got a suspect who had opportunity, a suspect with a violent past, a suspect who is on the top of another agency's list in the disappearance of another vulnerable woman. I thought you were the one who never believed in coincidences."

Her eyes were still burning when Billy walked up.

"Sh-Sherry."

She put the photograph in the pocket of her slacks and extended her hand to meet his.

"You are l-looking great," Billy said, taking her hand in both of his and meaning, I knew, every word.

"Counselor," she said. "You were quite impressive in there. I'm

199

sure I'll get a call from the prosecutor for not warning him who he'd be up against this morning."

He stepped in and at first I thought he might kiss Richards on the cheek, but instead he whispered: "It's not personal, Sherry." And then louder: "I s-still need a good crew person on my Sunday b-beer can races. Diane is learning, but slowly."

"I'll see if I can get a weekend evening free," she said.

"Wonderful," Billy said and turned to me. "Ready?"

He stepped away and I turned to Richards.

"I'll guarantee it," I said.

"What?"

"I'll guarantee that no one will be in jeopardy while O'Shea is out."

She didn't answer. She just nodded. When I caught up with Billy I looked back and her hand was back in the pocket of her slacks.

We walked over to the county courthouse which was next to the jail. Billy said he needed to visit an acquaintance. As an attorney, he might never show up in court, but the man had more connections than a senator at a lobbyist's convention.

"It w-will take a couple of hours for them to process O'Shea out."

"You paid his bond, cash?"

"A cashier's ch-check," he corrected.

"You just happened to have it in the exact amount?"

"I anticipated."

"Pretty damned sure of yourself, Counselor."

He paused a second.

"It was n-not as unpleasant as I thought it might be, M-Max."

This time I paused, letting Billy consider what he was saying about his lifelong fear that his stutter was an intolerable flaw that society would forever hold against him.

"So if this goes to trial, you'll represent him?"

He stopped at the corner.

"They don't t-take aggravated assault to trial, M-Max. They deal them down and plead them out."

"I meant if they tag him for the disappearances," I said. This time he looked me in the eyes.

"Be careful, M-Max," he said without hesitation. "If they come up with enough evidence to indict O'Shea on homicide charges, w-we both may have made big mistakes."

CHAPTER 21

She knew she'd made a mistake, and now she was paying for it. Scared as hell, and paying for it.

They'd gone to dinner, his choice, the steak house that she was really getting sick of, but whenever she balked he gave her that look, the one that made her turn her face away, waiting, the skin on her cheek almost warming like she'd already been slapped.

But the dinner conversation went well. He was smart, no doubt about that. He kept up on current events and spoke intelligently about issues that she rarely paid attention to. They'd talked, like adults. Then they went to the movies, again, his choice. Again, somehow, they always ended up at the show he first suggested. Not that she hated them. It was just that if she mentioned another film, he'd say "Yeah, OK, that's a possibility. Let's see what else there is," and by the time they went through the listings in the paper, they'd be right back to his choice.

She'd thought about her father then, how they always "discussed" things but whenever it looked like she might get something her way, he'd pull his trump card: "Your holy mother and the Lord himself are looking down on us, Marci. Ask them. What would they do?"

Kyle didn't have to push those cheap buttons. His trump card was now the back of his hand. In the last two weeks he'd stung her a couple of times. She'd told herself that was it. Then he'd show up with apologizing flowers. Then there was that "love light" with the candle in it that he said he wanted her to hang in her window to remind him that even brushing his hand too close to the flame could put it out, and he would never do it again. Christ, she'd thought. How do you dump a guy like that?

She'd told him after the movies that she didn't want to go riding again. She was tired. She had another double shift coming up. He started driving out Broward Boulevard and pulled the flask filled with Maker's Mark from under the seat and didn't bother mixing it, just sipped it, right out in traffic.

"Come on, Marci. Just for a little while."

"Kyle, no," she said. He didn't like no. But she wasn't sure she cared anymore.

"Oh, I see. I take you to dinner. I take you to the movies. Then when I want to do something for me, it's no."

She was silent and he looked over. She sat there, slack-jawed. Then she let that half-grin come into her face, the one she knew pissed him off. The one he called her "It's almost amusing how stupid you are" look. Then she made her big mistake. They were already west of Dixie Highway, past where he should have turned to take her home.

"Christ!" she snapped. "Can't you give up this 'My way, my way, my way' all the time and give someone else a little say?"

She watched those marbles in his jaw start to roll, but didn't care this time.

"I mean, goddamn. It's not always about you, Kyle, and you ruin it when you're always making it about you!"

He still remained quiet, but she could feel the car accelerate as they passed the Fort Lauderdale Police Department building doing at least fifteen over the speed limit. But what were his friends going to do? Pull him over?

"Goddammit, Kyle. Take me home! Now!"

The movement was faster than she could catch in the soft darkness of the car. She didn't even pick up on it until the impact snapped her head to the side. He'd backhanded her with the speed and lightning-fast anger she'd seen him use on others. The sound of his skin and knuckles smacking her cheek and the bridge of her nose came a millisecond before the sting of pain.

For a moment she thought she hadn't even had time to close her eyes, and was astounded that someone's hand could be faster than a blink. Then she opened her eyes and oriented herself. She was against the door. Kyle was staring straight ahead, both hands on the wheel. She blinked through welling tears and looked out the windshield, thinking. Now they were pulling up to the I-95 entrance and she could make out the blur of colored traffic lights going from green to yellow. She felt the car slow, felt for the door handle and clack! The locks snapped down. He'd anticipated her move, flipped on his siren and lights and swung through the red light, gathering speed onto the interstate. She knew she'd made her big mistake. Now she was scared.

CHAPTER 22

After I left Billy I went across the street to the Barrister's Bagel and had breakfast. They had a special on a "Locks & Turnkey" sandwich. Maybe the food was better than the prison wit. I had coffee and watched the morning hustle. There were lots of ties and an equal number of wonderful women's dresses. There was an energy around the place, people moving, bumping, saying hello or even avoiding eye contact. A guy shuffled a briefcase from one hand to the other to dig for change. A woman watched the eyes of the cashier, waiting for them to catch hers and take an order. A too loud guffaw sounded from the knot of three suited men, causing the rest to turn and look. People moved with purpose and checked their watches. In my semi-isolation I had lost some of my people-watching skills. It had been a constant when I'd worked a beat, watching, and not always just for the pickpocket working his way through the tourists or the smack dealer hooking up with a new face on the corner. You had to have a suspicious eye as a cop. But you also had to remind yourself that ninety-nine percent of what went on around you were folks just living, working honest jobs, fill-ing their spot in the world. You got jaded if you weren't careful and did something stupid or just burned out. Richards's words were still stinging. She was right. She was the cop. I wasn't. But I resented her implication that I'd gone home and fallen back into the brotherhood of see-no-evil. I'd gotten jaded and left. The shadows followed, but I had left.

I bought another large coffee to go and walked back to the jail-house. I was on the outside bench when O'Shea came through the doors, automatically looked up into the sky and took a deep breath of air, and then spotted me.

"Thanks, Max," he said, shaking my hand, "and your friend Manchester."

His eyes were red-rimmed. He'd only been in overnight but looked like he'd lost weight. His clothes carried a stink that flashed me back to Philadelphia lockups that we as officers only had to stand for a few minutes and then joked about back in the squad rooms.

"You all right?" I said, watching his face.

"You see that bitch, Richards, standing in the back of the court-room?"

I just nodded.

"Took that fucking gloat off her face, your boy Manchester did."

"He's good," I said. "You need a ride home? Want to get some-thing to eat? It's almost noon."

O'Shea nodded and walked with me.

"What's with that guy's stutter, anyway?" he said after a few moments. "He puttin' that on for a sympathy factor or what?"

"Does he look like a guy who needs sympathy?" I said, sharp, snapping to Billy's defense even when he didn't need it.

"No. Shit, no. He kicked their ass," O'Shea said and took my tone and let it go.

We got to my truck and as soon as I started the engine I hit the automatic windows and pulled out of the parking to get some air circulating. I got on Andrews Avenue and headed north. O'Shea put his arm out his window.

"Back in the world. Isn't that what the cons say?"

"Yeah."

"Christ, only one night and you can feel it," he said. "I can't understand why they even take the gamble."

I looked over at the side of his face when he said it. She was wrong, I thought again, shifting more of my doubt. O'Shea wasn't the one. When I got to Sunrise Boulevard I started east and then threw a U-turn at the crossover and pulled into a small lot at Hot Dog Heaven. Chicago-style dogs. Best in the city. Plus tables outside in the breeze. I bought two with everything for O'Shea and couldn't help myself and got a third for me. We sat at a picnic table outside, only fifteen feet from the street traffic. I let him finish the first dog.

"So tell me about the photo."

"Oh, yeah. OK," he said, wiping relish off his chin. "Sorry, had other things on my mind." He finished chewing, took a gulp of coffee, exhaled and looked across the street like he was seeing it.

"I took the third seat from the end of the bar, figuring, like you said, he liked the last seat and I didn't want to crowd him if he showed. I was a couple of beers into it when some woman sat down on my left. Not my type and besides she was taking up the trap so I belched once, trying to dissuade her.

"She asked a question about the game that was up on the tube, trying to be friendly, so I asked her if she ever heard the joke that goes: 'What did one tampon say to the other when they met on the street?' "

"Did she wait for the answer?" I said.

"No. She got up and left," O'Shea said. "Then about eleven the guy in the picture comes in and sits at the end. I can tell there's something up between him and the blonde bartender. She ignores him at first and he just sits there, same look on his face, passive, not a bit bothered. I'm checking him in the mirror and he's playing the same game, watching me. Guy's got cop all over him. Tight haircut, like old Sergeant Rixson used to push on us.

"He's got that smell of talcum like we all did in the days after we had to wear the Kevlar every night. Get so goddamn sweaty you had to powder up even after you showered at the end of the shift."

"What about him and the bartender? Did they talk?" I asked, maybe a little too suddenly.

"You didn't say you were looking for a cop, Max," O'Shea said, putting both elbows on the table and bringing his coffee cup up with both hands.

"No, I didn't," I said. I wasn't going to offer that I hadn't known I was looking for a cop until Richards ID'ed the photo two hours ago. "Did they talk?"

He sipped and made me wait.

"She finally came down and put a Rolling Rock in front of him without being asked and they looked at each other for a couple of seconds longer than a barmaid and just a regular would. Now mind you, she'd been pretty friendly before he got there, worked the bar nice."

"Thanks, O'Shea. I know you're an expert in that area, but did they talk?"

"Not a word with me sittin' there but there was a hell of a lot being said, if that's what you're asking. They knew each other. She might be dealing for him from the bar. Might be something else. My take was he's trying to be contrite about pissing her off about something and she's making a plan that he ain't got a clue about."

O'Shea had been a good cop. He knew something about reading people. But he'd yet to prove himself a psychic.

"You picked all this up through their body language, Colin?"

"Some of it, yeah," he said. "The girl walks down to the other end and I say to the guy 'Nice ass on that one, eh?' and he looks at me like I just insulted his mother."

"And of course you let it go."

"Sure. I say: 'Well excuse me, pal, but if your name ain't on it, every paying customer in the place has the right to at least look.' "

"And?"

"Guy's got an eye, Max. Kind you see on the street that makes you want to take the baton out of your belt loop just for safety sake."

"He say anything?"

"No. But it was in his throat, twitchin'. I could see it there so I backed off, bought him a beer and made like I was calling someone on the picture phone. When the girl brought him the Rock, I snapped that shot of him," O'Shea said, obviously proud of himself. "That's when he got up and walked out through the back hallway. Left the beer and his money untouched."

O'Shea said he stayed in the bar and hadn't tried to tail the guy. I started to react but held myself; he was right, if the guy was a cop and made him as a tail it might have scared him off completely. O'Shea said he stayed put and waited for the bartender to close up and watched her get into her own car, just like I had the other night. When he got home to his apartment, two Broward sheriff's officers were waiting for him. He called Billy, sent the photo over the phone and went to jail.

When we got back into the car I asked where I could drop him and he asked me to go east. We got over the intracoastal bridge and he motioned me to pull over next to the Holiday Inn.

"You got a room?" I asked.

"Not exactly," he said, getting out at the curb. "I'll keep in touch."

I watched his back while he walked away. I knew the Parrot Lounge was just around the corner and I would have bet a paycheck that's where he was headed. Irish whiskey, straight up, and I'm not sure I could blame him after the night he'd had.

CHAPTER 23

He'd pushed the patrol car up to eighty on the freeway and blown through the toll plaza to Alligator Alley, and hadn't said a word since he'd slapped her.

She didn't know where the hell he was going, but she did know that if she pushed it the wrong way it was only going to make it worse. They'd done this dark stretch of straight road before at night. She remembered the turnoff that he'd taken, up a hard-scrabbled path that was barely a road at all and ended up in some kind of woods he called a hammock.

They'd done some necking and then screwed in the backseat of the squad car. She'd thought it was actually pretty cool at the time. When they were getting dressed she clicked on the switch for the swirling blue lights and it made him yell at her at first and then he'd smiled that goddamn smile.

"You are a pistol, girl."

He wasn't smiling now and she knew she didn't have a choice.

"Come on, Kyle. What're we doing?"

Nothing.

She was using a soft voice and brushed the hair off her face.

"Look, I'm sorry. Really. I just get tired sometimes and, you know, I say stuff I don't really mean."

He was still quiet, but in the dim light from the dash she could see that his jaw was loosening, the marbles of muscle settling. At this point she didn't trust what the hell he might do. She'd witnessed that anger and speed when he'd done it to others and now it was on her and she didn't know how far he might take it. And Jesus, look where they were now, way the hell out here where nobody was going to hear her scream and no way was she going to jump out and run if he ever slowed the hell down or stopped.

She'd been out here during the daytime when they'd taken a drive to Naples on the west coast of the state. The sawgrass and open land went on like a damn meadow for miles and miles and she knew enough about the Everglades to know that most of it was hip deep in water.

But she'd also had plenty of practice getting pissed-off men to calm down. When you're in the bar you use what you've got. Sometimes it's a free drink. Sometimes a smile. Sometimes a promise of something to come later. It was a small price to pay.

"Come on, baby. I wasn't trying to order you around," she said. "I was just thinking about going home and relaxing and being with you instead of driving."

Christ, she thought. Just like her father when he'd start crying about mom and saying how it wasn't worth carrying on and where was the Lord when you were the one in need, and she'd sit down on the floor in front of his chair and take his big thick hands in hers and tell him how strong he'd always been and how much she loved him and as long as they were together they'd be a family and everything would be all right.

She hadn't believed any of those words, either. But it got both of them through. It was the same thing, she told herself now while she forced back the bile that came up while she was apologizing for nothing. But this time she was scared and only trying to get herself through.

"Kyle. Come on, baby. I can't stand it when you ignore me. It makes me feel alone and you know I need you to talk with me."

She straightened up in her seat and squared her shoulders against the seat back, still watching his face, watching that right hand on the wheel, waiting for him to slap her again.

He cocked his head and tightened his lips and she reached out, slowly, thinking she'd try to touch him.

"You don't know how close you come, Marci," he said.

Yes, she did, she thought.

"You know I try to give you everything I can. And then you turn on me like that and how the fuck do you think that makes me feel?"

You're insane, she thought.

"I know, baby. I know and I'm sorry," she said.

He was easing off the speed and she thought that was good. They'd already passed the few cars and a tractor-trailer that had probably gone through the toll before them and now there weren't any taillights out ahead of them. Across the divided highway she saw some headlights going east, but only a couple of pairs. She reached out farther and touched his thigh and forced herself not to flinch when she felt the muscle in his leg quiver.

"I really am sorry, Kyle."

This time he turned his head and looked at her. The expression on his face said 'you poor pitiful little girl' and she absorbed it and bit the side of her lip and swallowed it and let him repeat himself: "You don't know how close you come sometimes."

He slowed nearly to a stop and then pulled onto what felt like that same dirt road and now they were moving into the trees and into the dark. When they came to a stop, she let him kiss her. She got out of the car with him and looked up at a smear of stars and thought 'Where's my goddamn fairy godmother when I need her?' and then she let him undress her and said she was sorry again, but this time she was apologizing to herself.

She heard the leather of the gun belt creak and then drop to the ground. He pushed himself against her and she let him take her on the back bumper. She picked a spot out in the darkness and focused on it, watched it, wished she was in it. Was this her fault? she thought. Did I do this to myself again?

When he was finished he backed off and she started to relax. She could take this. She could get through this, she thought.

But then he held her by the shoulders and turned her and pushed her chest down on the trunk of the car and she let him take her again. She closed her eyes and silently vowed: Last Time.

On the ride back home he sipped at the flask and actually asked her if she had liked the movie. She forced herself to say yes, especially the part when the SWAT team came in and cleared out the room of foreign terrorists without firing a shot. He'd just nodded. She tried to concentrate on the moon and remembered a storybook from when she was a child about a boy with a purple crayon and how the moon walked with him.

When they got a block from her apartment he parked and got out and opened the door for her. She stepped out and then stood facing him, looking into his face, her eyes as dry as parchment.

"I gotta go. I'll call you," he said, and she nodded and he leaned down and kissed her on the forehead.

She watched him get back into the car and pull out onto the street and she stayed still until the red glow of the taillights disappeared around the corner. And then she turned and threw up into the gutter over and over and over until her throat was raw.

CHAPTER 24

I walked into the bar late afternoon and the darkness and the odor of stale beer and a subtle hint of mildew stopped me. I took two steps in and waited until my eyes adjusted, pupils spiraling down from the brilliance of the sun outside.

There were three humped backs at the bar, men with their shoulders turned in as though the light that came through the door was a cold wind. There was a blonde head moving beyond them. Her hair was pulled back tight. Marci, working the day shift just as Laurie had told me over the phone. The manager had offered quickly that the girl had just asked to switch her shifts and get off the eight-to-two for a few weeks. Laurie became even more suspicious when I said I needed to talk with the girl and would rather do it in private.

"She came in with the strangest look. Said there was nothing wrong but I knew there was. Is she in some kind of trouble with the police?"

I told her again that I wasn't a cop and that I was only a consultant when detective Richards and I had met with her.

"But you didn't say that then, did you?" she reminded me.

I apologized for leading her on.

"It's OK," she said, brightly, like she meant it. "You get used to liars in this business."

I let the dig sit.

"So can I talk with Marci?" I asked.

"You don't need my permission. She's on four-to-eight all this week."

I made my way down the bar and took the end seat on purpose. I had called Richards the same day I'd given her the picture. I knew she would look up his name. Pissed as she was, she was too good a cop to turn away from it. What I was surprised at was that she gave me the rundown. Maybe it was in the form of an apology, maybe she was intrigued. It was hard to read her over the phone.

Kyle Morrison. Three years on the Fort Lauderdale Department. Came in from a small department in North Florida. Since he'd been here there were a handful of complaints in his file. Most of them gripes from arrestees about use of force, but not one that had stuck. Like most metropolitan departments, Fort Lauderdale had a strong union. They dealt with most complaints internally and even if they did think Morrison was heavy-handed, there wasn't much they would do unless he knocked around someone prominent and it went public. He was assigned to a night prowl car shift in the Victoria Park area. The only odd thing Richards said she noticed was that despite his experience Morrison had never taken the sergeant's exam. He seemed to be satisfied with what he had, which does not always endear you to the powers that be. Supervisors are wary of those who don't aspire to management like they did. It makes them second-guess themselves.

I complimented Richards on her thoroughness and her sources.

"I'm sorry for this morning, Freeman," she'd said and hung up.

Marci looked twice at me when I sat down and then she reached into the cooler. She brought out a Rolling Rock and pried the cap off.

"Hi," she said when she put the bottle in front of me and then stood back, waiting.

"How you doing?" I said, my tone conversational.

She stared at my face a couple of moments too long. Her eyes had a color like rainwater on a concrete slab and had about the same amount of emotion in them. She looked older than the last time, and not just by days.

"You on the job?" she said, like an accusation.

I took a sip of beer and couldn't hold her look.

"Used to be. Now I'm working as a private investigator," I said.

The other men at the bar were too far down the rail to hear me. I had the feeling it was as intimate a setting as I was going to get with her.

"But you were with that cop the other day, the woman with the hair?"

"Yeah. She's looking into a case that I was trying to help her with."

"What kind of case?" she said, all subtlety gone from her voice. I had the feeling she'd given up on subtlety.

"The disappearance of some women," I said. "Women who were all bartenders."

She actually stepped back, though I was sure she was aware of it.

"From here?"

"One from here," I said. "The others from a couple of places in the area that are pretty much like this. Small bars. Relatively quiet. Regular customers."

"What happened to them?"

"No one has been able to find out," I said. "They never turned up. They just vanished. No notes. No argument with family. No damage to their apartments. It was almost like they went out on a date and never came back."

When I said it I watched her face. I thought she was looking at the mirror on the wall behind me but I could see a paleness spread down her face like the blood was sliding down out of her cheeks, leaking somewhere below her throat. She stumbled like she'd suddenly fallen off a pair of high heels and I came off the stool and reached out for her.

She put up her palm.

"Don't touch me," she said, regained her balance and then turned and poured herself a shot of brandy from the back of the bar. When she tossed it back one of the boys down the way picked up on the movement and raised his tumbler of dark liquid.

"Cheers," he croaked in a raspy voice, downed the drink and went back to studying the wood grain on the bar top.

I waited for a hint of color to come back into her skin but I wasn't going to waste my advantage.

"You know a guy named Morrison, Marci? A Kyle Morrison?"

"Yeah," she said and I could see a flicker of fear in her eyes. "Why? Does he have anything to do with this?"

"It's possible," I said, using the fear. "How well do you know him?"

Now she was looking down into her empty shot glass.

"Maybe not as well as I should, huh?"

She motioned for me to take a stool down around the corner of the bar, behind the electronic poker machine, and we talked for an hour, breaking on occasion so she could tend to the others when they tapped their glasses on the African mahogany. At first she just listened while I described the cases that Richards thought were more than just disappearances. I gave her the details about the girls, all from places far away with no local family connections and not a lot of close friends outside the bar business. They had all lived alone. They were all single. She waited until I'd given as much detail as I was going to give and then she poured herself another brandy.

She hadn't known any of the women. She had heard some of the other bartenders gossiping, but hadn't given it much thought. Trading in rumor was all part of the business.

"So, you don't know if any of them was raped?" she asked, the question coming far too quickly.

"No. There weren't any reports made before they disappeared, no," I said.

The slightest tremor had set up in her chin. Scared? Disappointed? Heartbroken? I couldn't tell. She looked vulnerable for the first time, but I am not beyond taking advantage of vulnerable.

"Tell me about Kyle, Marci," I said, looking straight into her eyes.

"He's a cop," she said.

"I know."

"I've been dating him."

I let her eyes look past me again.

"You two have a drug thing going, him supplying, you selling to the customers over the bar?" I said.

"No," she said instantly. "Shit, no. Kyle doesn't do drugs. Neither do I. No."

But she was putting him somewhere.

"Then why are you so scared, Marci?" I said. She was shaking her head and despite her effort to stop it, moisture was coming into her eyes.

"You think Kyle did it, that he killed those girls?" she said.

I shook my own head.

"No one's sure of anything," I said. Marci had made the jump, suspecting Kyle, for some reason. And I did not peg her as a simple, paranoid woman.

"Why? Do you think he could have?"

I was watching her eyes to see if she was working back on days or nights or conversations with Morrison, putting him in a context that she had never before imagined.

"The guy we're talking about went out with these girls several times, knew where they lived and had some access to their apartments so he could cover up afterward," I said.

I knew I was leading her. But I didn't care. If my drug theory was out, I had to find something to get this Morrison guy off the list.

"Jesus," she said and her head dropped and she slowly shook it, letting strands of her hair swing loose. After a few seconds her chin came up and it was set, back teeth tightened down.

"Kyle," she said and nothing more.

"Do you think he's capable?"

"Goddamn right he's capable," she said, now letting the anger into her voice.

"Why? Did you see anything? Did he say anything that makes you believe that?"

She shook her head.

"Too smart," she said, again with the look over my shoulder, seeing him and all his motives and moves through a whole different looking glass. "He'd be way too smart for that."

I still didn't know for sure where she was coming from, but I did know there was something under the surface. Even if your boyfriend has jerked you around and done you wrong, you don't accept the accusation that he's a killer this easily.

"But he wasn't smart enough with you," I said, hoping it would come.

"No, he wasn't," she said, and the anger she was holding flashed into her eyes. "He raped me. And I let him."

Christ, I thought. As a cop, I had heard the accusation of rape fly from the mouths of a lot of women. The word still stung, just the thought of it, even when it had a ring of untruth. But this wasn't an accusation. It was an admission. Marci turned her face away from me. Some guy at the other end of the bar banged his glass on the wood. I looked down at him and the expression on my face made him return his attention to the bottom of his glass for further study.

Marci did not move, no sobs, not even a snuffle. The blonde ponytail, for Christ's sake, made her look like a college girl. I put my hand on her shoulder and she did not flinch, just rotated the stool back to me and her eyes were dry.

"So what do you need to know?" she said.

The rape had taken place two nights before. She had not gone to the hospital, so there was no rape kit. She had come home and scrubbed herself in the shower after throwing up in the gutter. She had slept with Morrison several times over the last couple of months and it wouldn't make any difference, she said. They'd call it consensual, she said: "And they'd be right. I let it happen."

I kept shaking my head no. She was turning on herself, giving him a way out. I needed the strong side of her.

"Don't go there, Marci. Husbands get convicted of raping their wives. Don't go there," I said. "You can file charges against him."

I tried to make my voice sound convincing, even while she kept shaking her head no, no, no.

"Where did this happen, Marci?" I said, still thinking evidence, evidence.

"Out in the Glades," she said. "Way out past the toll booth on the Alley."

"All right. Do you think you could find it again, this place out in the Glades?"

She shook her head, still facing the length of the bar away from me and the other men now began to take notice.

"There's no way I would recognize it. It was dark when he took me there. It's an unmarked turnoff."

"Had he taken you there before?" I asked. Every human has a pattern, does what he does in a way or in a place that he considers a comfort zone. The bars, the women running the show in those bars, the night as cover.

She nodded her head and turned away, picked up the empty shot glass but did not move to fill it.

"You'll never find it," she said.

I looked across at myself in the mirror. I knew I could take this all to Richards. God knows she'd be all over Morrison if she thought she could substantiate another officer raping a woman. She'd shot and killed the last one.

But I also knew the system, the PBA lawyers, the disparagement of the victim, the drawn out court process with filings and cross-filings. My own mother had taken a more direct route to justice and I'd praised her for it. If there were other victims, they too would be buried forever in the paperwork. If Morrison was our guy, it might be the best chance to come up with evidence to give those girls and their families some justice. If Morrison wasn't our guy, at least we'd have the chance to nail his ass.

I knew I was freelancing on this. I'd have to tell Richards in either case, but not yet.

"All right. Then there's another way," I said. "But it would involve some risk—to you."

She turned around and her eyes were dry and hard.

"Then I'm in."

CHAPTER 25

I set up surveillance on Kim's across the street in the movie house parking lot. I could see the west side door to the bar and the two south exits of the shopping center. O'Shea had borrowed an unmarked Camaro from the security firm he worked for and was on the other side with a sight line to the front door of the bar and the east and north exits. Marci was inside, setting up her boyfriend.

As far as O'Shea knew, we were tagging Morrison and the girl with the chance of finding a drug connection. That's what I'd told him when I recruited him, but I wasn't dumb enough not to think he was stringing the pieces together. But I'd convinced myself that even if I was wrong, I wasn't giving him any outs. O'Shea would still be there, and the fact that he was willing to spend this much time with me was easing my doubts that he was the man Richards thought he was.

We had sketched out a plan that was simple and believable because the bulk of it was true. I'd learned a long time ago that the trick to getting confidential informants to lie well was to give them enough truth to sell it.

All I wanted Marci to do was to call Morrison, tell him that she had gotten a personal visit from the tall guy who'd been with the woman detective. When he asked her what I'd talked about, she needed to convince him she was too scared to tell him over the phone. That she needed to see him. I didn't need to instruct her to sound scared. She was tough, she was angry, but her fear was real. She did exactly as we had planned and Morrison told her he'd be by before the end of her shift. She called me. I called O'Shea.

O'Shea brought a couple of Nextel cell phones from his job so we could stay instantly connected. It was the way business was done. A high *tweet* came from the cell. I clicked back.

"Your boy is here," O'Shea's voice came over the Nextel. "And this one's got some balls, Freeman. He's in his goddamn squad car."

"You're sure?"

"Same guy I snapped the picture of. He parked the unit over on the other side of the lot and is walking into the front door of the bar now."

"He's in uniform?"

"No. Plainclothes."

"What's the number on the car?" I asked, and when O'Shea read it off I matched it to the number I'd scribbled down when watching the cop car in the parking lot, thinking it was security, knowing now that it was no such thing.

"When he comes back out, you're on him; if he leaves on your side, I'll follow and we can switch up the line."

"I know how to work a two-man tail, Freeman."

"Yeah, all right," I said. I was nervous. A two-tail was not a difficult technique, but South Florida was not a big urban city like Philly where parallel streets are a common layout and traffic moves like patterned waves that rush and stop at lights. But if I was correct, or better, lucky, most of this tail was going to be on the highway leading out to the western part of the county to the Glades.

If I'd read Marci right, she would be in Kim's now, down in front of the last seat, telling Kyle that I was a private investigator working for the family of some bartender from up north who'd disappeared down here months ago. In a way, it was a truth.

She would tell him that I had worked a theory that the girl had been picked up by someone who had dated her, killed her and then dumped her body. Another truth, and when I had gone over this part with Marci she had again blanched and the look on her face was exactly the look I hoped she was using now.

"And if he asks you why I think that, you tell him that I've found evidence, DNA evidence, and all I need to do now is find corroborating witnesses to set up a time line so the authorities will take the cases seriously."

The tricky part, I told her, would be if he didn't ask about where I got DNA. Then she was going to have to offer up the lie about my finding a body in the Glades. She had nodded at the instructions, said she could do it. But this wasn't some drunk she would be trying to convince. There was something raw about the way she used his name. I could not dismiss the feeling that she was too anxious to hurt this guy and if that showed through, no way was this going to work.

"Whatever you do, Marci," I'd said, "don't go with him." She'd tightened her mouth and I repeated my instruction. "Don't go with him or it's off."

Morrison was inside for forty-five minutes. O'Shea buzzed me when he came out.

"Guy's marchin,' Freeman," he said into the cell. "Looks like a man on a mission and hasn't looked left or right yet."

I started my truck, figuring his pattern would be the same and he would exit the center through the road in front of me just like he had the night his headlights had caught me on the stakeout.

"Headin' your way, Freeman," O'Shea said. "I'll fall in behind."

I pressed my head against the driver's side window, using the frame strut to partially hide behind and watched as the cruiser swung around the corner and onto the street. Morrison pulled a rolling stop through the first stop sign and I had to come out fast to stay within a reasonable distance. Either he was so focused he wasn't paying attention, or he was just arrogant. Both were good things. He wouldn't be thinking of a tail.

We were heading west through a residential area, then he took a right back toward Sunrise Boulevard to catch a light. It was the same way I would have gone to get on the main strip west toward the expressway.

"O'Shea, head up the back way to the park so you can get in behind him," I said into the Nextel. "I'm going to have to stop at the light with him and he's going to get a good look at my truck and I'll have to fall back to keep him from getting familiar."

"Roger that, big man."

"If he keeps westbound to I-95 you'll fit in with the rest of the traffic heading that way. I'll stay back a couple of blocks."

"We got this one, Max. Not a problem."

Christ, I thought. I'm partnered with Colin O'Shea. I could only hope he wouldn't hold to form and somehow screw this one up.

Morrison stopped at the light. It was difficult to see his silhouette through the dark glass of his back window in the daylight. The advantage to police cars in Florida was that they almost all had tinted windows so they were obscured from the outside. The treatments used to scare the shit out of us as patrol officers, pulling over some van or tricked out ghetto cruiser when you couldn't see if some banger inside was sighting up a shotgun at the window. Now law enforcement had followed the trend themselves. I again leaned into my driver's door behind the strut, hung my elbow out of the open window like I was a tired worker going home for the evening. I didn't think Morrison could have gotten much of a look at me when he slipped out of Kim's that first time I glimpsed him, but I was trying not to underestimate the guy.

He took a left at the light change as I expected and I followed but fell back. We were heading into a setting sun, the flare of orange spraying strong up into the clouds, and there was enough white light left to cause everyone to drop their visors a couple of inches. It was past commuter time, but South Florida traffic never seemed to ease. It was good for cover, bad if Morrison got nervous and made any quick moves.

"I'm in behind him coming up on the Sears curve," O'Shea reported over the Nextel.

"I'm three blocks back," I answered.

I had to think that Morrison would believe most of what Marci had reported to him. I wasn't exactly going out on a limb with this but maybe we could get lucky. If he wasn't our guy, he'd go home, or to the station, or to some poker game for all I knew. But if he was our guy, I was betting the mention of somehow finding a woman's body in the Glades would spook him. He wouldn't believe it, but the thought of it would get into his head and twist it. If he was as careful as we made him out to be, he would have to confirm it. I was betting on the Glades. Marci had just added to it with her description of someplace off Alligator Alley. Dumping bodies in the Everglades was a tradition in South Florida. The Indians had done it to early explorers, the ruthless farm bosses to slave labor. The mob had done it with their enemies in the twenties and the myriad criminals from dope runners to child abductors had done it in the modern era. Two and a half million acres of open land, shifting water, canals and sawgrass and plenty of reptiles to eliminate all traces: a perfect disposal site. I figured he'd head straight for the Alley and use the failing daylight to his advantage.

But maybe I thought wrong.

"Freeman, I'm losing him up here," O'Shea snapped into the Nextel. "Some asshole is trying to make a left over two lanes and I'm trapped and your boy just put his blue lights on and went up around everybody in the right lane."

I immediately pushed up my speed and moved to the right, passing through a crosswalk, forcing a hulking black man with a shopping cart to yank his load back and spit a string of tobacco at my pickup. I was sitting high enough in my cab to see the flashes of blue from Morrison's light bar and kept pushing. I cut off another driver moving too slow over the railroad tracks and gained another half a block. I saw O'Shea twisting his wheel and cursing out to my left as I went by and gave him a hand sign that I was chasing now.

I blew a red light at Ninth Avenue by barely a second and picked up Morrison's cruiser a block and a half in front. I sped up to get in the same traffic herd so we wouldn't get separated by another light, and exhaled. No big deal. This was why you did two-mans. It was the old way before every metro P.D. had helicopters and the undercover guys hid locators in their cell phones.

I was watching Morrison's light bar and was anticipating his shift into the left lane when he suddenly went right without a signal onto Thirteenth heading north. Shit. Where the hell was he going? An SUV and a sedan made the same turn and I swung behind them and watched the squad car making distance on me and I punched up O'Shea.

"Our guy just took a north route on Thirteenth. If he makes a couple more turns he's going to make me," I said.

"I'll cut up on Twelfth and try to catch him parallel," O'Shea answered.

I was trying to keep my speed but the sun was now on the left side of my face, glancing off my hood, and before I could adjust my focus I realized Morrison had slowed, and when the fat SUV between us swerved around him into the left lane, only the small car was a buffer. The squad car kept its speed and rolled on and I was too far back to see if Morrison was checking his side mirrors. We were on our way up to Oakland Park and I started thinking about what we could do if he simply went home. I was prepared to just sit on him. But tailing him out to some spot in the Glades would be even tougher at night. Out there in the flat expanse you could see headlights for more than a mile. I was grinding and watching the next traffic light burn green when Morrison's car slowed a little more than normal and then suddenly cut over to the far left and took a hard turn into the sun. I had to make a decision: O'Shea was still east, he wouldn't be able to tag on and Morrison was heading west, the direction I'd wanted him to go. Should I call it off or take a chance?

"He's going west on Twenty-eighth," I barked into the Nextel and I went left, caught a horn from an oncoming taxi driver, cussed under my breath and was then partially blinded by the streaming light of sunset.

I caught a glimpse of the police lettering on Morrison's back bumper as he cut another left turn and when I hooked onto the same street I slammed on the brakes. There were two patrol cars parked nose-to-nose blocking the street and Morrison's brake lights beyond them. When I stopped I took a futile look into my rearview and another cruiser was crossing the T behind me. The Nextel tweeted.

"Sorry brother, you know I can't take a chance gettin' into that beehive," O'Shea said from somewhere back there. "Call me when you can. Out."

I tossed the cell under the seat like you might roll an empty beer bottle after getting pulled over. If they wanted to find it bad enough, they would. The three officers in front seemed to climb out of their cars at the same time, like it was choreographed. The fourth, behind me, stayed behind the wheel. Classic drug stop. Don't ever try to tail a cop without installing a police scanner, I thought. You miss that call for backup, you're screwed.

CHAPTER 26

When she called him, he didn't know for sure whether she'd learned her lesson, or she was fucking with him somehow. All he knew for sure was that he didn't feel right. Maybe he should have just done her when he had the chance and moved on.

"Hi, Kyle. Hey, I'm at work, baby, and you know that big tall guy who came in the other day with the blonde cop? He was back in here today, asking me questions and it scared me, you know, what you said, about you getting into trouble by hanging out here?"

"Whoa, whoa, whoa, Marci," he'd said, trying to calm her, though there was something in her voice that sounded more like she was acting spooked instead of being afraid. And he knew her well enough now to know she didn't scare easily. Hell, she wasn't even scared the other night. She might have been pissed. She might have even known that if she hadn't done what he wanted he would have killed her right there like the rest of them. But she didn't come off scared. He liked that in a woman.

"OK, listen. What the hell did the guy say?" he asked.

"He was talking about missing bartenders," she said. "Girls that had worked at a bunch of places, up on OPB and down off Seventeenth Street and even here that that blonde cop thinks were kidnapped."

Kidnapped, he thought. Christ, Marci, you're such a child.

"Yeah, well, those are a bunch of rumors, Marci. They're like urban legends that assholes like to sit around at the bar and yak about like it's all intriguing when it isn't anything more than girls walking away from their job, gone down to Key West or someplace. Don't tell me you never wanted to just walk away and get the hell out of there?"

That fucking Richards, he thought. Still pushing that shit and now she's got some goddamn P.I. into it because nobody in real law enforcement will believe her.

"But this guy says that he found some kind of evidence. Some kind of body part or blood or something that's going to prove who did it and all they had to do was find out when certain people were in the bar when Suzy disappeared," she'd said.

"Body parts? That's what he said? Body parts?"

Christ, he thought, don't lose it. Just get it out of her.

"He said a bunch of stuff but I don't want to talk about it over the phone, Kyle, you know. Can't you come over? I'm scared."

And this time when she said it, she did sound scared and he didn't want to hear the rest of it over the phone, anyway, he wanted to look into her eyes and hear it.

"I'll be over in an hour," he told her. "Just be calm, baby. I'm coming over." These goddamn women can get so emotional.

On the drive over there he'd let his own head start cranking. Body parts. That's bullshit. There's no way Richards or some P.I. went out in the middle of the goddamn Glades and found body parts. Shit, the gators out there would have taken care of that long ago. Sure, somebody might have found a corpse or part of one out there. Fucking mopes were dumping dopers or bad business partners out there all the time. Shit, that asshole who beat up his old lady and killed his own kid went and dumped the body in one of the canals at a boat ramp out there just last summer and a fisherman came up with part of the body. But that was stupid, in close, where people hang out.

So they might have found something, but why come and ask Marci about it? Marci didn't know shit unless they were trying to manufacture a case and were going to use her to set somebody up just to clear the case. That would be so typical of the detective bureau, use some poor innocent girl to make a case for them.

He'd parked at the shopping center on the other side and then walked over to Kim's. Don't be in such a hurry, he told himself. You draw attention to yourself. Why the hell did you bring the squad, anyway? That wasn't too bright, somebody sees you coming into the place in broad daylight. Jesus, Kyle. What happened to careful?

Inside there was that group of magazine smart-asses at one end of the bar and the Schnapps guy in the middle. He went to the end and then around the corner, under the TV, instead of in his usual spot. Marci waited a minute or so before she came down and pulled a beer out of the cooler for him on her way.

There was something very tense about her. Maybe this guy really had shaken her up.

"OK, Marci. Tell me about it again, the whole thing, babe. Right from the point that the guy walks in here, OK? Nothing left out."

She pretty much repeated herself and he let her until she got to the mention of the so-called body parts and hesitated.

"Slow down now, Marci," he said. "You're sure he said 'body parts'?"

"Well, I uh, it was something that he said was DNA evidence. He might not have said 'body parts' exactly but where the hell else do you get DNA for Christ's sake?"

Jesus, he thought.

"Baby, it could be anything, hair from a comb, a goddamn toothbrush, a fucking Band-Aid tossed in the trash," he told her. "Did he say where he found it?"

"No. Just that he had it and they were trying to get some kind of verification."

"Did they ask you for any kind of sample? Blood or a swab of the inside of your mouth?"

"No. Why would they want something from me?"

That flash of tenseness was back in her eyes, he could see it in there, her fighting it.

"Exactly," he said to her. "He's fishing for stuff, baby. He's probably done this to every goddamn girl in town who serves drinks."

He took a pull on his beer, didn't like the taste and put it down. He tried to make himself relax, get her to match him. She excused herself and went down to the other end and made up some pansy-ass Shirley Temples or whatever the hell it was the alternative boys were drinking.

He tried to get a picture of the big, lanky guy who'd walked in that night before Richards. He'd sat at the other end and acted like he was friendly with Laurie. Tanned guy, he remembered. Not an office man. He looked more like a boat captain or construction foreman. All he'd noted was that the guy was drinking his brand of beer and then that bitch had come in and he had to bolt.

Marci came back down to him, exhaled, was more relaxed.

"No big deal, baby," he said. "Nothing for you to worry about. I'll find out from the inside what the rumor is and let you know, OK?"

She nodded her head.

"This guy didn't say anything about me, did he? I mean, he didn't ask if any other cops had been in here or drank regular here?"

"No," she said. "But I wouldn't have told him anyway."

"Atta girl," he said and she had an odd look on her face when he said it, one that held some kind of inside smile, like she'd accomplished something. He ignored it, thanked her in his customer voice and walked out into the late sunlight and back to his patrol car.

He was running a plan through his head while he sat at the first traffic light on Sunrise. Should he ignore the whole damn thing? If they had anything to connect him to the dead girls, wouldn't they be on his ass already? They'd have called him into his sergeant's office for a little face time to at least warn him that the Richards bitch was coming down on him.

But what if this P.I. was teamed up with Richards and they were trying to show she was right and prove everyone else wrong? Then why come to Marci? Showing up twice meant they didn't get enough from Laurie to keep them away, and that wasn't good. When the light changed he went west on Sunrise and pulled his visor down to block the glaring sun.

The P.I. said "DNA evidence"—he kept tumbling Marci's words in his head. Of course she didn't get the conversation exact. Body parts. DNA evidence. What the fuck did the guy have, if anything? Shit. He'd just ended it with Suzy. Her body would still be pretty fresh, even if the gators did get to it. He ought to just go out to the spot now, see if there was any sign that anyone had been out there. Answer the goddamn question so he'd at least know what he was dealing with. It'd be better than most of the mopes that he arrested who just sat there waiting for shit to come through the door and then it was too late, then you were already playing their game.

He was watching half a block ahead like he usually did and saw the traffic starting to jam up on the left and he knew some dipshit was trying to make a left against the light like they always did and he slid over to the right lane. He would have gotten snared up, too, but he used his lights and a couple of hits on the siren and skirted by the on the right.

"Fucking lemmings," he said aloud and then looked up into his rearview to watch the mess and registered in his head the midnight blue pickup truck that had just run a red light half a block back. He kept driving. Maybe he ought to wait. But shit, he'd be back on shift tomorrow and that would only give him the daylight hours to get out to the Glades site and back in time, and he was even more wary about doing anything in the daylight. Only bad shit happened in the light, he thought. Right now he could stop out there and check for fresh tire tracks or signs of disturbance with a flashlight and be a hell of a lot less conspicuous.

He went through the intersection at Ninth Avenue and glanced at the old bagman starting across the street. Christ, I just busted that guy for carrying dope two weeks ago and he's already back on the street, he thought and looked back to see for sure if it was the same guy pushing the same old grocery cart. That's when he saw it again, the blue pickup, charging through the intersection, but then easing back. Following.

At the next light he made a hard right and watched his mirror. He saw the pickup hesitate and then make the same turn.

"Son of a bitch," he said and slowed down, watching his mirrors, trying to see the single driver, his image behind the windshield high up over the one car between them. A minute later he snatched up his radio.

"Two-fourteen. Two-eighteen. This is two-oh-four in need of assistance. Switch over to tack channel three," he said into the microphone.

CHAPTER 27

I sat with both hands on the steering wheel at ten and two o'-clock. I didn't know what Morrison might have called in, but I wasn't taking any chances. Make no quick moves and keep your hands in full view. I watched the three cops in front of me huddle at Morrison's trunk, talking and cutting their eyes to me. It was Morrison's meeting and I watched him, trying to match him up with the figure I'd seen briefly at the bar. He hooked his thumbs into his polished leather belt, turned his face to me a couple of times for emphasis. It was the same face as in the photo. They talked for a full two minutes and I did not move my hands, not even to turn off the engine.

Finally, the two other officers nodded and started toward me, one moving to the left, the other to the right of my truck. Morrison leaned back against his trunk and crossed his arms and stared into my face. His eyes felt much closer than they physically were.

"License and registration, please," said the cop who came to my open window.

"What, uh, seems to be the problem, officer?" I said, truly interested in what they were going to come up with.

"License and registration, please," he repeated.

The other cop was at the passenger window, looking into the seat and on the floor and checking what he could see in the bed of the truck.

"May I go into the glove box?" I asked before leaning over to turn the knob.

"Sure," said the cop. "Turn off the ignition first, please."

I shut down the engine and then reached in and got my registration and insurance card. I asked if I could get my wallet from my back pocket. Again he agreed, but I noticed that he had flipped off the strap on his 9mm holster and was resting the web between his thumb and forefinger on the butt of the gun.

I handed him the documentation and he said: "I'll be right with you, sir."

He was a younger man, sandy blonde hair and skin that was too fair for the semitropics. He was wide in the shoulders and narrow in the hips and the short sleeves of his shirt were too tight to fit comfortably around his biceps. He nodded at the other one over the hood and then walked my paperwork back to Morrison.

We were a good forty feet apart and maybe I could feel his sneer more than actually see it. Morrison was cupping his elbows now, looking nonchalant, but there was something misshapen about his mouth that gave the effect that his whole head was tilted. He took the documents from the other one's hands and stared down at them. I got the sense that he could memorize the pertinent facts and did not write them down. In fact I doubted that he wrote anything down with the exception of work-related reports that were mandatory. He was a man whose secrets would all be filed inside his head.

After another minute, the two men nodded in affirmation and as muscle boy walked back toward me, Morrison turned and got back into his squad car.

I watched him do a three point turn as the younger cop approached my window and said: "Mr. Freeman, step out of the car, please. We are going to have to conduct a roadside sobriety test, sir."

As he drove out and past me, Morrison did not meet my eye.

He stared straight ahead and did not acknowledge me at all, as though I were something not worth his time or effort. He was leaving my detention to other, less important persons while he attended to something more pressing. He knew who I was now. But for the next twenty minutes, while I went through a small humiliation, I would shed an entire layer of doubt about his involvement in something ugly. And that, I promised, would not be a good thing for Kyle Morrison.

If they had tested me a few hours later at Billy's penthouse apartment, the cops might have actually been able to hold me. I was working on my third beer and it had been no struggle at all. Billy was sipping from his crystal wineglass and his fiancée was out for the evening, "clearing her head."

On the drive back north I'd called O'Shea and told him that our tail had called in his backup to make a bogus DUI stop and then split, ending any further chance of surveillance. He would be watching now, and he was no slouch when it came to paying attention. I had figured he'd be too caught up in Marci's story to notice what was happening around him and I had been wrong. I wouldn't underestimate him again.

"Sorry I had to leave you like that, Freeman. But you know my circumstances. Brushing up against rogue cops isn't what I need right now," O'Shea said. "So I figured if I got dealt out of the cop chase, I'd make myself useful and go back and set up on the girl."

It was the smart thing to do. O'Shea had to be given credit, but even when I did it it felt like begrudging credit.

"You're smarter than you look, O'Shea. "Are you good to stay on her when she leaves?"

"Fuck you, Freeman. And yeah, I'll hang with her. If you want, I'll tail her to her apartment and babysit all night."

Maybe he was just being a smart-ass, but I quickly agreed and told him I'd get back with him later. But before he could disconnect, I asked him one last question.

"You know what this is, don't you, Colin?"

"I'm not stupid, Freeman. You're figuring this cop for the abductions and ponytail is his next victim."

"No, you're not stupid," I said. "You're deductive."

"I'm not deductive," he answered. "I'm experienced, Freeman. I've seen this before, remember. But even if you're as wrong on this guy as they were on me up in Philly, I'm still willing to help you find out this way instead of sticking the guy's face into the official IAD toilet where innocence don't mean jack."

This time he was quicker on the button and the connection went dead. I might not like his attitude, but O'Shea was right. We were both hanging it out there. But I also took some peace knowing he was looking over Marci's back. He would call me if Morrison showed up. And I'd spell him in the morning.

When I called Billy it was late but he invited me over and I launched into the story of my botched plan to follow the cop on the long shot that he might lead us to something worth more than speculation. When I got to the part about the DUI trap he winced. We were on the patio with the black, colorless ocean out in front of us. He listened intently, like he always did, before offering a question or opinion.

"So you d-don't think they were in on anything t-together, this Marci girl and M-Morrison?"

"She doesn't strike me as a user," I said, shaking my head. "Or someone who'd get into the drug thing. She comes across too smart and too proud. When he raped her, he made one hell of an enemy."

"But you said she was s-scared of Morrison."

"Scared and pissed at the same time. She said she wouldn't press charges, that she knew she'd lose because he was a cop and she hadn't struggled enough."

We were quiet at the thought, looking out into a sea we could only hear and smell. The wind rustled the palm fronds and a crinkle of laughter from some balcony below found its way on the breeze up to us.

"W-What's your next move?" Billy finally said.

"Don't know."

He waited a moment.

"Liar," he said.

"OK. I'll have to talk to her again. Try to get something out of her we can use. Some detail she doesn't know she has that can trap this guy.

"It will be difficult. M-Maybe someone else should be the interviewer?"

"Richards?"

"It would m-make sense. Woman to woman."

I sipped at the beer, thought about the possibilities.

"Sherry is going to l-listen to a woman in pain, M-Max. No matter what."

I brought the bottle down.

"I'll call her tomorrow," I said.

"You can do it from here," Billy said and I could tell by his tone that he was leading me. I looked over at him and raised an eyebrow.

"S-Stay here in the guest room tonight," he said.

"No thanks. You know? You guys deserve some guest-free living."

"Diane w-went back to her place," he said.

This time I swung my legs off the chaise and faced him.

"Besides, I g-gave your bed away at the b-beach."

I'd just be wasting my time if I asked why his fiancée was sleeping away from the penthouse. He would tell me if he wanted me to know so I kept my mouth shut while he got up and went inside. When he returned he handed me a manila envelope and started to explain while I went through the contents.

"We got this two days ago, no p-postmark. It was somehow dropped on the front d-desk without anyone noticing."

The front of the envelope said simply: MANCHESTER. The name was written in block letters with some kind of black marker.

I pulled out a sheaf of five photos. One shot was of Billy and Diane, in front of the apartment building, both dressed for work in business suits. Another was a single shot of Billy in front of the West Palm Beach County Courthouse, carrying his briefcase, heading inside. Another single shot was of Diane, exiting her car in the federal courthouse parking lot only a few blocks away. Another was of her sunbathing on the beach, one knee raised as she lay on a blanket. Her skin was moist with lotion and her straw hat was placed over her face.

The final photograph was of a woman I did not recognize. She appeared to be of medium height and build and was also in business attire and coming out of a small shaded residence built in the old style of South Florida in the 1950s.

"When you told us the other day that you had s-seen someone outside with a camera, we weren't exactly sure whether to tell you," Billy said. "Diane had n-noticed someone on the b-beach taking photos in her direction, but didn't mention it until I brought up a concern. The p-political hierarchy was m-making noise about our marriage, the race issue. I had considered that s-someone was taking pictures to put up on some Internet site or d-distribute them another way to influence those of a like mind to second-guess Diane's judgeship."

I started to say something when Billy stopped me with a raised hand.

"I was b-being paranoid," he said and then handed me a type-written note sealed in a plastic bag. "This came with the pictures."

I held the bag by the corners, laid it smooth on my thigh and read:
GET OFF THE CRUISE WORKERS CASE OR ALL THREE OF YOU LAWYER FUCKS WILL BE GATOR FOOD

"Eloquent," I said. I glanced at the evidence tag that was stripped and dated on the corner of the bag.

"Brody come up with anything?" I said, guessing at the precise tag markings.

Brody was a former FBI forensics expert who had quit the agency when his entire government lab was smeared as incompetent by the general accounting office a few years back. He'd moved to South Florida and opened his own private lab and did uncompromising work for a variety of attorneys, investigators and the occasional freelance operator who needed his services with no questions or paperwork.

"I assume the stranger is a lawyer?" I said, holding up the photo of the single woman.

"Sarah O'Kelly," Billy said. "I know her, but I was unaware that she was doing work with cruise ship workers from the Port of Miami.

"She lives in Fort Lauderdale and when I called her, her secretary said she had been traveling in Panama doing research on the cruise cases and had been gone for ten days. The assistant had not opened her mail, but nothing unposted or of similar size to this one had arrived at her office."

"If she got it, it's probably at her house," I said.

"If our new friends are c-consistent."

I turned the photos over and scanned through them again. The shot of Diane seemed uncomfortably pornographic, knowing someone had stalked her and taken it without her knowledge with the purpose of a threat.

"The Hix brothers?" I said.

"I can only imagine," Billy said. "I asked O'Kelly's assistant to pass on my number as soon as she contacts her and preferably before she gets home. She said she's due in tomorrow."

I put the photos and letter back into the envelope and handed them back.

"You tell Rodrigo about this?" I said, thinking of the scared man and his decision to go home.

"That's w-why you'll have to stay here tonight, M-Max," Billy said. "He's out of the hospital, b-but I gave him your bed down at the Flamingo."

"Hiding?"

"For now."

"And Diane?"

"She is not the k-kind of woman who is used to threats," Billy said. "I asked her to st-stay at her place because it is g-gated and secured and she did not argue."

I wasn't sure what it was in his voice: Disappointment? Guilt? All I did know was that I wasn't going to probe there. Not without an invitation.

He was still standing, leaning against the railing now and, unlike the analytical and focused man I had always known, he was preoccupied. I gave him space and looked out where I knew the horizon was, where dark sky met dark water, and searched for the light of a trawler or overnight fisherman, something to give the blackness a reference point. I finally found one far to the south, winking on and off with a rhythm that I knew had to be the roll of the swells.

"So what's the plan?" I finally said. "Do we take this to the authorities as a written threat and let them handle it?"

"Huh?" Billy flinched and looked down as if just discovering the glass in his hand and stepped back from the slosh of wine that had spilled to the deck.

"I'm sorry, M-Max," he said and looked embarrassed. "I, uh, well, certainly that's an option. B-But I think I would rather wait until we get the chance to t-talk with O'Kelly. I'd like to s-see if she too has b-been contacted and what her take on all this is. If I recall correctly, she is an amiable and thoughtful lawyer and I w-would think we'd want her opinion since she is obviously intimately involved."

"Spoken like a true attorney," I said, razzing him for his quick little soliloquy, spit out with style even though it had been far from his thoughts.

He smiled and raised his glass. "I have been threatened b-before. This will wait. I think you have more p-pressing matters at hand. Let's go over your scenarios with a true attorney's perspective on all of this."

CHAPTER 28

The smell of wet green earth and the sound of rain pattering through high trees woke me and I was startled in the way you are when you can't register where the hell you are. I blinked the dream away and pushed my hands up into my face and realized I was already sitting up on the edge of a bed.

Billy's, I recalled, noting the deep ivory color of the wall in front of me and the chill on my bare shoulders from the air-conditioning. I was in his guest room. I was still wearing my canvas pants and looked around to see that I had not pulled the bed covers back and had simply fallen asleep atop them. I rubbed my eyes and again caught the smell of turned and rotted soil on the palms of my hands and stared stupidly down at them. Clean.

I pushed myself up and walked into the bath and stood at the basin and splashed water up into my face and the odor disappeared. When I was a child my mother described how my dreams had seemed so vivid and my recollections of them so detailed that it made her uneasy. She said she would walk to the Italian Market in South Philly or to church and half expect to come around the corner and see the shear cliffs or talking dogs or some falling child that I had foretold from a dream the previous night. There were times now that I fell back into that vividness when dreaming or daydreaming of past experiences. As a cop who saw too many ugly scenes I often considered it a curse. Still, they were dreams. I had never had them portend the future before.

I dressed and went out to the kitchen where I found the coffeemaker loaded with fresh grounds and ready to flip on, and a note from Billy:

"I have gone to check on Diane and will be in my office later. I will call O'Kelly and contact you. I checked on Rodrigo and he is fine. Can you stop in to see him?"

Even though we'd stayed up well into the morning hours, Billy was an early riser. He would have consumed the *Wall Street Journal* and that horrid fruit and vitamin concoction of his and then been out the door dressed in Brooks Brothers before seven.

I looked at my watch. It was almost noon. When the coffee was brewed I took a cup out onto the patio. There was a nor'easter starting to kick in. The water was gray-green and moving like an enormous blanket being shaken from four corners at the same time, waves of varying sizes swallowing each other and an uneven chop strewn with foam. The sky was overcast and tightened down and the wind was blowing hard enough to snap the single American flag that the faux British manager had raised at dawn. Before my first cup was empty I could feel a film of warm, clammy moisture on my skin. I went back inside and my first call was to O'Shea. He gave the same report he had when I called him at three in the morning, before I passed out: Marci was in her apartment. No sign of Morrison.

"How you doin'?" I asked.

"You ever trying sleeping in a Camaro?" he said

I didn't answer.

"Hey, I'm a security guard, Freeman," he said. "I can handle security."

My next call was to Richards's office number. Her answering machine was on and I left a message telling her I had more information about Morrison and one of the bartenders who we had recently met who might know more than was offered. I hoped at least the bartender reference would cause her to call back.

I finished the coffee and left, pulling Billy's apartment door closed and checking the automatic locking mechanism before taking the elevator down. Outside in the front lot I instinctively scanned the cars, looking for one backed into a spot with signs of a cameraman. Now I wished I had confronted the guy the first time.

I took A1A south and traffic was light. It wasn't a beach day and the tourists and regulars would stay inside or inland somewhere out of the wet wind. The grayness gave the dunes and seaside mansions a look like old antique oil paintings, the colors dimmed and the landscape lonely. I was pulling into the Flamingo Villas when my cell phone rang.

"Yeah."

"It's Sherry, Max."

"Hey. You got my message?"

"No. I haven't been into the office yet. What did you need?"

If she was calling me unsolicited, I immediately wondered why. To offer me something? To ask for help? If I let her go first, it would put me in a better position to state my own case. I hesitated, then realized I was playing the info-for-info game and shook my head like I could just toss off a million years of human social behavior like a bead of sweat.

"I uh, wanted to get with you and tell you about a conversation I had with the bartender," I said. "Marci, at Kim's. The younger one who is fairly new."

"OK. Has this got anything to do with patrolman Morrison?" she said.

"Yeah, it does. How'd you know?"

"Well," she said, and now it was her turn to hesitate, and maybe for the same reason I had.

"I understand that you two had a bit of a face-to-face yesterday," she said. "I know that's your method of operation, Max. And I'm interested in what that finely tuned perceptive gut of yours told you when you looked him in the eye. But wasn't that a little outside the envelope, trying to tail a cop while he's in his squad car?"

There was a bit of a lilt in her voice, like she was smiling when she said it, and not a smile that held a comeuppance.

"Yeah, I suppose it was. But how did this information come to your attention?"

"O'Shea called me," she said, flat and matter-of-fact.

"You're kidding," I said, spinning the conversation I'd just had with O'Shea.

"He was concerned about you. He thought you were working something that was going to get you into trouble on his account and he said he didn't want to be responsible. He said he figured that I should know the truth before the facts got twisted around to suit the uniforms."

"The truth?" I said.

"Meet me over in the covered parking lot at the Galleria at two, under the west side," she said. "It's raining like hell down here."

I told her I would be there by two, as soon as I checked on another client.

It was still only gray here. The clouds were heavy and had not yet opened up but I could hear the surf beginning to slash at the beach as the wind increased. The fronds of the rubber plants and white birds of paradise that sheltered each bungalow were clacking and the smell of salt and flotsam was thick in my nose when I came around the corner and stopped.

The door to Billy's hideaway was standing open. There was a light glowing somewhere behind the front window. Probably the one over the sink in the kitchen, I thought, putting the layout together in my head while I squinted and tried to pick up any movement inside. I stepped closer to the sea grape tree next to me and knelt with one knee in the sand. The wind swung the door a foot more and I could now see a bar stool on the floor and the small dining area light was missing from its spot suspended above the table, only a bare cord left hanging in the air. I was unarmed. My 9mm was back at the shack, wrapped in its oilskin cloth where I had re-tired it.

Don't jump to conclusions, I told myself, and then got up and took a couple of steps closer, listening through the rumble of the ocean and wind. There was still no movement from inside. I looked around for neighbors but the weather had sent most people in-doors.

On the flat concrete stones that started a path in front of the patio I picked up on a trail of dark droplets and one didn't have to be a CSI to recognize blood, and that's when I moved faster. At the door I peered around the corner. The front room had been tossed and glass and half a bulb from the hanging light lay shattered in one corner. The blood trail led to the couch and joined a stain there that formed the shape of Italy in the fabric. I was about to step all the way in when the panicked voices of women came from behind me in the wind.

"Help! Somebody help him!"

I turned and jogged toward the beach and saw three women, one with children huddled into her skirts, waving their arms and point-ing out to sea.

I had my shirt off by the time I hit the railing of the bulkhead and then used the top rung to swing over and down. I kicked my Docksides off after landing in the sand and I was honing in on a splotch of yellow that was bobbing fifty yards out. The shape ex-panded at the top of a crest to something human and then disap-peared on the backside of the wave and a prayer seemed to bring it back to the surface again.

I hurdled the first three waves and then launched myself like a spear down into the next one, grabbed a handhold of the bottom sand, pulled myself into a crouch and used my legs to launch again. Each time I dolphined I tried to catch a breath and a glimpse of the yellow shirt. Sometimes I got one, sometimes the other.

When it got too deep I started to freestyle, looking forward each time a wave picked me up to the top of a crest. It didn't take long to close in on the shirt. When I got to within ten yards I could see it was Rodrigo, one side of his face a pale white, the scarred half an angry red. But his eyes were still wide and he was flapping with one arm, trying to stay on top in the oxygen while the white water tried to drown him. I went to a breast stroke and got into the same swell with him and yelled his name. There was no recognition in his face but he saw hope and grabbed for it.

I'd learned enough about water rescues to keep a struggling swimmer off your body. If you let them get a choke hold, you were both going down. I grabbed his wrist when he reached for me and held him at arm's length.

"OK Rodrigo!" I yelled. "You're OK, you're OK!"

I was looking to find his other arm when a wave broke over both our heads. While we were under I reached for his other arm and held it. When we both cleared the white water Rodrigo was screaming in pain like he'd been hooked with a sharp barb and I realized the arm I'd grabbed was hanging limp.

"Broke, Mr. Max! Broke, broke," he spit out, his face twisted in agony and I let go of the arm.

"OK, OK. Let me pull you Rodrigo. Let me pull!"

He may have understood me or maybe he went into shock but I was able to hook him under the pit of his good arm and turn his back so it was on my hip and I began sidestroking for shore. The waves had no rhythm and in the white water it felt like all I was doing was pulling at air bubbles and getting nowhere. I was breathing heavily and trying to scissor kick each time a wave pushed us, and then I'd rest when it left us bogged down in the swell. It seemed like thirty minutes and I started counting strokes to give myself a goal.

In the middle of my second count to fifty I felt my right foot touch the ocean floor and the next wave pushed both of us onto solid sand. I struggled with Rodrigo's sudden weight and then heard yelling, "We got you, man! We got you!" and we were suddenly surrounded by hands and arms and other bodies in the water around us.

"Watch his arm, watch his arm, it's broke," I said as two men took Rodrigo from me and I felt another strong arm around my own waist.

"Oh, shit, man and his leg, too, watch his leg, man!" another voice said.

On the beach there was a red-and-white rescue truck with a red gumball light spinning on its roof and the lifeguards lay Rodrigo down in the lee side out of the wind and had me sit beside him. The little Filipino had an unnatural lump in the side of his arm where his bicep should have been and from the thigh of his left leg a stark white splinter of bone was protruding, blood trickling from the gash and mixing with the water and running a spiderweb of red down through the hair on his leg. One of the guards wrapped a blanket around the leg and someone draped one over my shoulders.

While my heartbeat tripped down I heard the sound of a siren growing and two of the guards brought out a backboard, strapped Rodrigo onto it, and then carried him to the street end, where an ambulance was backing up to the bulkhead. After they took him away a guard crouched down next to me. It was Amsler, the guard who chinning bar I used.

"You want a ride to the E.R., Mr. Freeman? Let them check you out?"

"No," I said. "I'm all right. Swallowed a little salt water is all but thanks, thanks for helping out. You, uh, know what hospital they're taking that guy to?"

"Probably North Broward," he said. "Man, I've never seen anyone break bones like that in the surf. That guy was messed up."

"Yeah," I said, "he was."

When I stood I could see up over the Royal Flamingo's bulkhead where the group of women whose call for help had set me off was talking with a uniformed Broward sheriff's office deputy. One of the women pointed to me and the cop looked up. I didn't recognize him. He was writing on a pad that looked like a reporter's notebook and the pages were flapping in the wind. I started toward the bottom of the stairs as he passed out cards to the women and by the time I reached the top he was heading for me.

"Excuse me, sir."

I stood near the shower and waited.

"Excuse me, I'm Deputy Cardona. You are the rescuer?"

He was a young man with a tight Spanish accent but his English pronunciations were careful.

"Sure," I said, offering nothing more and looking down at my soaked pants, now covered with a crust of sand from sitting wet on the beach.

"The ladies there," he said, tipping his pen back toward the group, which had not moved. "They say they were calling for help when they saw the gentleman in trouble and then you came flying in from nowhere and into the water."

"Yeah, a real Superman," I said, not really meaning to be a smart-ass but coming off that way while I was trying to piece together the sight of the smashed bungalow, Rodrigo's broken bones and whether I wanted to talk about any of it with this cop.

"OK. First of all, I will require a name, sir," the officer said and raised his pen to his pad.

"Max. Max Freeman. Look, do you mind if I shower this stuff off?" I said, dropping my fingers to my pants and nodding at the shower. He said "Not at all, please," and stepped back to the windward side and let me turn on the water.

I let the stream run over my head and kept my eyes closed while I thought of what I was going to say to the guy. I rinsed the sand off my pants as best I could and when I couldn't stall any longer I cranked the valve shut. The cop stood patiently by, looking out to sea and then to the bulkhead, and if he was perceptive enough he would pick up the deep impressions that my landing on the beach had made and then follow my running footsteps leading back to the bungalow. The door was still wide open.

When I stepped away from the shower one of the ladies was there with a towel.

"Thank you," I said, caught off guard.

"You were marvelous," she said. "That man owes you his life."

I started to say something but she held up a palm and then

walked away to join her friends. I turned back to the cop, raised my eyebrows and then motioned to the chickee hut nearby.

"Can we sit?"

I picked up the shirt I'd tossed on the ground when I'd bolted for the ocean and pulled it over my head. I ducked under the dried fronds that formed the roof of the open shelter and took a chair facing my bungalow so that the officer's back would be to it. It didn't help. He was perceptive.

"You live here, Mr. Freeman?" he said, pointing the pen over his shoulder.

"Actually, it belongs to a friend. I was just borrowing it for a while."

"Was the drowning man your friend?"

It figured that I'd get one of the bright ones.

"Why do you ask?" I said. It was one of those sophomore techniques; answer a question with a question. He checked his notebook.

"One of the ladies, she says she saw the drowning man limping down to the beach and saw him go into the water with his clothes on."

No question had been asked, so I didn't respond. I used the towel to dry my hair and avoid eye contact.

"She also says a larger man who appeared to be chasing him came down these steps with anger and with a baseball bat in his hands."

David, of the infamous Hix brothers, I thought. I could picture him in the bungalow, taking down the dining room light with a single swing.

"The limping man appeared to escape into the water because the other refused to follow."

I draped the towel around my neck and then stretched out one leg and reached into my pants pocket. The cop did not tense. He had already seen me without a shirt and knew I wasn't carrying.

"Do you mind if I make a call?" I said and pulled a dripping cell phone from my pocket but then looked dumbly at it when I saw that the power button brought no light or noise.

Cardona seemed patiently amused. He reached into his own shirt pocket and took out an even smaller cell phone and handed it to me.

"I will take it that the call is local?" he said.

I nodded my assent and dialed a number while he watched.

"Lieutenant Sherry Richards?" I said for the cop's benefit when she picked up on the other end.

"You stood me up, Max," she answered.

"No. I've had an unexpected emergency up here, Lieutenant," I said, loud enough for the deputy to hear.

"Are you OK, Max?" she said and the concern sounded real.

"Uh, yeah, there's already an officer here at the scene," I said, and Cardona was now looking into my face.

"What scene are you talking about?" Richards said, now letting worry creep into her voice. I ran through what I figured had happened, that Rodrigo had been tracked by David Hix, who saw his chance to impress his ugliness on the little man and scare him out of the country. I talked loud enough for both Richards and the cop next to me to hear. He looked skeptical.

"Here, I'll let, uh, Deputy Cardona explain," I said and handed the officer his own phone. He turned away and I looked out at the whitecaps, hoping the concern I'd heard in Richards's voice meant she wasn't so pissed at me that she would leave me swinging. After a minute, Cardona snapped the phone shut.

"The lieutenant says she wants you down at your prearranged meeting place, asap, Mr. Freeman."

"I think this will go much better this way," I said to him, and without another word I went inside to change my clothes.

CHAPTER 29

O n the drive to the Galleria in Fort Lauderdale I called Billy on the cell and told him about Rodrigo.

"How is he?" was his first question.

"Broken leg and maybe the same for his arm," I said. "Probably with the baseball bat."

"Hix?"

"No doubt on the loose," I said.

"Max, how did they find him? How did Hix know about the Flamingo?"

It was the more difficult question. There was no way bat man was sophisticated enough to be extrapolating cell phone signals. It took expensive equipment to pull that off and he and his brother just didn't come off with that kind of juice. Since Billy had been the one who picked Rodrigo from his last hospital visit in West Palm and drove him to the beach house, the only guess I had was that he'd been followed. He was an attorney, not a street investigator. He could have led the Hix brothers straight to the place where he thought Rodrigo would be safe. But I wasn't going to put it on him.

"I'm not sure, Billy. But he's in North Broward Hospital now, and I doubt he'll be going anywhere soon."

"So you're there with him?"

"Ah, not right now," I said, the admission sticking in my throat. Billy had put me on the cruise worker case. He expected certain things from me. I was letting him down by chasing after Morrison and O'Shea.

"I'm driving down to meet with Richards now," I said. "She took a report from the deputy at the Flamingo and I'll ask that they put a guard on Rodrigo's door. He's been the victim of the same attacker twice now, it's gotta pull some protection."

My excuse sounded lame. Billy let it sit there in my mouth, forcing me to taste it by not answering.

"OK, Max," he finally said. "I hope, my friend, you know what you're doing."

Me too, I thought and punched off the cell.

When I met Richards in the parking garage, I wasn't in the mood for any more questions or some pissing match over O'Shea. She said he'd called her, after all this time trying to avoid all contact with "the bitch." The last time I talked to him he said he wanted to help me find the truth about Morrison before any internal investigators got in on the rape charge, a charge that Richards would want to file as soon as she found out.

When I pulled up to her unmarked car she got out and walked around to stand at my door. She was in jeans and a collared blouse with a cotton jersey underneath. Her detective's shield was clipped to her belt and her 9mm was in a holster on the other hip.

"We going on a raid?" I said in greeting.

"I'm not sure what we're going to, Max."

I got out and leaned back against my closed door. She crossed her arms. The ball was in her court.

"O'Shea called me at the office," she started. "It was nearly midnight but he talked dispatch into giving me his cell number by telling them he had information about the missing girls I was tracking."

I nodded my head. At midnight O'Shea would have been on the

stakeout of Marci's apartment for several hours. Long enough to do some thinking.

"When I reached him he was cryptic as hell. Told me he thought you were getting in deep chasing down Morrison and that the only way he figured he could really help you was by coming out with the truth."

I couldn't react. It was too much to grind. I could still feel the sand in my shoes from pulling a guy out of the ocean, a guy I should have been guarding. I was less than twenty-four hours from getting caught trying to tail a cop, a cop who might be guilty of multiple homicides.

"So what's the truth?" I said.

"That's where we're going, Max. He gave me an address," she said, pulling an orange 'While You Were Out' message note from her pocket. "He said not to get there until after two. He told me it would be safe and in fact kind of begged me not to bring anyone but you. He said bringing you would be proof that it wasn't some kind of setup that would be dangerous."

I looked around in the garage like I was searching for the SWAT boys.

"And you're going to trust him?"

"You did, Max," she said.

We took her car and I rode shotgun. The address was a few blocks to the north along the Middle River. She was nervous. I knew because she always had to talk when she was nervous.

"So tell me about the scene at the Flamingo," she said.

I told her the story in more detail, how Rodrigo had somehow slipped out of the bungalow and took his chances in the water.

She stopped at a light to cross Sunrise and rolled down the window.

"I'd have to agree with Deputy Cardona," she said. "Those spots of blood on the walkway would make me nervous, too."

I shook my head and told her that from the impressions left in the walls and the descriptions that the women gave Cardona, it had to be David Hix.

"This is your union-busting guy? The one who took on you and O'Shea in the alley with his brother?" she said.

I nodded and then told her about the photos and the threats that Billy and Diane had received at their home and the additional photo of the Fort Lauderdale attorney.

"You do know how to get your nose into the shit, Max," she said.

"It is a talent," I said.

She cut her eyes at me and I thought I could see a smile play at the corner of her mouth. I took advantage of the moment.

"And since Mr. Colon has been attacked twice by this baseball bat–wielding felon, can we get an officer to watch his room over at North Broward Medical Center?"

She looked over at me and then picked up the radio. She made the arrangements with dispatch, only asking me the spelling on Rodrigo's name and then checking a computer screen attached to the dash in front of her and finding the case number.

We turned east for a few blocks and then made a right onto Middle River Drive.

"Thanks," I said.

The address on the note was a small, two-story apartment building. Eight units in all. Painted a powdery light green. There were three cars parked in spaces at the front, older models, a four-door Caprice, a small SUV, a Volkswagen beetle, the original, with rust spots on the rounded corners and door seams. We sat quietly and watched for a minute. Richards wrote down the license plate numbers in her notebook.

"Not the Ritz," I said.

"Unit C has to be on the first floor, huh?"

"That'd figure."

Richards pulled the 9mm, checked the load, slid it back in the holster.

"Let's go find the truth," she said and we got out together.

The tiny pool in front of the complex wasn't much larger than a hot tub. The shrubbery was dry and needed clipping. Unit C was in the middle and we stepped under an overhang and flanked the door. Inside I could hear the sound of a television, the tinny words of a game show host, the canned applause. When Richards knocked someone turned down the volume. There was a peephole in the door and Richards stood in front of it but I could see by the cant of her hip that her weight was all on her right leg, ready to push off to one side if she didn't like what appeared. We heard the snick of a lock and the door opened only as far as the safety chain would let it.

"Yes?"

The nose, full mouth and expectant eyes of a woman filled the crack.

"Can I help you?"

"Hi," Richards said. "Uh, Colin O'Shea sent us over. He said that you might have something for us."

The woman's eyes were dark brown, wary, but not afraid. She looked straight into Richards's face and then down to the badge, maybe the gun.

"Do you work with Colin?" she said, shifting her sight to take me in, but did not meet my eyes.

"Yes, in a way, we do work with him," Richards said. "May we come in?"

"Uh, yes," the woman said. "Yes."

She closed the door and while she slipped the chain Richards and I exchanged raised eyebrows.

Richards stepped in and to the right, I moved automatically to her left, like an entry team. Inside, the sun struggled to lighten the place. I marked the pass-through serving opening to the kitchen first, then the short hallway. Nothing. When I scanned back to Richards she was looking past the woman to the windows and the long couch pushed flush against the wall. Her hand moved off the butt of her gun and I almost expected to hear someone yell, "Clear!"

Then I focused on the woman. It was after four now and she was dressed in some kind of uniform. Waitress, I guessed. She was barefoot and there was a stain on her apron. Her hair was pinned up but strands were leaking down onto her shoulders.

"My name is Sherry Richards. I'm a detective with the Broward sheriff's office," Richards said. "And this is Max Freeman."

The woman nodded, looking at Richards and still avoiding my eyes.

"Hi," she said again. "Um, Colin said you were going to come here, just to talk, he said."

She stepped back and at first I thought she was just getting distance between us but then I realized she was shielding something. Behind her was a playpen. A child was standing up with her hands knuckled around the top bar.

"Well, what a beautiful girl," Richards said, a lilt in her voice that was far too convincing to be faked. The woman turned as Richards took a step forward and a smile was coming into her face.

"Oh, this is Jessica," she said, moving to the playpen. "She just woke up from a nap because Mommy's home." Richards sat down on the end of the couch and reached out to touch the girl's hand. The woman bent and gathered the child up in her arms and held her on her hip, letting her look out at us. She had flame red hair and wide blue eyes and when the contrast with the woman's coloring struck me, I stared closer at her face and knew who we'd been sent to meet.

"You're Faith Hamlin," I said, and the astonishment in my voice caused her to finally look into my face and she nodded.

"You're the one from Philadelphia, right?" she said. "Colin told me. You were a cop."

I nodded my head. Richards looked from me to the woman and her mouth had opened slightly but nothing came out.

Over the next hour Faith Hamlin told us her story, how Colin O'Shea had come to tell her that she needed to leave Philadelphia because the officers she knew from the store were in deep trouble and everything that she had done with them was going to come out in the newspapers. At first she told him she wanted to stay. She wanted to help them. She didn't care what the news said.

"But when I told Colin that I knew I was going to have a baby, he said I had to leave and that he had to leave and that and everything would be better if we left together."

She'd left with nothing, on Colin's word, and they came here and he set her up in this apartment.

"He paid for everything and then he went back and said he'd come back when the police department was done with him. And he didn't lie. We talked on the cell phone every day until he did come back."

She was holding the girl on her lap until she fought her way loose and started a regular three-year-old's search around the room for favorite toys to show company.

"Is Colin the father?" Richards said, looking up after being presented with a stuffed Barney.

Faith shook her head no and lowered her face for a second and then looked up at her daughter and smiled.

"No. She looks just like her daddy, but we don't use his name here," she said, going serious.

"So Colin doesn't live here?" I said, and again she shook her head.

"Colin got me my job at the restaurant. He said it was under the table so no one could find me. I work the early morning shift, just for tips. I don't work at night anymore," she said and I winced at the words. She knew what I knew. Nothing good happens at night.

"Colin comes over to check on us and he plays sometimes with Jessica, but I'm a single mom," she said, sounding proud of the designation.

"Don't you know that people in Philadelphia are worried about you?" Richards said. "That your family doesn't even know you're alive?"

"No, they aren't," she said with a finality that locked down any further conversation. "Colin was the only one who ever really cared and it's better this way."

I thought she was just echoing O'Shea's words but then we watched as she snagged her daughter and folded her arms around her and put her face in the child's hair and whispered something in her ear that made both of them laugh.

"You're sure?" Richards said, and Faith nodded, her cheek moving up and down against the little girl's ear while she looked straight into our faces.

CHAPTER 30

Richards couldn't start the car. We sat outside the apartment in silence and looked straight ahead, putting mental dominoes in a row.

"OK, Max," she finally said. "Was that the truth?"

"That was her. I saw her portrait in Philly, on the wall of the store where she worked. It's only been three years. That's her."

"Damn," Richards said, and all I could do was agree.

She finally turned the ignition. The start of the motor was something, an action at least, while we both tried to line up where to step next. We started back in the direction of the Galleria, to my truck.

"You know I'm going to have to report this," Richards said and her voice held as much question as statement. "I mean, she's officially missing, and we found her."

I knew what that report meant, both to Faith Hamlin's life and to Colin O'Shea's, and so did she.

"Yeah, I know," I said, pulling out my cell phone. "But do you think we could wait until we get Colin's side of all this before you do that?"

I flipped open the phone but paused. Richards chewed the side of her lip and then nodded. I punched in the numbers to O'Shea's cell.

"You're not going to pull an 'I told you so' on me are you, Max?" Richards said while I listened to the ring in my other ear.

"No," I said. "And you wouldn't have done it to me, either. There are more important moves to make here."

I was now hearing a recorded voice telling me that the customer I was trying reach was unavailable at this time. I left a message for O'Shea to call me as soon as possible.

"Morrison?" she said and I nodded while we sat at the light.

From memory I replayed my conversation with Marci the bartender, her admission that she had been seeing Morrison for a few months, that the romance had gone wrong and that the officer had raped her. The word itself caused Richards to recoil.

"She told you this?"

"Yeah. I thought I was going to talk her into opening up on some kind of drug connection the two of them had," I said. "I told her about the missing bartenders and that we were looking at Morrison as a possible supplier who might have been responsible for their disappearance."

"We, Max?"

"Yeah," I said, ignoring the question. "Then she just spilled it. She said she didn't fight him and it might have saved her life."

"And let me guess, she's not willing to press charges and testify," Richards said.

I didn't have to answer. I watched her hands flex on the steering wheel. She was controlling her anger, keeping it at bay while she ran the scenario. She might even have been seeing the image of a dead deputy lying facedown in her front yard, the gun still in her hand.

"The rape took place out in the Glades, Sherry," I said, trying to pull her back. "Some spot out off the Alley."

She reconnected her eyes to mine.

"But she couldn't lead you to it, right?" she said and I must have had some look of stupidity on my face again.

"So somehow you get it in your head to tail the guy? How long did you think you'd have to pull that off?"

"It wasn't that blind," I said, defending myself. "I talked with Marci and got her to pass on a lie to Morrison that we had physical evidence on one of the missing bartenders."

"So what you're telling me is that you used her to set him up?"

"It was just an attempt, Sherry. It might have stirred up something to cause him to make a mistake, give up a lead. O'Shea was covering her," I said. "It didn't work out and if Morrison did have someplace to go, he'll stay the hell away from it now."

We both went quiet as we pulled into the parking garage and up next to my truck.

"Maybe not," Richards said and I looked at her. "I put a tracker on his patrol car the day after I told you about his file."

Now I was staring.

"You know, those GPS trackers that the delivery managers and armored car guys use on their vehicles so they can monitor their fleets or individual drivers? It clocks their stops and mileage and maps out every damn place they go during the day."

"Yeah, yeah," I said. "I know what they are. How the hell did you manage that?"

"Internal affairs," she said. "Morrison was already on their screen. I just gave them a nudge. They called in his car for a bogus maintenance check and stuck the tracker in there the other day."

"So you believed me," I said.

"I was opening myself up to possibilities," she said, not looking away. "I checked it this morning and last night after Morrison caught you up in his little DUI trap he went home to his residence until about midnight and then took this long drive out on Alligator Alley.

"He got about fifteen miles out past the toll booth and then turned north on some kind of trail, I'm guessing, because the map doesn't even show a road. He stopped there for thirty minutes. Then it appears he turned around and came back."

"Christ," I said. "That's where he takes them."

I could feel the blood in my veins, the adrenaline chasing it. Sherry saw it too, the scenario, the possibilities.

"And you've got the coordinates of this place where he stopped?" I said, opening up my door.

"I've got a mapped printout. It's in my briefcase."

"You know where he is now?"

"I can find out," she said.

I tried O'Shea again, got the recording. While I called Kim's, Richards handed me the printout of Morrison's trip to the Glades.

"I have a friend in dispatch," she said and then made a call of her own.

When I finished I looked in at her and she raised a finger to me, said thank you to someone and clicked off.

"Marci didn't show for her two o'clock shift," I said. "It's the first time she's missed since she was hired and Laurie can't get her on her cell."

"Morrison checked in at roll call and will be on patrol for the next eight hours," she said.

"All right, I'm taking this with me," I said, waving the printout. I expected her to stop me, to tell me to wait for a crime scene team, to at least demand that she come with me.

"You make that run, Max," she said instead, a sense of urgency in her voice. "I'm going to find this girl."

CHAPTER 31

I was ten miles west of the tollbooth, doing eighty in the rain and watching both the darkening roadway slide out under my headlights and the truck's odometer to mark the turnoff. Richards would be checking Marci's apartment and the hospital E.R.s and doing it without having anything broadcast out on the police radio band. She'd keep checking with a friend at dispatch to confirm that Morrison was still working in his Victoria Park zone. I was out after physical evidence only.

My wipers were running a delayed beat, a one-step brush and then silent. Sunset had long been shrouded by the cloud cover. The rain was light but had turned the freeway into a ribbon of asphalt that shined wet in my lights and then dulled and disappeared out where the beams could not catch up to my speed. The hiss of tires slinging water up into the wheel wells sounded just above the deep rumble of my engine. When I'd stopped to hand the toll-taker a dollar I'd noticed the cameras and knew that there would be yet another piece of evidence against Morrison if he tried to deny his trips out here.

When the woman gave me change I tossed it into the cup holder and punched the trigger on my trip meter. I was now watching for 21.7, the exact distance Richards's planted GPS tracker had recorded. As I got closer, I slowed to 50 mph, then 20. When the odometer crept to 21.5 I pulled over to the shoulder and crept along, looking out into the darkness on my left for a sign of disturbed gravel or a light-colored wheel track in the vegetation. Almost to the exact mileage mark I spotted a streak of matted grass leading off to the north and I stopped. I put on my slicker and took the long-handled flashlight from its place behind my seat and got out. It was a two-track, unmarked by anything official. But clearly it had once been used for some kind of access to the other side of the canal that ran the length of the freeway. I walked twenty yards out and shot my flashlight beam out to the north. A man-made earthen bridge had been built across the canal over a culvert which allowed the water to flow. Even in the dark my eyes could pick up the difference in black shades that showed a tree line. There was a hammock extending out from the freeway. There were no reflectors or fences or signage, just a path to nowhere.

I went back to the truck cab and dialed Richards.

"Your map was on the money," I said when she clicked in. "I'm going to walk it in and see what I can find. Any luck with Marci?"

There was a scratchy delay over the transmission and then it cleared.

". . . to her apartment but nothing seems out of place. Her clothes are still there and her makeup. The manager said he doesn't remember ever seeing a marked police car out in front of the place. He said the last time he saw her was when she drove away Wednesday morning and he didn't notice her carrying a bag or suitcase."

While she talked I watched a set of headlights grow out of the east. The sound of low and powerful engine noise reached me before I could make out that it was a tractor-trailer rig. It blew past me, leaving a swirl of rainwater and wind in its wake that I had to turn my face away from. Its passing drowned out the first part of another sentence.

". . . don't want to put the plate number out on the radio in case

Morrison could recognize it but we're going to have to do something soon," she was saying.

"Look. The map shows it's only a half mile from here to where he stopped. I'll let you know," I said.

"Max?"

"Yeah."

"Be careful, all right?"

"Yeah," I said and hit the End button and stuck the phone in my raincoat pocket.

Before starting in I got back in the truck and parked it lengthwise across the entry to the trail. With the canal on either side, no one would be able to drive in and surprise me. On the other hand, it was a marker that I was here and on foot. I reached into the glove box and took out a handful of plastic ziplock baggies for evidence and stuck them in my back pocket.

I locked the doors by habit and started out with my rain hood off so I could hear the sounds around me. I had been living on the edge of the Glades for a few years now and trusted my senses. Morrison might know the tricks of the streets but I felt sure he could not match me on this turf. This had become mine.

I stepped carefully down the slight incline and used the flashlight to trace along the flattened grass and rut of the left track. When I got to the other side of the canal, I stopped when the beam glistened dully on the ground and then bent to look at a recent impression in a patch of clear mud. The tire track was not one of the wide, chunky off-road types that hunters and gladerunners used. It was a street tread. If it didn't rain too much more, it might be lifted with a mold and then matched against an existing tire. I filed the thought away and moved on.

Once I got used to the footing, it was easy going. I kept sweeping the light beam in a circle, up to judge the reach of the gumbo limbo lining the path and then down in front of me from one track to the other to check for any drop-off. The rain had stopped and I had not gone far before the sounds of passing traffic behind me were absorbed by the thickness of vine and fern and leaf cover. The hiss of the tires was replaced by the sound of wind in the tree branches. Off to the west I thought I could even hear the rush of acres of open sawgrass being pushed and folded by the breeze, the long stiff blades softly clattering. Twice the trail became enclosed in a tunnel of overhang and melding branches. If there had been a chirrup of frog or cicadas before my arrival, they were quiet now. I had learned from my late canoeing that the animals of the swamp were highly sensitive to any unnatural stirrings of water and air. The night dwellers would have sensed me long ago. They also would have marked Morrison's presence each time he came here. Nothing goes unwitnessed in this world.

After twenty minutes the trail opened up into a clearing and the track curved to a stop. To the east the hammock fell away and went flat, melting into the sawgrass. To the west the black mangroves grew thicker, almost like a wall. I was studying the tire track, tracing it with the light. It formed a three point turn in the opening and I thought of Morrison's move at the DUI stop. I was sweeping the light beam on the ground, looking for trash or some sign of carelessness and bent to examine what might have been the impression of a foot heel in the earth when I heard the grunt.

The sound caused a breath to catch in my throat and I turned to it. I cupped my hand over the lens of the flashlight and froze. Thirty seconds of silence, then it came again, low, like a cough into the emptiness of a big wooden barrel. It was a living sound. I stared in its direction, searched the darkness inside the wall of mangroves for movement, imagined whatever it was doing the same to me.

I looked down at my hands; the ring of light from the flashlight lens was glowing red against my palm and I snicked it off.

The next sound was a snort, and a rustling of vegetation that was deep into the trees. A big male gator makes such sounds during mating season. It is a call to the females meant to impress them by indicating size and power. I had heard them many times on my river. If it was a gator he would not be frightened away by my skimpy noises. If it was something else I still couldn't just sit here in the open. I moved to the edge of the tree wall as quietly as I could. Again I wished I had my gun.

I knelt and strained to hear, trying to raise my senses, and I felt the wind change. It had been rotating during the walk in, clearing the sky and stirring the leaves as it swung to come out of the west and now it had gained strength. I heard the snort and heavy rustle again and then on the breeze came an odor that washed over me and made me involuntarily twist my nose and squeeze my eyes shut. It was the stench of death, rotted in earth and water, never dried to dust by the sun but left putrid on the moist ground.

Now I knew the snorting noise and I stood and snapped on the light and searched for an opening in the tree wall and stepped in. The terrain went down at an angle, covered in the soft detritus of fallen leaves and loose soil that in the flashlight beam appeared to have been disturbed already. I had to crouch to get through and under the limbs and found a footprint, big enough for a man, pointing back up in the direction I had come. I was thirty feet in and flicked the light beam back up and there was a pair of luminous eyes staring at me. It was a wild boar, its ugly face frozen in the sudden circle of light, its massive body looming black and glistening behind. Strings of gristle and dirt hung from its mouth and I yelled, half in fear, half in disgust and anger. The beast startled and I yelled again and crashed through the trees and my upright and aggressive assault caused the damn thing to scream from its throat and flee the other way.

I stayed still and listened until I could no longer hear the sounds of the animal splashing and snapping twigs in retreat. Then I waited until I couldn't hear my own heart banging in my chest. But as I settled, the smell came back into focus and it was stronger. I wished I'd had the tin of Vicks we used at homicide scenes to dab inside my nose. Instead I pressed my left hand to my nostrils and pointed the flashlight to where the boar had been snuffling.

In a slight depression at the base of a clump of black mangrove roots my light caught a torn strip of yellow plastic first. The animals had shredded it and parts were still pushed down into the thick muck. When I fanned out with the light and got down closer, even I could identify bone fragments. Out here in the wet heat where insects and microbes flourish, a corpse could be consumed in a matter of a few days. Scavengers like the boar and gators and even birds would cause a certain amount of destruction and drag evidence for yards, maybe more, spreading out the crime scene. Non-biodegradables like plastic and clothing would last much longer, but even they would eventually disappear.

I did not want to disturb more than I had to, so I stepped up onto the tree root and bent to pick up a strip of the plastic. It was a medium thickness like the kind used for police tarps. I'd used them myself to cover bodies, to give them some dignity in death while the news camera crews in Philly flocked around homicide scenes. "Bastard," I whispered aloud.

I shined the flashlight down into the pile again where the boar's hooves had dug down and the light found something metal the size of a penny. I snapped a twig from the tree and poked it loose. It was a snap button, still rimmed by frayed blue-jean material with the word GUESS stamped into it. I put the button and strip of plastic into a ziplock baggy and then I widened the search, not panicked but intent. If it weren't edible the animals wouldn't have carried it.

I studied the muck in concentric circles at first, like I'd seen crime techs do. Then I took a chance and looked back from the pile shaped like a cone where the digging boar would have flung the muck and bone as it was pawing.

I picked up the glint of shiny metal six feet back. It was lying in a patch of standing water, just below the surface, and shimmered in the beam as I moved closer. The water had cleansed it of dirt and it gleamed up at me. It was a flat chrome bottle opener with a handle at one end, the kind of opener women bartenders slip into their back pockets, the kind men watch and the girls know that they watch. But this was never supposed to be a part of the game.

CHAPTER 32

"**I**'m bringing the evidence back," I said. "Where do you want to meet?"

"At Kim's," Richards said. "She's back."

"What?"

"Marci, she's back and I've got her working."

I was in the truck, driving, fast, for the city. It had taken me half the time to get back to the roadway. I stayed in the middle of the two-track to keep from messing up any tire prints for the impression techs but there wasn't anything else to look for. With what we had, Morrison's documented trip to the burial spot, a trace of a police tarp and obvious property belonging to the missing girls, we could squeeze the hell out of this guy. And that was before the crime scene guys got out there to match his tire tracks and go through the forensics at the site. In daylight there was no telling what they might find. The son of a bitch had gotten cocky. That had been his mistake.

When I got back to my truck I'd used a marine rope from my truck and strung a barrier across the entrance just in case someone should come along. When I got Richards on her cell phone I told her what I'd found and she'd gone quiet long enough to make me think I'd lost the connection again. Then she came back.

"I'll call the Florida Highway Patrol and have them put a trooper out there to secure the scene," she said.

"You're still on Morrison, right?"

"Yeah. I've been checking with dispatch. They've been in touch with him by radio and have been sending him out on regular assignments," Richards said.

"So what's with Marci? Where the hell was she?"

Richards lowered her voice.

"She won't say. When I asked her she just said, 'Wait and see.'

"I was still in the office working the phones and the computer using her social security number to trace her folks in Minnesota but they'd both died—her mother when Marci was young and her father of a heart attack three years ago. Then Laurie called me and said she'd just shown up for work, begging to make up her time on the night shift."

Instead of sounding relieved, maybe even giddy over Marci's safety and my report on what we'd gotten from the Glades site, Richards sounded wary.

"So where are you now?" I said, slowing as I moved into a more populated section of Broward County. I didn't need to get stopped now.

"I'm at Kim's. I pulled a stool back into the hallway and I'm watching her work. She keeps answering the phone and looking out the windows," Richards said. "I'm not letting her out of my sight and if Morrison comes in here I'm going to arrest his ass myself."

"Look, Sherry," I said. "If that happens, call for backup first, OK?"

"Right," she said, and the phone clicked off.

It was one in the morning when I got to the bar. My jeans were wet up to the middle of my thighs from the swamp. My shirt was smeared with muck and I thought I could still smell the stench of death in the material. I parked in a spot on the back side of the shopping center and walked through the pool-room entrance.

Richards was still sitting in the hallway that linked the two rooms, her back up against the wall. Another patron was making his way to the men's room and said to her: "Hey, honey. You still here? I told you I'd be glad to give you a ride home."

"My boyfriend will be here any minute," she answered.

"That's what you said an hour ago, sweetheart."

"I was being polite," she said and then noticed me walk in. "And I still am."

The guy shrugged and slid by me.

"What's up?" I said, looking beyond Richards to see Marci behind the back bar, working at the register, closing out the paper tabs that were piled there.

Even here in the shadows I could see the gray in her eyes. She'd let this whole mess boil too long in her head.

"I woke up the damn prosecutor and he said the evidence is circumstantial," she said, the bitterness snapping off the words. "He said we'll have to take it to a grand jury if we want to go after a cop."

I put my back to the wall opposite her and leaned into it. I was tired.

"He said if forensics comes up with a blood match out there in the morning, maybe. If we run a photo spread past some other women who pick him out as trying to take them out there, maybe. The fact that he might have driven his squad car out there to look at the stars isn't criminal. Even if you're right and those are my girls out there, it's still circumstantial. No judge will order an arrest warrant."

Everything she said, I'd heard before and she had probably heard every time she'd gone to the same prosecutor's office for the last several months on her disappearing girls. She was looking at the floor, trying to hide her tears. I was looking down, trying to think of something to say.

"He raped me."

We both looked up at Marci. She'd come out from behind the bar and was standing in the hallway opening. Her arms were folded across her chest. Her chin was up and she did not try to wipe the tears from her cheek.

"He raped me out there in the Everglades, where he goes. I went to the sexual assault treatment center today. That's where I was. I thought they would just go and arrest him but they didn't."

Richards and I looked at each other but let her continue.

"They taped an interview and made me sign a sworn statement and when I asked them what they were going to do they said they had to send everything to some internal office because it was a cop and that they'd get back to me. I thought that meant a couple of hours so I stayed away from my place all day and they never called but he did," she said and a tremble was setting up in her voice and a paleness I had seen before when I had first told her of Morrison's motives.

"So I came to work because I was afraid and he's still calling and he's still out there and he's going to be out there when I get off and . . ."

This time when she stumbled, Richards jumped forward and caught her. She reached under the girl's elbows to support her and this time Marci did not wave off the help and instead leaned into Richards and sobbed, and then they wrapped their arms around each other and Sherry looked up at me and her eyes were filled with tears.

"We're going to arrest his ass now, right now," Richards barked into the cell phone. "We've got a witness to an attack perpetrated by him, the same witness that your office has had all goddamn day and sat on your hands with for the sake of goddamn protocol. We also have evidence of at least one other homicide at the same site where this witness was attacked and we're picking him up. You can meet us out there if you're fast but we're not waiting."

We were in my truck, Richards in the passenger seat, Marci in between us. When Richards had called dispatch, they told her Morrison was helping to set up a perimeter on the east side of the city park. Another officer was in foot pursuit of an aggravated battery suspect. She had pulled out her police radio and switched channels to the Fort Lauderdale P.D. frequency and we were following their call out directions.

Richards had asked if the battery was of a woman and the dispatcher had answered, "No, it's a, uh, Ms. O'Kelly, out in front of her home in Victoria Park. She reported that someone threatened her with a baseball bat."

The name set a lump in my chest and I asked Sherry to turn the radio up.

"Description of the suspect, four-eighteen?" dispatch asked.

"White male . . . heavy, six-foot . . . wearing, wearing gray cut-off sweatshirt . . . uh . . . dark pants . . ."

"Four-eighteen? Four-eighteen, what's your location?" the dispatcher said, worry now sneaking into her voice.

I turned off from Sunrise Boulevard into the main entrance of the park and could see other spinning cop-car lights coming in from two other directions.

"Four-eighteen. Suspect in custody," the winded cop on the radio said.

"Ten-four, four-eighteen. Location?" said the dispatcher.

"On the soccer field, north end of the park."

We followed the patrol cars and came to a stop in the parking lot of the soccer field. Richards held her door handle and we both scanned the squad cars, looking for Morrison's number or someone in uniform that looked like him. When we couldn't spot him, we got out.

"Stay inside for right now, OK, Marci? We need you to point him out, give us a positive identification. Just wait here," Richards said and reached out and touched the girl on the leg before closing the door.

We walked over to the line of cars together, looking in both directions, closely. The officers had aimed their headlights out onto the field and then gotten out. There were six of them.

The rain had stopped and the grass out in front of us was glistening in the low trajectory of the headlights and then someone yelled, "There they are."

Out on the field two figures were walking and appeared to be half dragging a third.

We stood and looked out along with the rest of the arriving cops and as the three came closer I recognized two of them.

They were twenty yards away when Morrison stopped, jerking the whole procession to a halt. He was staring at me with my stained shirt and jeans soaked to the thigh, and then at Richards and then farther to her left. Marci had walked up and stood beside her.

At first his face looked confused and then tightened like a fist into anger. He dropped the man I knew as David Hix and pointed his finger at Richards.

"What's that bitch doing here?" he yelled, to no one in particular.

The officers around us seemed to stop moving.

"Yo, Kyle," someone next to us started but Morrison stopped him.

"No," he yelled. "I want to know why these fucking people are here!"

A few of the cops looked at us, at least one recognized Richards.

"Hey chill, Kyle. It's command, man."

Richards turned and said something I could not hear to Marci. The girl nodded yes and Richards stepped forward.

"We need to talk with you, Morrison. It's as simple as that. Let your colleagues handle this arrest and come with us."

She took another step forward and I matched her.

"No. I don't think so," Morrison said, looking down at Hix and over to the running cop who seemed to be frozen by the turn of events. "You don't order me around, bitch."

I heard a jostle behind me and then a large, broad-chested man in uniform with sergeant stripes on his arm pushed through.

"I'm sorry, Lieutenant," he said to Richards as he passed her and then turned. "Goddammit, Officer Morrison, you are screwin' this up for everyone. Now surrender your weapon. I call the god-damn shots on this shift."

The collection of uniforms, polished leather, bristling chrome and brushed-steel weaponry was uncharacteristically caught up in indecision. One of their own was freaking. One of their own was way out of line, right in front of them. There was no standard procedure for it. No chapter in the manual.

Off to one side and behind Morrison, a figure came out of the dark and then stopped. I could tell by his size and shape it was O'Shea, on foot. But he too froze at the sight before him and no one on the line seemed to notice him.

They must have been watching as Morrison used his right hand to deliberately and slowly unsnap the leather guard on his holster.

"Officer Morrison," the sergeant said again, thinking it was a calming voice, thinking the cop's beef had to be with Richards for some reason. "I gave you an order, son. I'm the officer in charge here."

No one on the line said a word, but I saw the cop next to Morrison move away and I heard the clicks of several holster snaps behind me.

"No sir," Morrison said. "I beg to differ."

He pulled his 9mm and raised it, barrel first, and pointed it in our direction and just as every cop is trained, and just as every one on the line knew, it was a death sentence that Morrison now controlled.

At least a dozen rounds exploded from behind and to the side of us, many of them hitting their mark only twenty feet away and Morrison went down without once pulling his trigger.

Marci screamed and turned away. David Hix yelped and curled up into a ball on the grass. I looked down the line at Richards and she had not moved to draw her own weapon.

CHAPTER 33

It was early morning and the sun had broken white and molten like a heavy bubble stretching up and then off the horizon. I was in my beach chair, sipping my coffee, watching the sky and water absorb the blue light of refraction over the rim of my cup.

There was not a ripple of breeze and the ocean lay flat like a hot sheet of glass. The black-footed terns were working the shoreline, pecking and dancing. I would have at least another hour before the electrician came to install a new light over the dining room table. I had not been able to sleep on the couch with the smell of fresh paint in my nose so I had camped out on the beach since long before dawn.

Billy had called me late last night, amusement in his voice over the receipt of official notice informing him as the legal representative of Colin O'Shea that all charges had been dropped against his client. It had been weeks.

"The wheels of justice and paperwork," he'd said and left it to me to fill in whatever ending I wished.

David Hix had been arrested and charged in both the assault

on Rodrigo and attorney Sarah O'Kelly. Our Filipino friend stayed in the hospital for several days but neither Billy nor I could convince him to stay. He went home to Manila with his wife, who had accepted the cruise lines' money to come to America and retrieve him.

"I thank you with my life, Mr. Max," he had said when we had gone to see him in the hospital. "But your America is not a safe place. All I wanted to do was work and bring money to my family."

He was holding his wife's hand when we left and in the parking lot Billy stood at the window of my truck while I got in. I had been beating myself up over the man's injuries, one heaped on top of the other, because no one had been there to protect him.

"You are not r-responsible for the world, my friend," he said. "Even though you may think it is so."

I had stared out past him into the vision of the taped-off crime scene out at the end of a desolate road in the Glades where technicians and assistants from the medical examiner's officer were meticulously sorting out what would turn out to be the partial remains of four young women, including Amy Strausshiem and Suzy Martin.

The cause of Morrison's death had been ruled a suicide by cop. His choice. But I was not displeased with the ending. As far as the families of those young women were concerned, their daughters' killer was just as dead, and perhaps more forgettable without the drawn out process of law.

Billy's statement about responsibility and who carried it had stuck in my head for days afterward. We had all met a man in Colin O'Shea whose shoulders had been widest.

Colin had kept up his surveillance of Marci for nearly twenty hours until she had gone to work. There he recognized Morrison's squad car in the parking lot and was trying to move to another position when Morrison suddenly accelerated out toward the park. He tailed him. He was following on foot, crossing the field when he saw the line of cops open fire. From his distance and with Morrison's back to him, it had looked, he said, like a firing squad.

"Even the brotherhood of blue gotta break at some point, Freeman," he said later while we both sipped our whiskeys at Kim's and neither of us, with our histories, was smiling. O'Shea said he had never been a part of the sex games his fellow officers had played with Faith Hamlin. It had in fact disgusted him. "But I didn't have the guts to turn them in," he said.

But he knew the girl and her adoptive family. She had told him that her stepfather, an Irishman himself, had labeled her a whore, when IAD began snooping around the case. "And I also knew the married redheaded son of a bitch who fathered Jessica," he said. "Her life would've been hell there. So I took her away."

He had helped support and counsel Faith Hamlin ever since and had never looked back "until you came along and partnered up with me again, Freeman."

His rescue of the girl had been an act of redemption for him. Of his own volition, he'd stepped over the line more than a few times as a cop; his decision this time was to save her and let the pieces fall where they may. There was a look of resignation in his face when I told him there was no way Richards could keep it a secret. She'd have to report the discovery of a missing person to the Philadelphia department. He'd have to go back and face it.

"Guess your ex-wife ain't gonna get those captain's bars after all," he said, smiling as he thought about it.

"She'll find a way," I answered, trying not to.

It would be a media circus when the news broke. Someone would get a photo of the little girl. Someone else's life was going to crash. We were both quiet for a few drinks.

"It's a hell of a thing to do, lad," Colin suddenly said, using his old Irish brogue. "Goin' home again." We both drank to that.

Now I was thinking about sleet and spitting snow while the sun traveled higher in front of me and a sheen of sweat began to form on my chest. Beside me I picked up a movement of bright yellow and green in the corner of my eye. The young boy with the blue eyes was standing beside me, his sand bucket and shovel in hand.

"Josh," a woman's voice called from behind me. "Go down to the water, honey, and wash your bucket."

The boy turned and skipped toward the ocean and I looked up as a pair of legs stepped into his place.

"Good morning," the woman said.

I had to shield my eyes to see her face. She was young and very tanned and her dark hair was tucked through the back of a baseball cap.

"It is," I said.

"You know," she said, dropping down to face level, her knees resting in the sand, "you have my son infatuated."

I raised my eyebrows and pointed out to the boy. While she nodded I glanced at her left hand.

"Yes," she said, but her dark eyes were smiling. "He has come to me a couple of times with questions about a man, who I assume is you, and he wants something cylindrical and green that he thinks is somehow used to dig in the sand."

I knitted my brow, thinking of my previous encounters with the kid, and put it together.

"Rolling Rock," I finally said.

"Ahhh," she answered. "One of my favorites."

We both went quiet and watched the boy.

"Do you live here?" she asked, scooping up a handful of sand and letting it sift through her fingers.

"Yes, uh, on and off," I said.

"I noticed your housekeeping skills." She tossed her head back toward the bungalow.

I smiled. She was talking to me, but watching closely every movement of the child and I realized I was, too.

"Do you have family?" she said, and I did not answer at first.

I looked south down the sand to the edge of the water where two women were approaching. The taller one had long, tightly muscled legs like a cyclist's. The younger one was carrying a new sunburn. In the bar that night Sherry and Marci had found a connection. A woman's need to mother. A young lady's need of comfort. Over the past few weeks they'd spent hours talking and running the beach together and even when I was not invited I somehow felt part of it. As they came near, Marci leaned into Richards and flipped her ponytail onto her shoulder and put her arm around her waist and said something that made them both laugh.

"Maybe I do," I said, watching them. "Maybe I do."

ACKNOWLEDGMENTS

Thanks to Marie and John Cusano for letting me into their lives and that of their daughter, Cindy, and to Women in Distress, the South Florida shelter and center for victims of domestic violence. Thanks also to Lieutenant Sherry Schlueter of the Broward Sheriff's Office for her dedication to the most vulnerable and for her inspiration; Laurrie Pood, the finest bartender in South Florida; Erika Kahn for her patience and reading; and Anne Newgarden for catching my many errors.

A continuing debt of gratitude is owed to Marlene and Russ Parks for affording me "The Cabin" where the foundations are written.

Deepest thanks to my agent, Philip Spitzer, and to my editor, Mitch Hoffman, whose discerning eye made this one better.

ABOUT THE AUTHOR

Jonathon King is a former journalist and the author of three previous critically-acclaimed, award-winning novels. His debut, *The Blue
Edge of Midnight,* won the Edgar Award for Best First Novel. He
lives in South Florida.